AF225945

Twelve Coffins

By
Lewis Pennington

Silver Lining
PUBLISHING

Silver Lining

PUBLISHING

159 Waightstill Dr.
Arden, NC 28740

Copyright © 2024 Lewis Pennington

All Rights Reserved. No part of this publication may be reproduced, stored in a retrieval system, or transmitted, in any form or in any means – by electronic, mechanical, photocopying, recording or otherwise – without prior written permission.

ISBN: 978-1-7364239-8-1

For Scott
My rock, my brother, my Drew

Chapter 1
(1963)

I tugged on my grandfather's sleeve. "How come the black horse doesn't have anybody on it?"

My question hung unanswered within my grandparents' living room. Usually full of joy and revelry during the Thanksgiving weekend, it was now as solemn and subdued as the funeral procession playing out on their tiny black-and-white TV. For the entire week all that anyone could talk about was the shooting. And for the entire week the questions mounted as to why it had happened and who was behind it all. As an eleven-year-old with a curious nature I had my own list.

"Why does the black horse only have those empty boots on its back like that? Whose sword's on its side? He's way prettier than Mrs. Clegg's horse. How'd he get so—"

Mom tapped my shoulder and shushed me. "Not so many questions Cody. Just watch."

A second later, PaPa, the man I admired more than any other, a man who, at fifty-nine years of age could drive an eighteen-wheeler two days straight with no sleep, was kneeling beside me with his arm around my waist. He held me tight and whispered into my ear.

"First off, Mrs. Clegg's horse is a mule. This horse is a thoroughbred named Black Jack. In the wagon in front of him is a coffin, or casket as some call it, and in it is our president. Black Jack's following it to show he's no longer with us.

"He sure must've been liked a bunch. There's a lot of people there."

I looked into PaPa's eyes. I'd never seen him cry before but there it was, a tiny tear finding its way down through his gray stubbled beard.

I turned back to the TV and the image of a little boy standing beside a lady in a black dress with a black hat and see-through lacy black cloth over her face. Even through the lace I could sense her sadness. As Black Jack passed in front of them, a line of soldiers saluted the flag-draped coffin that preceded him. The little boy raised his hand to his forehead, fidgeting as he waited to lower it along with the men in uniform. Suddenly urged to do the same, I lifted my chin and followed with a salute of my own, holding it as the room filled with the sniffling and muted weeping of family and friends who had gathered to pay respect to President Kennedy.

My mother stroked my hair. "Why don't you go outside and play with your brother?"

The word "outside" instantly had me squirming free of my grandfather's embrace. I bounded through the house, into the kitchen and out the back door, shedding the gloom as I ran into my grandparents' backyard. It was on this magical plot of land where my brother and I spent six of our most formative years, the years where every minute was an hour long, every find of a new leaf or bug a major scientific discovery, and every flicker of mica in a piece of gravel a gold rush in the making.

Situated on the fringes of the small southern town of Burlington, North Carolina, our block was one of the biggest in the county mainly because we shared half of it with our K-12 school. Next to the school was the first of five houses that occupied the other half, the home of Mary Libowskenstein, whose sandy-blonde hair always looked like someone had chopped at it instead of styled it. A tenth grader like my brother, she was as rough and tumble as any of the boys, favoring overalls or jeans to dresses and preferring to be called "Mary Lib." She didn't want to burden anyone with the mouthful of "Libowskenstein." What she lacked in femininity, she made up for with an infectious positive attitude, the type Mom usually pointed Drew to when thoughts of our father turned him blue.

In her backyard was a small, mossy-stone koi pond. Chained next to it was a fearsome beast with a disagreeable disposition. Bullet, a perpetually snarling black mutt, was Ms. Libowskenstein's deterrent to any unlawful pond-dipping.

Next to Mary Lib's was my grandparents' house where Drew and I lived for the six years it took our mother to become something called an anesthetist, a tongue twister of a job. I always avoided the name and simply said she put people to sleep. For all those years she drove six hours in a tin can '56 Chevy to spend every other weekend with us, and every other Sunday evening I rang the front porch chimes as she headed out the driveway back to school. Her time away, however, didn't come close to PaPa's absences. As a long-haul trucker, he was gone two to three weeks at a time, leaving a dark cloud over my brother for the first couple days. I was only three when my father was killed, so my memories of him were faint, but for Drew, they were ever present. When PaPa was on the road, I had him to look to while he had no one.

The one mainstay of the household and the rock of the family was our grandmother. Dubbed "Gonny" by the oldest grandchild for no reason other than lacking the verbal dexterity to say "Granny," she was written into her high school yearbook as the Burlington Bulldogs' "Littlest Angel," a moniker that referred not only to her five-foot one-inch stature, but also to her staunch religious beliefs. Following her biblical teachings, she adhered to the proverb that taught, "spare the rod, spoil the child." She was always quick to keep my brother and me in line with a good switching, the practice of whacking our bottoms with a stiff reed from a despicable bush that lurked at the darkest corner of the house. Our love for Gonny ran deep, faltering only during the times when our misconduct called for us to fetch our own switches. The death march, as my brother and I called it, required us to walk to the bush, pull off a reed switch of at least three feet, then deliver it back for her to carry out our corporal punishment.

Calling my grandparents' house modest was a modest exaggeration. A postwar, one-story, three-bedroom home with no air-conditioning, separate cold- and hot-water faucets and a telephone party line shared with Hilda Harwell and Leona Kunkle, it stood in stark contrast to the house on the other side of the driveway. Located on the corner was an opulent, two-story Victorian where my great-grandmother Maudie lived. Full of turn-of-the-century manners, she was as regal in character as the great house itself. Minus her occasional habit of sniffing snuff, she was every bit the grand dame of the neighborhood, even though a stroke left her paralyzed from the waist down and confined her to a wheelchair.

If you turned the corner onto Tucker Street, you would come to the home of Mrs. Clegg, a reclusive widow who only communed with her mule, Julius, and spent every sunny day tending to her award-winning tomatoes in a garden that butted up against the back corner of our school's baseball field.

Smack-dab in the middle of our little village was a two-acre patch of earth that consisted of a one-acre open field facing another acre of pecan trees and three rows of muscadine grapevines. Except for the school, which was fenced off, a narrow one-car-wide gravel road wound its way throughout our complex, connecting everything. On this twisty stretch of rocky highway, our imaginations transformed us into fellow truckers like PaPa. Envisioning his big rig's trailer, we used our bikes to pull wagons carrying empty boxes of make-believe cargo from house to house. Other times we found ourselves traversing an intercoastal waterway, or sailing down an angry river in search of lost treasure in a remote jungle that most often came in the form of an unruly magnolia bush bunched up against Mrs. Clegg's house.

On most days, if I needed to locate my brother or any of our neighborhood buddies, I had only to run out to the open field and spin around once. Within a second, either through sight or sound, I'd find them climbing trees, racing along the gravel road, or playing tag, roller-bat, or any of the hundred games of pretend we devised. Today was different though. Leaving the president's funeral behind me, I ran out into a crisp autumn afternoon. The sun shone brightly, the birds chirped, but no kids were to be found.

"Drew! Where are you?" I waited with no reply. "Drewwww, where are youuu?"

"Not so loud." Mary Lib's voice came from the back of the house.

I turned to find her jagged blond mop of hair sticking out from behind a partially hidden door next to the switch bush. "What're you doing down there?"

"Come on," she said, waving me in.

Eager to be included in whatever was happening in the dungeon, our pet name for Gonny and PaPa's root cellar, I raced toward her.

She held a finger to her lips. "You gotta be quiet. We're conjuring."

"What's conjurin'?"

"Just come on in and be quiet. You'll see."

Halfway above ground, halfway under, the dungeon was a dark, dank cinder-block room tainted with the smell of oily rags from days of PaPa working on Mack trucks and a newfangled powered lawn mower that never seemed to run right. It was where Gonny stored her crates of fruit and vegetable preserves and where PaPa kept cases of his homemade muscadine wine along with an assortment of musty old tools and discarded items from the house that just couldn't be parted with. The only light came from a missing brick in the foundation and the cracks around the sagging door. On the brightest day a flashlight was still required to see. On other days, such as this, a day when my brother held court with one of his many spooktacular shenanigans, a candle was used.

I took one bold step in and a cautious half step back. "What're y'all doin'?"

"Just sit down, squirt," Drew said with an authoritative air.

Four and a half years my senior, I had always looked up to my brother. With the wit and wisdom of our elders, he was the centerpiece of all our juvenile exploits, usually commanding us with a cool hand and unnatural patience. Wicked smart for his age, he was especially patient with me, particularly when it came to school and learning. He said he wasn't about to go through life with a dufus by his side. Whether I liked it or not, or even when I wasn't aware of it, he was also working to shape not only my vocabulary but my character. It was for these reasons that I fiercely protected our relationship.

I surveyed the room and saw everyone bunched shoulder to shoulder, circling the candle. Drew sat crossed-legged with Mary Lib and two other kids from across the street: Jessie Limberg, a spunky, pig-tailed redhead also known as "Cackles," thanks to her raucous, over-the-top way of laughing; and Peeps, short for "Peepers Petey," a thick-rimmed, bifocaled fellow sixth grader with a split-tooth grin and fidgety nature. A year younger than me and Peeps, Cackles loved teasing him and spouted off anything that came into her little red noggin.

"Where you want me to sit?" I asked.

"Between me and Cackles," Mary Lib said.

I immediately plopped to the dirt floor and squeezed my way in between the girls, tucking my knees into my chest to take up as little space as possible.

"So, what's a conjurin'?" I asked.

"You promise you're not gonna get scared, are ya?" Drew said.

I looked across to Peeps and into the large, distorted orbs his thick lenses created.

Cackles ripped off a squawky, high-pitched laugh. "Don't be lookin' at Peeps. He always looks scared."

Mary Lib patted me on my knee. "Nothing to be afraid of, Cody, we're just summoning the dead is all."

"What!" I said, jumping to my feet.

"Would you sit back down," Drew said sternly. "He's the one who's gonna be scared."

"Who's gonna be scared?" I said, inching back to the floor and fighting the urge to bolt out into the sunlight.

"The president," Drew replied. "We're doing a séance to bring him back."

"Say who?"

"A sé—ance," he said, drawing out the syllables and hoping to nail the definition.

"It's a ritual that brings somebody's ghost back where you can talk to 'em," Cackles said.

"Why do we want to talk to him? He's dead. He ain't gonna want to talk."

"Oh, he'll have plenty to say," Drew added.

"Peeps, do you think he'll come back?" I asked.

"Sure he will," Drew said, cutting in. "He'll want to know who shot him. And we'll tell him it was that Lee Harvey fella. Now come on, we're gonna miss our chance. He'll be in heaven before long and won't want to talk to anybody. Now everybody hold hands. I'm going to say the chant once and then you guys repeat it with me." He cleared his throat. "Here goes…President Kennedy, hear our chant. Fly away, buzzard. Fly away, crow. Wherever you're at, where the cold wind blows, come, Mr. President, come."

"I can't remember all those words," I said.

Cackles snickered under her breath. "What's buzzards and crows got to do with anything?"

Drew sighed. "Gosh darn it, they're just to get his attention is all, and Cody, you can just move your lips like you're saying it. Now let's do this. Start when I say *go*. Ready—set…"

On *go* I began mouthing the words as the others performed a dysfunctional harmony of Drew's homegrown chant, wondering to myself why anybody's ghost would come back because of those buzzards and crows.

For a long minute we sat in silence, eyes darting around the room in anticipation of the appearance of the president's apparition.

"I-I don't think…" Peeps began.

"Shush," Drew whispered. "Give him time."

Another minute passed, and our eyes went from scanning the room to scanning each other as we waited for Drew's next directive.

"Maybe we should do it again," Mary Lib said.

He nodded. "Good idea. On *go*, okay? Ready—set…"

Another round of chanting followed with more silence and increasing skeptical glances around the room.

"One more time," Drew said. "Ready—set…"

This chant ended with a different result. Following the final *come,* a loud bang sent us all jumping out of our skins.

"Didja hear that?" Drew exclaimed.

We all sat wide-eyed, unable to answer. A moment passed as the sound of my heartbeat pounded in my ears. Then slowly it came, the sound of dead feet dragging across the ground. It reminded me of the sounds of the mummy's walk in the horror flick we'd all gone to see the week before—the same movie Drew got his séance idea from, I found out later. Louder and louder the footfalls came—then nothing. The room fell silent once again. I could hear only the sound of our panicked breathing. Suddenly someone hollered.

"Kids! Are you in the cellar?"

A collective sigh—part relief, part frustration—went up among us.

"Yes, Gonny, we're down here," Drew groaned back.

"Well, come on out. We're all going over to Maudie's for lunch."

"Yes ma'am," he replied halfheartedly.

One by one, we filed out with Drew bringing up the rear. On our way to Maudie's, I looked back over my shoulder to see him eyeballing the back screen door that had slammed and caused us all to nearly wet ourselves. I couldn't be certain, but I would've bet a dollar to a donut he was wearing a smile and not a frown. If there was one thing Drew Edwards loved more than anything else, it was a good joke—a trait that would ultimately bring more than just laughs.

Chapter 2

The following week, school was canceled to give all the grieving parents and kids more time to mourn the president we'd failed to conjure. As for mourning, I was decidedly against the practice, preferring to occupy my days with more entertaining things like a trip on an imaginary rocket ship or sneaking behind ole Bullet's back to take a plunge into Mary Lib's pond. Drew, while also loving his fun, leaned more toward more spectacular endeavors, especially anything that could raise the hair on one's arms, which is why I knew he relished how his séance had ended.

It was during that particular week, when all flags began flying half-mast and his boredom reached its limits, that my brother upped his game. On that Friday he called the entire neighborhood gang together to watch him do something of heroic proportions. Like a circus acrobat who defied death by walking a hundred-foot-high tightrope, he too would perform his own daring feat. He would walk across Tucker Street and enter the one building none of us had ever dared to step foot in—the coffin factory.

Two stories high, constructed of rusty-colored bricks and with a black overhanging metal roof, it took up half the block, making Maudie's house appear almost doll-like. Where her home was ornate and inviting, the factory was anything but. With the exception of a row of tiny, four-pane, black-framed windows running across the second story, the only other openings were two entrances on the first floor. The main entrance was a set of double metal doors on the corner with tall stained-glass windows on either side. A simple wooden sign dangling above the doors read "Fletcher and Son Coffin Company, established 1912," the year the *Titanic* sank. According to legend, Herbert Grandel, one of old man Fletcher's best friends, was aboard the ship that fateful night, thus ending up as one of the factory's first customers. Unfortunately for Mr. Grandel, times were lean in the company's early days, and corners had to be cut. Because Fletcher had been unable to provide the quality of coffin Grandel's family requested, it was said his ghost, feeling slighted by his friend, began to walk the corridors in protest while seeking an upgrade to his eternal resting place.

The other entrance was a simple, single black wooden door set in the middle of the building; it appeared to be permanently shut as no one was ever seen going in or out. Fittingly, the entire structure was more like a giant mausoleum than a business. Only the constant sound of the buzz saws ripping through lumber all day gave away its function. At night it would disappear into the darkness and Grandel would supposedly float through its halls. Occasionally a flicker of a candle could be seen through one of the tiny second-floor portals and one of the machines would crank up then quickly stop. Those were the nights our minds turned shadows on the bedroom walls into ghoulish intruders and the wind hissed and moaned. Those were the nights even Drew lay awake until the morning light.

Just after lunch that day, Maudie's back porch, which directly faced the factory, became the staging area for my brother's grand adventure. One by one, kids arrived with the same simple question: *Are you really going into that place?*

"Of course he is!" I would say. "Drew ain't scared of anything."

The sound of metal wheels clunking along a wooden floor suddenly filtered down the hall and Maudie appeared in the doorway. Always pressed and pristine and smelling of honeysuckle talcum, she sat in her chair as if it were a mobile throne. I can't remember ever seeing her out of sorts or disheveled in the least. Her hair was always done up in a tidy, snow-white bun, a six-inch silver hair pin holding it together. The necklines of all her dresses were bordered with a fancy lace wrap that looked peculiarly like any one of the hundred doilies scattered throughout her house.

"*Ain't* is not a word," she chided me, "and it certainly is not befitting a member of the Edwards' lineage."

I had no idea what lineage was but was sure Drew would inform me later. What I did know was whenever she used our last name, it was usually with a point of pride and worthy of our attention.

She swiveled her chair left and then right, studying our youthful get-together. In addition to Cackles, Mary Lib, Peeps, Drew, and myself, there was Irvin-Dell, a shy little kindergartner from a couple streets over, and Reubin, a stringy young black boy roughly the age of Cackles. He showed up out of the blue one day with a worn-out leather bag of tiger-eye marbles and a happy-go-lucky demeanor, and for some odd reason no one, not even the grownups, ever questioned him about where he lived or who his parents were. As shameful as it was, we didn't even think to ask what his last name was. He was simply Reubin, our friend with the marbles who came and went on his own schedule.

"My heavens," Maudie said, "to what do I owe the privilege of having such a handsome congregation at my home on this fine day?"

My great-grandmother's prim and proper ways always tickled our gang of commoners.

Cackles snorted back a laugh. "We're here to watch Cody boy's brother go off to the dead-box building."

"I beg your pardon?"

"He's gonna go into the coffin factory," I said.

Maudie arched an eyebrow toward him. "Do you have business with the Fletchers, young man?"

"Well, uh, not really. I uh—"

"He's just bored and needs something to do," I said. "We're all bored."

She smiled at him. "So then, you're the entertainment of the day."

Mary Lib pushed to the front. "I told him he should go up to the second floor. That's where the stairs are."

"But it's only a two-story building, my dear."

"I know, ma'am. I meant he should go look for the stairs that lead up to heaven. They're on that floor."

"Not the first floor?" Maudie said, biting her lip.

"Oh no, ma'am, that's where—pardon my language—the gates to hell are!"

Peeps' hands came together in front of his mouth. "Ye-yeah, you gotta stay clear of all the dark places, Drew."

"And if you see fire or pitchforks," I added, "you just

run straight back outside. No need to be ashamed, you just run like the devil's at your heels."

"'Cause he will be!" Cackles crowed.

Maudie grabbed the wheels to her chair and heaved herself forward. We respectfully divided our number into halves as she rolled toward Drew. She lifted her hand, gesturing with a crooked finger for him to come near.

He walked over and bent down.

"So, none of you have ever been in the coffin factory?" she said.

"No ma'am."

"Then what is it you want from this venture?"

"Nothing, I mean I just want to see what's inside."

"That's all?"

"Yes ma'am. I'm just curious."

"You're not going to take anything, are you? Something as a souvenir or anything like that?"

"Oh no, I just want to look around. Like I said, I'm just curious is all."

"You know what they say…"

"Say what, ma'am?"

"Curiosity—killed—the cat," she replied, strategically timing a wink with the word *killed*.

He swallowed hard.

Maudie's eyes narrowed on him as she worked to determine the sincerity of his objective. She motioned him farther down until his ear was beside her face, then leaned into it and whispered, "Ask for Avel. Tell him you're my great-grandson."

"Who's Avel?" he whispered back.

"He's the foreman. He'll show you around. And whatever you do, don't go wandering off."

"Yes ma'am, I'll be sure not to. How do you know this Mr. Avel?"

"Never you mind." Her voice grew serious. "You just do as I say. Don't—go—wandering. You understand?"

"Yes ma'am. I promise."

"Good!" she said, straightening up in her chair. "One last thing. On your way out, grab a handful of those pecans in the bowl on the kitchen counter—not the ones in the shells, but the unshelled ones." She spun her chair around and whizzed back into the house.

"Why do I need pecans?" he said, casting his voice after her.

I could barely make it out, but her stately tone suddenly reflected that of a schoolgirl's giggle. "You'll see," she said over her shoulder. "You'll see."

Drew turned to us.

"Well?" I said.

"Well, what?"

"What'd she say?"

"She wants me to ask for some guy named Avel. That and to bring nuts."

"Whose Avel?" I asked.

"And why nuts?" Mary Lib added.

"Heck if I know about either," Drew replied.

I reached into my pants pocket and pulled out my Mickey Mouse head Pez dispenser I'd carried with me since my previous birthday. "Here, I just filled it with peppermint bricks. You can chew on 'em if you get nervous in there."

"No thanks. I'm okay."

"You want me to go with you?" Mary Lib said in the hesitant voice of someone offering up a gift while hoping it wouldn't be accepted.

"No. I-I'll be fine," he replied in a tone equally less than enthusiastic. He started to the porch's edge, then stopped. "Shoot, I need that handful of pecans from the kitchen. I'll just go back and—"

Cackles grabbed him by the sleeve. "Oh no you don't. You're gonna go in there then skedaddle out the side door. I'll go get 'em," she said, running back inside and reappearing less than a minute later with two heaping handfuls of both shelled and unshelled pecans. She held them out to him. "Here ya are," she laughed. "Nuts for a nut!"

He stuffed them in his pants pockets. "Well, I, uh, I'm going now." He stepped into the backyard toward the dusty road that separated our little world from the factory, each step a tad slower than the last. "Here I go. I'm going now."

"Good luck!" we all shouted in random succession.

He hesitated as he looked back to the safety of Maudie's porch.

"We'll be waiting right here," Mary Lib said with a reassuring smile.

Drew nodded, produced a meager grin, turned and slowly walked across the street. When he reached the entrance, he stopped and looked back once more. I prodded him on with my own exaggerated smile to which he returned a modest wave before pushing the door open and disappearing inside.

For a long minute we all stood in silent reverence. Peeps rubbed the lenses of his glasses with his shirttail to make sure he'd seen correctly. "He's in. He's actually in the coffin factory, right this very minute!"

Had Neil Armstrong already walked on the moon, it would not have equaled my brother's accomplishment that afternoon.

Mary Lib sighed. "He's soooo brave."

"He's a nut," Cackles said. "A nut with a pocketful of nuts."

The sudden, gravelly rumble of a throat being cleared turned us around. "Miss Maudie wants to know if you children would like a refreshment." Without us knowing it, Miss Bloom, one of Maudie's part-time caregivers, had snuck up behind us. In one hand she held a pitcher of lemonade, in the other a stack of paper cups.

"Yes," we all said in unison.

Ten minutes later everyone except Mary Lib had finished their drinks. Hers sat untouched. "I thought he'd be out by now," she said, walking to the porch railing where she began unconsciously drumming it with her fingertips.

"You don't think he's lost, do ya?" Peeps said.

"He ain't—I mean he's not lost. He's—whatcha call it…casing the joint."

Fifteen minutes passed and then Reubin pulled out his leather bag of tiger eyes. "Wanna play a game, Cody?"

"Nah," I said as respectfully as I could while still concentrating along with Mary Lib on the factory's front door.

Cackles jumped from her stool. "I'll shoot with ya."

Reubin took Irvin-Dell by the hand. "You can play too," he said, leading him out to the backyard.

Cackles grabbed Peeps. "Come on. Me and you'll be a team."

As the game commenced, Mary Lib and I took turns pacing the porch. Another ten minutes passed, then another ten. When an hour came and went, my nerves erupted. "Something's wrong. I'm going in!"

"I'm coming with you!" she exclaimed.

Just as we leaped off the porch, Drew appeared, not from the main entrance but from the black door in the middle of the building. Even from a distance it was obvious he was different than when he'd gone in. He radiated. He wore a strange, quirky smirk and his eyes were wide. He was looking toward us but not at us.

"He made it!" Mary Lib said, wrapping her arm around me then quickly pulling it back. "Sorry about that," she said.

"You made it!" I yelled as I raced to him.

Mary Lib followed a half step behind, meeting us dead center of Tucker Street. A few seconds later the rest of the gang swarmed in on him. All at once the questions came gushing.

"What'd you see?" I asked.

Mary Lib touched his elbow. "Why were you in there so long?"

"Were you afraid?" Peeps asked.

Cackles bounced like a pogo stick. "Did ya see the stairway to heaven? What about the gates to hell? Did God come down or did the devil come up?"

When the questions finally ran dry, we stood staring at him, our mouths hanging open, wanting to ask more but needing answers. As his lips parted, we all leaned in.

"It was…"

"It was what?" said Mary Lib.

Drew's faraway gaze faded as his focus turned back to us. "It was…" His voice suddenly fell off as his hand found the inside of his right pants pocket. He pulled out a pecan. The corners of his eyes crinkled. He chuckled to himself, ignoring our presence.

"Come on, would ya!" Cackles groaned. "Tell us what happened already!"

In an instant he was somewhere else, his eyes distant again. He jerked his head back to the factory door. "I gotta go back!" He cupped both hands around the pecan, protecting it as if it were a robin's egg. "He'll want it. I gotta go back." Before any of us could form a thought, he had turned and was sprinting across the street.

"Drewwww, wait!" I started after him, but it was too late. He'd already vanished through the black door.

We all stood in the middle of the road, dumbfounded.

"What did he mean, *he'll want it*?" Mary Lib asked.

I shrugged, waiting for him to reappear. She grabbed my hand and squeezed it. "Should we—"

"You children get out of that road this minute!" Gonny's voice came from around the corner of Maudie's house. In an instant all the kids scurried back to the porch while Mary Lib and I remained stuck in the middle of Tucker Street.

"Cody! Mary Lib! Are you deaf? Get out of that road—now!"

The rise in my grandmother's voice suddenly registered with me and I realized that one octave higher would ensure a death march to the switch bush.

Back on the porch, we all trained our eyes across the street.

Gonny walked up beside me. I could feel her following my eyes to the black door where Drew had vanished. "Where's your brother?" she said.

My arm slowly rose, my finger stretching to the door. "In there," I said flatly.

Her gasp snapped my attention to her. I looked up, waiting for her to tell me to go fetch him, but all she did was stare along with the rest of us, her head tilted at an angle that projected either an uncertain level of concern or amazement. Either way, at that moment, she was one of us.

Chapter 3

The minutes spent focused on the black door dragged on until finally Irvin-Dell broke ranks when he heard the inaudible voice of his mom telling him to come home. "I'll see you guys later," he shouted as he dashed off.

Gonny blinked away her own fixation with the factory and instructed us to disband and do something other than gawk at an old building. "You children need to either be playing or doing your chores. Staring off like a bunch of zombies isn't healthy." At that directive, we instantly abandoned waiting for Drew's return, and everyone, including Mary Lib, headed off in different directions.

A tap on my shoulder caused me to look up.

"Time you crossed the River Jordan and retrieved your kin," Gonny said.

My puzzled expression indicated her biblical reference to the holy river fell flat with me.

"You need to go get your brother now. Play time at the coffin company is over."

"You—You want me to go get him?"

"Yes. Now trot on over and tell him I've got cookies right off the stove for you two."

"But that's th-the coffin factory. There's dead people in there. Hell's in there. The devil's in there!"

Gonny's chin disappeared into her neck as she reared back at my assessment. "Child, I know there's all kinds of rumors about that place but that's all they are—just rumors. Besides, a coffin factory is just where they make the box they put people in when they die. The folks who get these boxes have already passed on and are already in heaven or—unfortunately—in hell. And I assure you Fletcher's is not the entrance to either of those places."

"Where'd everybody go?"

"Drew!" I said, spinning around to find him stepping up to the back porch. He wore the same weird expression he'd had when he left the factory the first time. "What happened to you? Why were you gone so long? Why'd you go back?"

His smile grew to proportions I'd never seen his lips produce before. "It was incredible." He paused. "No, it was awesome. It was awesomely incredible."

"I knew it!" I said, slinging a sideways *I told you so* glance up at Gonny. "You saw heaven. You walked up the golden stairs and you saw it, didn't you?" I bounced in anticipation of hearing the details of how the steps glistened, how the fluffy white clouds floated above them, and how sweet the angels' harps sounded as he approached.

"No! I didn't see heaven and I didn't see the devil either."

The wind suddenly left my sails, leaving me disappointed and baffled as to what else could possibly have produced the spell he was under. "Then *what* did you see?" I demanded.

"Happy."

"Happy?" I said, scrunching my face the same way I had when I tried to figure out Gonny's River Jordan comment.

Equally puzzled as I was, she bent down and looked deep

into his eyes, examining his pupils like old Doc Kurnodel always did before whacking our knees with his rubber hammer. "Are you feeling okay, my boy?"

"Yes ma'am. I'm fine." He began fidgeting, his feet shifting side to side as if he was about to wet his britches. "I'm fine as can be."

Her words came measured and gentle so as not to upset the delicate state of mind he'd begun to display. "You can't see happiness, Drew. Happiness is an emotion. You can see people being happy though. Is that what you meant?"

"I didn't say I saw *happiness*. What I said was I saw *Happy*." He grabbed my arm. "And you can too! You can—"

"Now now," she said, laying a hand on his shoulder, "just settle down and breathe." For a minute she stood over him, gently stroking his hair, then broke the silence. "What'd they do over there in that factory, pour your pants full of ants?"

"I-I'm sorry, ma'am. I can't help but—"

Just then Miss Bloom burst onto the porch. "Come quick! Ms. Maudie's taken a spill, trying to get out of her chair by herself."

In an instant Gonny was gone, leaving Drew and I ogling the back door. The ants in his pants seemed to depart with her. The strange excitement he'd brought back from the factory had been replaced with concern. "Stay here," he told me. "I'm going to see what's happening."

Never having witnessed anyone in such a tizzy and knowing how fragile my great-grandmother was, I began biting my fingernails. Several minutes passed until I couldn't take it any longer. I quietly made my way into the house and was tiptoeing down the hall toward her room when Drew popped out.

"Shhhh. Let's go," he whispered.

Back outside, Drew freed a breath he'd been holding. He closed his eyes and exhaled.

"Maudie's not dead, is she?"

"No, buddy, she's alright. Banged up a bit, but she's okay."

"Phew! I started thinking about it while you were gone and, well, I-I don't want to think about it anymore."

"Gonny said she's going to sit with her all afternoon and that we should go on about our own."

"So we can go play?" I said, transitioning from the potential tragedy to another day's adventure.

Drew's eyes slowly rolled over to meet mine, the corners of his mouth inching upward. "That's right."

I followed his eyes as they left me and moved across the street to the coffin factory.

"You're not thinkin' about going back in there, are you?"

"Nope."

"Good," I said.

"I'm thinking *we're* going back in there."

"Ohhhh no." I took a step back. "You ain't gettin' me in that place."

"Come on, little brother. You gotta come see it."

"I've seen enough of the outside and I've seen how goofy you came out. That place put a hex on you. You're lucky Maudie snapped ya out of it."

"No, she didn't. Besides you don't know what I saw."

"I saw enough to know a spell when I see one."

"Oh, for heaven's sake, it wasn't a spell. I promise there's nothing to be afraid of. I'll be right beside you the entire time."

"I said—I'm *not* going."

"Tell you what, if anything happens that's no good, I'll give you my G.I. Joe. What do you say?"

I was stunned. Ever since Drew declared his action figure the best birthday present Mom had ever gotten him, he had treated it like gold. "You'd really give me your G.I. Joe?"

"Sure I would!"

"You wouldn't be funnin' me, would ya? You promise me it'll be alright?"

"Cross my heart, hope to die."

"Don't say *die* for crying out loud!"

"Cross my heart then."

"Well, I guess if you've already cased the joint."

Drew snickered. "You've been watching those detective shows again."

"Alright then." I turned toward the pecan orchard, where Mary Lib was swinging from one of the tree branches. "Should I go get her?"

"No, I think just you and me should go. Any more might be too much."

I could feel my chest puffing with pride. My brother had already walked on the moon and now he was willing to share the glory with me by asking me to co-captain the rest of his adventure. Our daring deed would be the buzz of Maple Avenue School for decades to come. "Well, okay. I-I guess I could go. But wait! We need somebody to see it."

"You want a witness?"

"Whatever you call it. If I'm gonna risk my life, I need somebody to see it."

"Alright then," he replied reluctantly, "I'll go get her. While I do, go to the kitchen and get some more pecans."

A moment later I met him and Mary Lib huffing their way back up on the porch. I held out a handful of nuts, two still in the shells and two without. He plucked the ones without shells from my hand. "You can keep those other ones."

"What're you gonna do with them?"

"You'll see."

"You guys are crazy," Mary Lib said.

"Go on and tell her what I get if this cockamamie adventure gets me killed," I said.

Drew placed his hand over his heart. "I, Drew Edwards, hereby promise to give my G.I. Joe to my sissy-boy brother if he dies, so help me God." His cheeks bulged holding back a laugh.

Mary Lib frowned. "That don't make a lick of sense."

Drew shrugged, his jaw muscles relaxing.

With my frazzled nerves, I failed to see the flawed logic in my brother's last will and testament and I stepped toward the backyard. In a welcomed surprise, Drew wrapped his arm around my shoulder, giving me a sudden sense of calm. Still, the thirty-second walk to the factory seemed like an eternity. Pausing in front of the main entrance, he patted me on the head and smiled. "Ready?"

I swallowed hard then nodded sheepishly.

Like an actor coming back onstage for his encore, Drew parted the doors with an equal push to each.

A second later my eyes adjusted from the bright outdoors to the dimness of the foyer. The stained-glass windows filtered in the light, washing the room in a rich rainbow of warm hues. Centered in the room behind a chest-high mahogany desk was a lady, though I could only see her horn-rimmed glasses set beneath a huge jet-black beehive hairdo. "Did you leave something, Mr. Edwards?" she said in a spritely voice.

"No ma'am," Drew replied. "I just wanted to bring my brother back over, if that's okay?"

The lady's towering beehive teetered backward as she

raised her glasses for a better look at me. "Sure. Just check in with Avel."

"Yes ma'am," he said, pulling me around the desk to another large metal door on the opposite wall.

As we approached, I could feel a soft hum vibrating through from the other side into my chest. Upon opening the door, a wave of maple, mahogany, and other hardwood scents filled my nose. The sounds of buzzing saws and boards banging against one another and onto huge wooden tables bombarded me. Hammers pounded nails while riveting machines clamped metal to metal. Dozens of workers scurried back and forth, moving plain pieces of wood from one station to the next where they slowly transformed into crude, rectangular boxes before being carted off to the other end of the factory.

"See all this?" Drew shouted above the noise. "This here is what's called the raw staging area. It's where they make the basic boxes." He pointed to the back side of the factory floor to where they were taking the unfinished wooden containers. "There's another room back there where they do all the fancy stuff, like putting in the padding and shellacking the outside and putting on the handles. They even put art and stuff on 'em."

"How many have they made?"

"Dunno, but it's a lot. There's a tiny code on the bottom of each coffin that Mr. Merriweather puts in a ledger. That sucker's about four inches thick."

I spun around, amazed at the commotion, marveling at how efficiently the workers went about their tasks, when suddenly I realized there was really no second story. What some might consider a second floor was actually a deck that wrapped around the entire building and looked down into the middle. Along the upstairs walls were long racks of boards and other materials.

Unless the stairway to heaven came in the form of a fire escape or one of the tall ladders leaning against the wall, the coffin factory had no access to the pearly gates. This left only one other entrance into the other world, the one I feared could be waiting around any corner.

"Are you sure the gates of hell aren't in here?" I said.

"I already told you. It's just a factory."

"Are you sure?"

"Sure, I'm sure. Now come on. I want you to meet Avel." Drew tugged at my elbow and began quickstepping across the factory floor, dodging in and out of the workstations while dancing around the workers like he was just another one of the fellas heading off for a coffee break. Several men even acknowledged his passing with a smile or nod. Each time my level of pride for him rose a notch. At the same time my anxiety began to dwindle.

"Where'd you say we were going?"

"Here," he said, stopping at a narrow door tucked into the far corner, opposite the foyer. To the right was a large set of double doors. A sign above them read "Finishing."

"Is this where they do all the fancy stuff?" I asked.

"Yeah, but we're not going in there just yet," he said, giving the narrow door several loud whacks.

Just as he raised his fist again, the door slowly opened. Drew took a step forward and leaned inside. "Mr. Merriweather?" he called out.

I peered around him to find an office not much bigger than a few broom closets. Facing the door was a tiny desk. Behind it was a wall of shelves with stacks of papers all neatly placed in symmetrical piles. On the bottom shelf, centered in the middle by itself, was a thick black leather-bound book the length and width of a man's arm from elbow to palm. To the left of the desk was a two-foot-high door that was opened to the outside. To the right of the desk was a normal-sized door.

"Mr. Merriweather?" Drew repeated as he took another cautious step inside.

"H-how'd the front door open like that?" I said, searching the room.

Just then a fraction of an elderly gentleman, five feet four or less, shuffled in. Unlike the rest of the workers who were dressed in coveralls, he wore neatly pressed black slacks and a stiff-collared white shirt with an equally stiff black bow tie. Almost completely bald on top, his remaining hair resided on his cheeks in the form of two woolly gray sideburns, the kind I'd only seen on soldiers in Civil War picture books. He was all angles with a hunched back and upturned nose that kept a pair of tiny round glasses teetering at the end. Seeing Drew standing in the doorway, he pushed them up with a knobby finger. "Mister Edwards. Back already!" he said.

"I hope it's okay, but I wanted to bring my brother to meet you."

The old man adjusted the tilt of his head toward me.

"Oh, I'm sorry," Drew said, springing out from in front of me. "This is my brother, Cody."

"Ahhh, yes! I see the resemblance." His voice crackled with a chipper tone that matched a broad smile that revealed a field of butter-bean-sized teeth.

As impressive as his sideburns happened to be, they were no contest for the magnitude of his smile. I thrust my hand forward. "Pleasure to meet you, sir."

"The pleasure's all mine, young fella. The name's Avel Merriweather."

"Tell him what it means, sir," Drew said in a way that made him sound like they were old friends.

"Wish I had a nickel for every time that request has been made. Well, sir, 'Avel' means wind and 'Merriweather' means pleasant weather." He smiled again. "Compliments of a long line of sailors."

"Wow!" I said. "You're a sailor?"

"Oh no, my boy. My father and his father before him were the sailors. I'm just a modest craftsman for the departed."

"Uh, what?"

"I make coffins," he said, winking at Drew.

"Mr. Merriweather is the foreman of the factory, Cody. He runs the place."

"Thank you for the promotion, Mr. Edwards, but that's not quite right. I do oversee things, but it's the junior Fletcher that owns it and handles all the legal matters and such."

"But you do the real work," Drew continued.

"And it's for the love of the craft that I do so," he replied.

I couldn't help but smile at how he mashed up his words, like a kind of poetry that I mostly understood.

"Can you let him meet—"

Before Drew could complete his request, something bounced off my ear and landed at my feet with a tiny clink.

"A peanut?" I said, looking down in amazement. "Where in the…" I searched the ceiling for where it might've come, but there were only large oak beams. I looked to Drew then Mr. Merriweather, who both wore the same mischievous grin. Mr. Merriweather bent his head forward, his eyes moving past me into the corner to my rear. Without moving my body, I craned my head behind me, following his gaze to a small pedestal table. On top of it, smiling just as broadly as my brother and Mr. Merriweather, was a small furry creature.

"It's a-a monkey," I muttered.

He sat motionless, his hands clasped together and holding his long, fluffy tail under his chin. He probably weighed less than ten pounds and had a white face and short golden hair surrounding it and his shoulders. The rest of his body, including the top of his head and forearms, was black. His eyes were closely set, and although his fur was dark, it seemed to sparkle. To my delight, and without a cue, he began to bob his head in rhythm with what sounded like a squeaky little laugh.

Mr. Merriweather beamed. "Allow me to introduce you to Happy."

Chapter 4

My mouth hung open as I stood spellbound.

"Now you know why I said to get the pecans," Drew said, holding out a nut between his fingers. "Give him one."

I turned to Mr. Merriweather.

"Go ahead. He likes those more than the cheap peanuts I give him."

Except for inside the *National Geographic* that showed up at our house once a month, I'd never seen a monkey before, let alone a live one that was only a foot away. My smile stretched wide as I held it out to him.

Like a furry flash of lightning, he dropped his tail and snatched it from me. He rolled it feverishly between his hands as he teetered side to side, dancing merrily on his tiny pedestal. He paused, flicked his tongue over it, then gnashed away at the morsel until a minute later it was no more. Unable to take my eyes off him, I reached into my pocket and pulled out one of the pecans still in a shell. I offered it to him. This time there was no lightning-quick grab, just his bushy eyebrows coming together and his thin lips pursing. He held back another second then snatched it from me and tossed it back while sticking his tongue out at me.

I swiped in front of my nose in a pathetic delayed reaction. My brother and Mr. Merriweather burst into laughter. "What just happened?" I said, stumbling backward.

"You found out your new friend likes his meals prepared," Merriweather said.

"Here," Drew said, handing me a naked pecan. "Make good."

Happy sat eyeing my new prize. Instead of doing his little dance, he patted the tips of his slim little fingers together like a grown man waiting to dive into a sirloin steak. The moment it was in his grasp he leaped to the floor and ran to the miniature door. He paused before triumphantly waving the nut in his hand then grabbed the doorknob and pulled it shut as he bounced outside.

I snapped my head toward Drew. "He—He's the one that let us in?"

"I told ya you'd like this place."

I turned to Mr. Merriweather. "What kind of monkey is that?"

"He's a Panamanian white-faced capuchin."

"No, I mean is he magical or something? He opens and shuts doors, throws peanuts and laughs like a kid. Heck, he even throws tantrums like our baby cousin."

"He's different alright." Merriweather paused. "As for magical…well, let's just say he's more…spiritual."

I looked back to the tiny door and smiled at a little brass plaque on it that read "Happy's Place." "Aren't you afraid he'll run off?"

"Not a'tall. He's got a couple big oak trees out back he likes hopping between and an old barrel he plays in, but he prefers being indoors most of the time. Besides, he's not run off once in the twenty years I've had him."

I continued staring at the little door. "Wow, I just met a real, live monkey."

Mr. Merriweather chuckled then picked up the black book from behind his desk. "I'm afraid I have to go to a meeting, but I should be back in about twenty minutes." He turned to Drew. "If you'll stick around, there's something I'd like to ask you."

"Sure," he replied.

"In the meantime, feel free to show young Mr. Cody around. All the workers will be at the meeting so now's a good time."

"What about Happy?" I asked.

"Don't worry. He'll be back shortly."

"Come on," Drew said, pulling me through the door marked "Finishing."

For the next twenty minutes my brother played tour guide, walking me around a part of the factory that was so big we could have fit the pecan orchard in it. In each corner was a different station with one or two coffins being worked on. We walked from station to station while he recited verbatim all the things Mr. Merriweather told him during his initial visit.

"This is the staining and paint station. Some people want their coffin painted; some want stain."

"You mean people pick out their *own* coffin?"

"Most of the time they don't, but Mr. Merriweather said sometimes they do. Like if they know they're gonna die they might. Now this area over here is the shellacking area." He continued with an in-depth explanation of why so many coats of the shiny stuff were applied. "And this is where the padding's put in," he said, giving me another lengthy explanation on the quality of the material. "Silk's the most expensive kind. Usually, it's just the rich people who get it. And the last part is over here," he said, leading me to a corner where a little white coffin sat on a table. A set of four brass handles with screws and bolts lay next to it. "This is the hardware section. It's where they put the handles and hinges on." He ran his hand over one of the curved pieces of metal. "Check out how much detail's on these."

"Are those leaves on the ends?" I asked.

"Yeah, they're maple leaves. Pretty neat, huh?"

I jumped up on the table and laid stiff next to it, crossing my arms like I'd seen in the Dracula movies. "It's almost my size." I hoisted a leg over the edge. "I'm gonna try it out."

"Oh, no you don't!" Drew said, yanking me back. "If Mr. Merriweather came in and saw you clowning around, he wouldn't let us come back."

"Now why would I ever do such a thing?" The old man's voice crackled from across the floor.

"Oh, h-hey Mr. Merriweather," Drew stammered.

"Did you get to the showroom yet?" he asked.

"No sir, not yet."

He bent down in front of me. "You see those two big doors over there, Cody? On the other side is where we display our coffins to the customers. Why don't you go take a gander? I'd like to talk to your brother."

"After that, can I feed Happy again?"

"Of course," he said, patting me on the shoulder. "Just come back to my office after you've had your look around."

Unlike the rest of the factory, the showroom was serene and brightly lit. Sunlight radiated down from a skylight onto a huge oriental rug. Plush, overstuffed high-back chairs and a tufted leather sofa circled a thick mahogany table stacked with brochures. Twelve different models of coffins lined the walls, ranging from a basic pine rectangle to a gold-plated, black walnut one with platinum handles. Each was open to display their comfy interior. The idea of hopping into one floated by me then I remembered Happy. I rushed back to Mr. Merriweather's office where I found him and Drew in the middle of a handshake.

"Welcome aboard, my boy!" he said, slapping Drew on his shoulder.

"Where's Happy?" I asked.

A tiny poke in my back instantly revealed my new friend's whereabouts. I spun on my heels. Like a little Oliver Twist, he stood crouched over, peering up at me with his arms stretched out, his hands cupped together in hopes I would deposit something tasty in them.

"Hold on, little fella," I said, reaching into my pocket and pulling out the one that was still in the shell. "Shoot, all I've got is this one. Can I get one of yours, Drew?"

"Sorry, buddy. I gave him my last one a few minutes ago."

I turned my palms open to him. "I'm sorry, Happy. I don't have any more."

He blinked pitifully at me.

"But I don't have any more." I dug my hands back into my pockets and pulled them inside out, producing a single piece of lint along with my Pez dispenser which fell at my feet. "Sir, can Happy have candy?"

"Come to think of it, I don't think he's ever had any. But sure, you can bring some with you next time."

"I've got some right here." I pulled the dispenser's Mickey Mouse head back and popped out a quarter-inch candy brick.

"Well, I'll be. Is that—"

"It's candy, Mr. Merriweather. A peppermint one. So it's okay to give it to him?"

"Sure!"

I knelt in front of Happy, hoping to make my offering more sincere. I dropped my treat into his hands, still cupped together.

His head rocked side to side while his hands rotated back and forth as he studied the sweet little rectangle. Instead of chomping down on it, he sniffed it then raised it behind his head as if about to dispose of it as he had the pecan in the shell.

"No, no, it's good!" I quickly tossed another one into my mouth. "Mmmm, yummy," I said, tempting him on.

He eyed me suspiciously then slowly raised the peppermint to his mouth. His tongue swiped it once followed immediately with a shake of the head that made his lips flap. Another swipe of the tongue followed, then another and another. Each new lick came with a bounce that turned into dancing, that turned into a joyous romp around the office. He finished by leaping onto Mr. Merriweather's desk where he plopped down onto his rear end and proceeded to gnaw his treat into oblivion.

"Sweet Jehoshaphat!" Mr. Merriweather exclaimed. "I've never seen him so excited over anything."

"Did you like it, Hap—"

Before I could finish, he flung himself across my chest and wrapped his arms around my neck. He rubbed his fuzzy little face against mine, then with a tilt of his head, he pressed his lips to my cheek and gave me three quick pecks before jumping down and running out into his Happy Place.

Mr. Merriweather and Drew stood staring at his exit.

"Wow! That was awesome! Did you see that? He gave me a hug. He actually gave me a real, honest-to-goodness hug."

"I think he even kissed you," Drew said.

"He's *never* given me a kiss," Mr. Merriweather added with a hint of jealousy.

I continued gazing down at the door. "Wowwww…"

"You wanna hear what else is wow?" Drew said.

"What?"

"Can I tell him?" he said, turning to Mr. Merriweather.

"Of course."

"Listen to this, little brother. Beginning tomorrow afternoon I'm going to be an official employee of the Fletcher and Son Coffin Company."

"That's *if* your parents agree to it," Mr. Merriweather added.

"That's soooo awesome."

"As soon as school's out, I'm coming straight here and working until quitting time. Mr. Merriweather's going to be my boss."

The old man smiled warmly. "Remember, that's *if* your parents agree."

"It's just my mom," Drew said.

"Oh, I'm sorry to hear that."

"That's okay," I chimed in. "He, uh, well, my dad was…" Drew's blank expression halted my stuttering, causing me to change direction. "Can I have a job too? Maybe I could take care of Happy. He probably needs a helper, don't you think?"

Mr. Merriweather patted me on the head. "As much as I'd like to hire you both, I'm afraid I can only take on Drew since he's old enough. We'll talk about you later." He leaned down to me. "But you can come over anytime you want while he's here. I'm sure Happy would love the company. Especially if you bring your Mickey Mouse friend."

"Yeah, I can do that."

"Then it's settled. Drew, if your mom's good with the arrangement, I'll see you back here tomorrow after school. And it would be my pleasure to have the young Mr. Cody in tow as well."

I giggled at how Mr. Merriweather worked my toe into his sentence, but I was pleased to know it was okay for me to tag along.

The coffin factory's spell had both Drew and me smiling like a couple of idiots as we made our way back to the foyer where Drew proceeded to announce his hiring to Ms. Haverstach, the lady with the beehive hairdo.

"Mr. Merriweather told me to tell you I'm to report here tomorrow to fill out some paperwork."

"What kind of paperwork would that be, Mr. Edwards?"

"The hiring kind."

"Is that right?"

My brother's chest couldn't have been puffed any larger. "Yes ma'am!"

"Well, alright then. I'll be expecting you at…"

"Three thirty," Drew said, opening the front door. "Right after school. Bye, Ms. Haverstach!"

When our feet hit the steps, our excitement poured out. "What'd I tell you! It's nothing like what we thought it was."

"I know. It wasn't scary at all. It was—nice. It was more than nice. It was…"

"Awesome!" we shouted together.

"And how about Happy?"

"Boy, howdy! I can't wait to tell the gang. First thing I'm gonna do is…" My thought suddenly faded as I watched a long silver car slowly pull to the curb and stop directly in front of us.

"That's one of those Cadillacs," Drew gushed, "like the mayor drives around in."

We watched as a large man in a black suit and matching black captain's hat stepped out of the driver's seat. He walked to the back door as ramrod straight as the soldiers at President Kennedy's funeral. A second later he pulled it open, immediately stiffening back into attention as a tall man with slicked-back, salt-and-pepper hair and wearing a long black overcoat emerged. Everything about him was squared off with the kind of solid good looks I knew Mary Lib would have gone gaga over.

"He could be from the movies," I whispered to Drew.

While he straightened his collar, a younger man stepped out behind him. A half foot shorter, he had the same handsome features and tight frame. The only other difference was his dark, buzz-cut hair style, a teenage replica of Drew's G.I. Joe come to life.

With the factory as their target, they made a beeline to the front doors, brushing past us without so much as a nod, leaving the driver standing guard by the Cadillac.

"Let's go ask the big guy who that was."

"No, let's not," Drew said.

"I'm gonna go ask him." I turned to the man, who now appeared another foot taller. His eyes drew down into tiny slits as a corner of his mouth crept up into a snarl aimed directly at me. "Uh, yeah, I think we'd better just get on back home."

Chapter 5

The next day, Drew and I took every opportunity to share our coffin-factory adventure with anyone who would listen. Drew kept the story in line with every detail, down to the step-by-step order that it happened, while I provided the exclamation points with the biggest, most power-packed words I could muster. When Drew said Mr. Merriweather was nice, I added that his smile made you feel like you could fly. When he described the finishing room, I chimed in with, "Did you know there's more than a million things they have to do to make a coffin?" And when he began talking about Happy, I launched into a rambling tale of how I could swear I'd met a miniature furry kid with magical powers.

When my embellishments became too much of a burden to his story, he slapped me on the shoulder. "Would you please hush?"

"Sorry," I said, falling back in line with the rest of his audience, still hanging on his every word as if hearing it for the first time.

When the school bell rang that afternoon, most of our crew

had already assembled on Maudie's back porch, clamoring for admission to our new playground.

Cackles bopped from foot to foot. "What're we waitin' on?"

"Patience," Mary Lib said. "We gotta be patient."

"Wait for me," Peeps shouted, running across the orchard and waving a handful of nuts over his head. "I got something for—"

Into the air his glasses and pecans flew as he went bumbling onto the ground, thanks to Big Bertha, the orchard's largest tree root and main nemesis to our carefree romps.

"Dad blame it!" He rubbed his leg with one hand while scrounging for his spectacles.

Cackles gulped air, ready to unleash a building belly laugh, until Drew held out his hand and squelched the eruption. "I'm sorry, guys. I'd like to take you, but I can't."

Mary Lib's shoulders fell. "How come?"

"It's my first day and I gotta learn what I'm doing. Besides, I need to ask Mr. Merriweather if I can bring anybody else."

"But I can go," I said, raising my chin to a noble height. "I'm helping take care of Happy. I'm gonna—"

Drew gave me the hidden look Mom always used when she wanted us to hold our tongues.

"Don't worry. I promise I'll ask him and then maybe tomorrow. Okay?"

"Okay what?" Peeps said, bending over to catch his breath from his sprint to the porch.

"What happened to your glasses?" I asked.

"One of the lenses popped out when I tripped over Bertha. That's okay, I got another pair. Are we ready to go?"

"He can't take us," Cackles groaned. "His stupid boss man won't let us in."

"That's not it. I just have to ask him."

"Come on, guys," Mary Lib said. "Let's play roller-bat. Peeps, can you see out of one eye good enough to pitch?"

"Sure. I'll just close the one."

"Make sure you don't close the wrong one," Cackles cracked.

Mary Lib smiled at Drew. "Tomorrow though, right?"

He returned a gentle nod. "You'll be first," he mouthed.

True to his word, the next day Drew had Mary Lib meet him early so they could sneak over to the factory with me following along. The fun of watching him play tour guide again was almost as entertaining as my first day. What made the afternoon truly special was seeing her reaction to how Happy and I played together. While Mr. Merriweather had Drew counting coffin handles and hinges, I used my Pez candy to manage my one-monkey circus. With my Mickey Mouse dispenser as my secret weapon, I brought her to tears from laughing as I coaxed him into performing his little jig. Making it even funnier was how he giggled just at the sight of Mickey's head bending backward to spit out his treats.

So it went for the next few weeks. Every day Drew and I went to the factory accompanied by a different one of our gang. Mr. Merriweather said he'd allow more later, but for now he didn't want to give Happy too much to think about. So, like our softball games, we rotated through our lineup of friends for their time at the factory. Only once did the order alter when Peeps had to forego his turn for an appointment with the eye doctor.

Day by day Drew's friendship with Mr. Merriweather grew stronger as did his knowledge of the factory and its workers. It wasn't long before he knew most of them by their first name as well as every stage of the coffin-making process. Mr. Merriweather loved to show off Drew's knowledge to new employees by having him provide their introductory tour. When asked how old his protégé was, he would simply say, "Old enough."

Meanwhile, my relationship with Happy was also growing to where he would do just about anything for me, even without the treats. I would laugh and he'd laugh with me. I'd pretend to cry, and he'd ball up his fist and rub his eyes. I'd say, "Let's go outside," and he'd bolt out into his Happy Place only to come back a little later and pretend to tug me through his private little doorway. I would even mess with him by giving him a pecan in its shell, which he'd pretend he was about to throw back at me then stop and giggle.

For the remainder of the school year Drew and I rarely missed a day at the factory and neither did our friends. The rotation continued into the first week of the seventh grade when, out of the blue, Mr. Merriweather informed us it was time to invite all our friends over that Saturday.

"You want them to come all at once?" Drew said.

"Of course. If you're going to have a birthday party, you want all your friends there, don't you?"

"It's your birthday?"

"No," he said with a cheeky grin. "It's Happy's!"

Both our jaws dropped with a singular gasp. Just as we'd

never thought to venture into our friend Reubin's family life, we never thought to ask about a monkey's birthday.

"That's fantastic! Are you sure?"

"Absolutely. Can you get them here by noon?"

"Sure."

"Perfect. Since we shut down at one o'clock, we can celebrate the last hour of the day."

I grabbed Drew's arm. "Man, oh man, do I have the perfect cake—well, it's more of a pie than a cake." I started to pace in circles when Happy climbed onto my shoulder. I reached up to give him a pat. "You're going to love what I'm gonna get for you," I giggled, and he patted my head and giggled along with me.

Just before noon that Saturday, Gonny walked me out of the house with a white box. "Don't let him eat too much—he'll get sick."

"I won't."

She began wrapping a blue ribbon around it. "Did you know dogs get sick when they eat chocolate?"

"No ma'am," I said, tapping my feet, eagerly awaiting her wrapping to be completed.

"Well, they do. So mind you watch the little fella's appetite." She wiped her hands on her apron. "Now off you go. And tell him Gonny said, 'Happy birthday!'" she shouted as I sprinted off to Maudie's where the gang was waiting.

Drew flashed me a knowing smile upon seeing the box. Before he could say anything, everyone was off to the races, with Peeps and his skinned-up knees and handful of nuts leading the way, and Mary Lib and her mother's Polaroid camera close behind. Before Drew and I even reached the street, they were already at the entrance, jockeying for position to be first in.

Drew cut his way to the front. "Gee whiz! You guys act like you've never been here before."

"This is different," Reubin said, appearing from around the corner. "This is Happy's birthday."

"Hey, buddy! Glad you could make it," Drew said.

Reubin displayed his marble pouch. "I got him a special tiger eye."

"I don't think I'd do that," I warned. "If he tries to eat it, he'll get upset and you don't want him chunkin' a tiger eye back at ya."

"Come on," Drew snickered. "Let's get this show on the road."

As he was reaching for the door, it suddenly swung open and startled him. He stumbled back on me, causing me to drop my box. I stomped my foot as an obnoxious whiff of musky cologne suddenly filled my nostrils.

The man responsible for Drew's stumble and my box being grounded came huffing outside, the overpowering scent trailing behind him like an invisible cloud.

Forgetting my box, I looked up just in time to leap out of his way as he marched to the street corner. Over his shoulder he barked, "This isn't a playground. It's a business." A moment later a long silver Cadillac pulled up and he disappeared inside.

"Drew, that's the guy. Remember—the movie guy from way back?"

"Yeah. Wonder why he's so mad."

"Maybe somebody died in his family, and he was here buying a coffin," Peeps said.

"That's probably it," Mary Lib added. "People either get sad or mad when—"

"You gotta be kidding me," I groaned, staring down at the footprint that now appeared dead center on my box. I picked up the smushed container and pulled the crumpled bow off. My eyes glared back at the Cadillac as it rounded the corner out of sight. "Dead relative or not, you don't have to be a jerk," I muttered.

Drew put a hand to my shoulder. "Come on, little brother. He won't know the difference."

"I reckon," I said flatly.

As we walked inside, Ms. Haverstash was seated behind her desk with the junior Mr. Fletcher leaning over her and whispering in her ear. She held a handkerchief to her nose and appeared to be studying the floor.

Upon seeing us, he bolted straight. "Why hello, young people," he said cheerfully. "I assume you're all here for Happy?"

"Yes sir," Drew said.

"You can head on back. Mr. Merriweather should be waiting for you."

"What's wrong with the place today?" I said as we made our way through the factory. "It's not quittin' time yet and none of the machines are running and why's everybody just standing around talking?"

"Search me. Maybe it's got something to do with Happy's birthday."

When we arrived at Mr. Merriweather's office, we found him sitting behind his desk and staring down at Happy's tiny door. Dozens of balloons and streamers were scattered about the office. A cardboard sign hung from the shelves behind his desk read, "Happy Birthday, Happy!"

Cackles poked my arm then pointed to the board. "Looky there, he stutters when he writes," she giggled.

"Mr. Merriweather?" Drew said.

He continued gazing at the door without a reply.

Drew knocked on the wall. "Sir, we're all here. Mr. Merriweather—"

"Oh my!" He spun in his chair, blinking away whatever was occupying his thoughts. "I'm so sorry. I-I was just—well—I was just thinking about today's party." He smiled. "Children! Welcome!"

"Is he outside?" I asked.

"Yes. He just went out, so let's give him about fifteen minutes then you can call him in, and we'll sing to him. How's that sound?"

"Sounds good to me."

"Why's everything so quiet?" Drew asked. "The men aren't working. It's not quitting time, is it?"

He scratched his sideburns as he gazed back at the door to the factory. "Uh—no, it's not," he said, his mind appearing to wander. "Listen, I need to go out on the floor for just a bit. Make yourselves at home. There's lemonade on the table. I'll be back shortly."

Mary Lib began laughing. "This is going to sound so funny."

"What is?" I asked.

"Singing 'Happy Birthday' to Happy. Is there something we can say instead of, 'Happy birthday, dear Happy'? Sounds kind of—"

"Stupid?" Cackles blurted.

"It's his name, people," I said. "Besides, he won't know who we're singing to unless we use his name."

Mr. Merriweather's stooped frame always made him

appear every one of his seventy-two years, but when he came back in, he looked like another five had just been added.

Drew helped him to his desk. "Are you okay, sir?"

"Yes, yes, I'm fine. Just a busy day is all. If you don't mind, I might sit during the festivities."

"Of course. You rest. I'll take care of everything."

With my brother's nod as my cue, I poked my head out the tiny door and shouted for the monkey of the hour to come back inside. In less than five seconds Happy was bouncing back into the office and jumping up into my arms. "Happy birthday, fella!"

Mary Lib motioned toward me. "Everybody bunch up around them. "Come on. Closer now." She squinted into her Polaroid viewfinder. "That's it. Okay, here we go. One—two—three!"

"Happy birthday, Happy!" everyone yelled.

In a flash he was on my shoulder, bouncing and clapping his hands along with the rest of us.

"See, I told ya he'd know it was his birthday!"

Drew handed me my newly flattened box.

Placing it on Mr. Merriweather's desk, I slowly lifted the lid. "Okay, boy, here you go…"

"That's not a cake," Peeps said.

"It's a flattened pie, is what it is," Cackles added.

"A pecan pie," Reubin said, almost drooling. "My favorite."

Happy dove off me and landed smack-dab in the middle of his treat, splattering syrup-covered pecans and crust onto Mr. Merriweather's white shirt. His little hands were a blur as he furiously began shoveling it into his mouth.

Mr. Merriweather flicked a piece of crust from his breast

pocket. "I think he's rather fond of pecan pie. How clever of you to think of it, Mr. Cody."

When Happy had eaten half the pie, Drew closed the lid. "Sorry, Happy, you'll get sick if you eat any more."

To my surprise he was okay with Drew cutting him off, deciding to use his sugary high by pouncing on every balloon until it popped. Each burst sent him bouncing and us laughing raucously, all except Mary Lib who stood frowning at the square image that slid out from her camera.

"Mr. Merriweather, would you mind if we get some pics in the showroom? This one didn't come out so good. The background and lights are so much better in there."

"Sure. I sent everybody home earlier, so you've got the run of the place."

"You want to come along? I'd like to get some with you."

"No thank you, honey. I'm feeling a little peaked. I'll stay here if that's okay."

"I think I'll stay too," Drew said. "I'm going to clean up. I'll come when I'm finished."

She smiled. "Alright, lead the way, monkey boy."

With Happy clinging to my back, we marched through the finishing room and into the ornate world of the showroom.

"This is perfect," she said, scanning the space like a movie director. "Here's what we're gonna do."

For the next ten minutes we followed her instructions, posing against the walls, doors and windows. We even lay on the huge oriental rug while she stood on a chair shooting down on us.

As we began running out of poses, Cackles began running out of patience. "This is getting boring," she said.

"I know what we can do," Reubin said. "Let's play

marbles on the rug. The circle in the middle can be out of bounds."

"No, I got it!" I said, clasping my hands together. "Let's lie in the coffins. We'll pretend we're dead."

"What a great idea!" was the resounding response from everyone.

Mary Lib checked her camera. "I only have two pics left, so we gotta make 'em good. We want everybody included, so we've got to move four coffins side by side. Can we do that, Cody?"

"Easy-peasy, their tables have wheels. Peeps, why don't you take this brown one? I'll help you move it next to the smaller white one there. I've got dibs on it."

"How come?"

"It's just so neat. It's about my size and it's got those fancy gold maple leaves on the handles."

"I'll take this super-fancy one," Reubin said, heaving the gold-plated onyx model into place.

"Okay, mister snazzy pants," Cackles huffed, "I guess I'll have to take the el cheapo pine box there."

"Let me help," I said.

"No, no, you high-and-mighties take care of your own. It probably only weighs five pounds."

Sure enough, by the time we had ours lined up, hers was already in place.

Mary Lib clapped her hands. "Okay, hop on in!"

Cackles suddenly belted out a tidal wave of uncontrollable laughter.

"Hush!" I said. "If Mr. Merriweather catches us, he'll skin us alive. Worse, he'll never let us come back."

Cackles jammed her fists into her cheeks. "I'm sorry, Cody boy," she squeezed out. "This is just so weird."

"Hurry up before she blows again," I said.

"I can't see your face because Happy's on your chest," Mary Lib said. "Can you nudge him down?"

I pushed him to my stomach. "How's that?"

"Good. Okay, on three. One—two—three. Got it! Alright, one more and that's it. Ready, one—"

"Wait, can you take Happy? I want to do it like a vampire. All you guys keep your lids open. I'm gonna close mine but have my hand sticking out."

"Oh yeah. That'll be spooky," Peeps said.

I tossed my Pez dispenser to Mary Lib. "Pop out a candy and he'll come to you."

As soon as he saw the peppermint drop to her palm, he was out of the coffin and bobbing up and down on the table next to her. "Here you go, little buddy."

Seeing him take the bait, I closed my coffin, leaving just my fingers out.

The last thing I heard was Mary Lib's muffled voice. "No! Happy, stop!"

Chapter 6

"You can come on out now, Mr. Dracula." The words softly rose through the darkness, pulling me back. The moment Mary Lib raised the coffin lid, my eyes flashed wide.

I stared straight above me into the ceiling, not moving my head. The silhouette of her choppy blonde hair hovered above me.

"Come on. You don't want us to get caught, do you?"

"Wha-what happened?"

"We took the picture," Mary Lib said. "I'm sorry it's not going to come out like you wanted though. Happy just can't bear being away from you."

"I don't get it. How'd I fall asleep like that?"

"Sleep? I kinda doubt it," she snorted.

"What do you mean? I was in there for a while. Long enough to have a dream anyway." I rose up to find everyone standing next to their coffins and staring at me.

"If five seconds is what you call a while," Cackles said, "then you need to go back to first grade."

Mary Lib's eyes moved across my face then up to the top of my head. "Did the lid hit you when Happy landed on it?"

"I-I don't remember." My hand found the back of my head.

"Here, let me see," she said, running her fingers through my hair. "I don't feel any bumps. You're okay."

My chest tightened. "How long were you out, Peeps?"

"I wasn't. I mean, I didn't fall asleep if that's what you're askin'."

"Reubin, Cackles, what about you guys?"

Both shook their heads, their eyes bearing down on me with the same curiosity we all had for the dead cat we found next to the root cellar the week before.

I slapped my knee and gave a hardy laugh. "You guys are too much. You really had me going." I took a deep breath. "Seriously though, how long was my snooze?"

"You didn't have time to sleep," Mary Lib said. "As soon as you pulled the lid down, Happy jumped on it and slammed it shut. I'm surprised you didn't get your fingers smashed. He did some kind of dance then bounced off."

"But—"

"Look here," she said, pulling the picture from the Polaroid. "That blur's him bolting."

"Maybe you're a speed dreamer," Cackles said.

Mary Lib rolled her eyes. "There's no way you can fall asleep in a second, dream for another second, then wake up the next. I say the lid hit your head and made you think it all happened."

"My granddaddy fell down a well once," Reubin chimed in. "He whacked his head on the way down and woke up an hour later and swore to everybody and the Lord Almighty he'd been down there for a year." He paused. "Grandaddy said his bottle of corn liquor helped him remember it all."

"What're you guys doing!"

Drew's sudden appearance in the doorway caused us all to flinch.

"Oh shoot, we're busted," Cackles said.

"Dang right you're busted! Lucky for you criminals Mr. Merriweather's still in his office. Now get those coffins back where they were. The factory's closed now and we've gotta go. Cody, take Happy back to him while I lead these hoodlums out of here. I'll see you back at the house."

"Can I at least tell you something first? Something that just happened that—"

"No! Just wait until we're home like I said."

Drew's demand jolted me. "I-I'm sorry. I'll take him back right now." I swung Happy onto my shoulder and ran him back to Mr. Merriweather's.

By the time I got home, I had rehearsed a dozen ways to begin my explanation of my experience in the coffin, not sure which one to go with. But when I found Drew on the front porch, I didn't go with any of them. He sat in a wicker chair, his head in his hands.

"What's wrong?"

His head lowered farther as he snuck his collar up to his eyes to wipe away a tear he didn't want me to see.

"Is something wrong with Mr. Merriweather?"

"Kinda."

"Is he sick? He's not sick, is he? Please don't tell me he's gonna die."

"No, it's nothing like that. It's the factory. It's shutting down."

"What! Why?"

"It's being sold. They're going to make it into a lumber company."

"Well, that's okay, isn't it? Either a coffin factory or a lumber company. They're nearly the same thing."

"I don't think so. At least I don't think the new owner thinks that."

"So what's it mean?"

"Mr. Merriweather said he'll probably lose his job. It won't be right away because they're going to keep making coffins for a little while until they switch it over. But whenever that happens, he'll have to move."

"When?"

"He said maybe six months."

"Will he take Happy?"

"Of course. Happy belongs to him. They're a family. He'll have to go with him."

"Stupid lumber company! Who are these people? Why'd they have to come here anyway? Stupid lumber people."

"Remember the guy who barged out the building when we were coming in, the one with all that smelly cologne, the one who got into the Cadillac?"

"The movie guy?"

"That's the one. He just moved into town a couple months ago."

"That's the jerk that smashed Happy's pie!" I kicked the porch railing.

"What's even worse is I can't work there anymore. Mr. Merriweather said the guy told him they were already overstaffed so he couldn't tell him about me."

I kicked the railing again. "Stupid, smelly lumber man!"

Drew's head dropped. When he raised it again, he calmly asked, "What was it you wanted to tell me in the showroom?"

I looked at him. His eyes were puffy, red, and sad. "Oh, it was nothing," I replied softly.

"I'm sorry I yelled at you."

"It's okay. I would've yelled at me too."

Several minutes passed without either of us saying anything. "I think I'll go inside for a while," I finally said.

Whenever I felt mopey, I retreated to my room and buried myself in a comic book, or if I was really feeling down, I'd write out my thoughts—a practice Mom had taught us for battling the worst cases of the blues. Not caring for a comic, I was ready to write. As I sat trying to piece together my feelings about losing Happy and the sadness of watching Drew mourn over losing Mr. Merriweather, my thoughts rolled over to the increasingly fuzzy images from the time I'd spent in the coffin.

The next day began in church as it had for as many Sundays as I could remember. Our whole family walked two blocks down Tucker Street to the Methodist church where we had fidgeted through so many hours of Pastor Wilson's sermons. There would be no squirming in the pews that day as Drew and I squeezed our eyes tighter and clasped our hands harder than we'd ever done before, praying the Lord would smite the lumber man's plans to kingdom come.

The following week was as dismal for our gang as it was for the grown-ups during the days that followed President Kennedy's assassination. Instead of rushing off to the coffin factory after school, we lugged our way through games of kick the can and Simon Says. There were no séances or conjuring of the dead, no gathering of pecans for Happy, just more hours of nothingness. We didn't think the week could get any worse.

We were wrong.

Just after recess that Friday, the shrill cry of a passing siren interrupted the usually cheerful chirping of birds around the schoolhouse lawn. Seconds later another came, followed by another, and another. Within minutes, the vehicles creating the blaring noise had congregated somewhere down the road, filling the air with their dreadful racket. Teachers halted classes, craned their necks out windows, then quickly pulled back inside with their hands over their mouths. When I tried running outside to see what was happening, my teacher jumped in front of me and ordered me back to my seat.

As part of some new routine, the principal dropped by our classes to confer with them in hushed tones, all of which ended with the teachers clutching their hearts—some weeping, some stumbling to take a seat.

When the final bell released us that day, me and every other student raced outside to find out where the commotion had come from. Spying Drew across the lawn, I ran up to him. "What happened?"

"I don't know. Nobody does."

"Nobody in the eleventh grade knows? I thought you guys knew everything," I said jokingly.

He looked up and down the street, ignoring another one of my attempts to bring him out of his depression. "Come on, let's go home."

Halfway there, I heard a car door slam from the other side of our house.

"I bet that's Mom!" I said, sprinting off without him.

My heart sank when I turned the corner. Instead of my mother, who I was hoping had come home early for the weekend, it was Pastor Wilson.

"Is it her?" Drew said, trotting up behind me.

"No, it's just the preacher."

A plump, bearded man noted for his good nature and easy smile, our pastor was Santa Claus in a vestment. Upon spotting us, however, all he could muster was a slight rise in a tense upper lip, the type he reserved for communion when giving out his tiny breadcrumbs.

"Why do you think he's here?" I asked.

Drew didn't answer; he just began walking faster. Both our paces quickened as the sounds of a woman's wailing suddenly poured out the back door and into the orchard.

"What's wrong, Drew? What's going on?"

He stopped short of going in, holding his arm out to prevent me from passing. "Just wait."

Together we stood on the back steps, watching our pastor through the screen door wrap his arms around Gonny.

"What's he saying?" I asked.

Drew angled his ear closer to the door. Holding his breath, he didn't blink. He stood motionless, focusing on the clergyman's words, straining to piece the syllables together into a clear sentence. "Oh no," he muttered. "Noooo."

"What is it?"

He backed down the steps, still staring at the screen door. I grabbed his arm. "What'd you hear? Tell me."

"It's Irvin-Dell."

"What about him?"

"He-He's dead."

"What!"

"He-He was hit by a car, walking home today."

I turned in the direction of his house. "All those sirens were…"

He nodded, then tried to say something, but all he could do was just shake his head.

Neither of us knew what to say. We just stood as the birds' chirping mingled with the sorrow of our grandmother's weeping.

For two days Drew and I walked on eggshells, fearful of saying or doing anything to upset the grown-ups. Our only job was staying out of Gonny's way as she helped the grieving family prepare for Irvin-Dell's funeral.

On the morning of the third day, our mother pulled into the driveway in her beat-up Chevy. Wearing her best black dress, she ran up to meet us, squeezing us in her arms tighter than she'd ever done before.

"Are you boys doing okay?"

"Yes ma'am," we replied.

She smiled. "I need to go help Gonny. In the meantime, you can stay outside and play."

"But that wouldn't be right," I said.

"You don't think Irvin-Dell would want you to play?"

"I-I don't know. Maybe."

"If it was you, wouldn't you want your friends to be happy?"

"Sure I would."

"Well then, Irvin-Dell would too. So you go on now. Go play."

I'd always welcomed those two words, but today there was no playing to be done. Today, "go play" felt like a chore. With no other kids around, Drew and I simply wandered aimlessly about the backyard, plucking an occasional muscadine from PaPa's grapevines, or picking up pecans only to toss them back into the orchard. Mostly we just searched the ground, biding our time as we waited for our mother to summon us back to the house in preparation for another trip to the church.

Chapter 7

Tired of my wasted attempts to keep busy, I finally found a productive use of my time by squatting next to an old tree stump on the far side of the pecan orchard and counting the rings. "You'll never guess how old this tree was," I called out to Drew.

A few seconds later he was trotting up to me. "I couldn't hear you. What'd you say?"

"I said guess how old this tree was."

"I don't know, forty or fifty years."

"Sixty-two."

"Wow, it was just a twig when PaPa was born." He started to reach into his pocket. "Guess what I just found?"

"The lens to Peeps' glasses," I blurted.

"How'd you know?"

I stared blankly at his hand as he pulled it out.

"I found it next to—"

"A sparrow's feather." My words continued to spill out without any thought. "It was lying on top of it."

He squinted back in the direction where the feather still lay. "How in the world did you see that itty-bitty thing all the way over here?"

"Boys!" Mom's voice rang out. "Time to get ready."

"You're not going to believe this…" I began.

"Come on!" she said, holding the back door open. "We can't be late."

Drew started for the house, stopped a moment as he began to speak, then ran inside with me on his heels.

My fifteen-minute grooming session ended with Mom attaching my clip-on tie then spitting into her hand and pressing it down on my cowlick. Drew, having mastered the skill of church prepping years earlier, stood pressed and ready to go in his matching dark-gray suit.

Several minutes later we were all out the door, the rest of the neighborhood falling in behind us. Together we made our way down Tucker Street in a somber march to the church where Irvin-Dell's body lay waiting for us to say our goodbyes.

By the time we got there, every pew was packed, leaving the last two rows for us to cram into. With this being my and Drew's first funeral, we sat ramrod straight, taking the lead from the grown-ups for how to behave. To my surprise it was much like a regular sermon except for the focus being on Irvin-Dell. At times it was even funny as Pastor Wilson told stories of his mischievous nature and his ability to make family and friends smile. But when he talked about how he made his mother laugh one day when she was feeling down by singing "Twinkle, Twinkle, Little Star" and substituting *wrinkle* for *twinkle,* I—along with the rest of the congregation—wept.

Following a short prayer, each pew filed out in a slow, orderly progression. With my mother behind me and Drew in front, I walked with my head lowered, watching his steps to know when to go forward. It was only when he'd finished his moment in front of the coffin that I raised my head. Lying across a small table, topped with a half-dozen white roses, the coffin looked like a snowcapped mountain. As I stood with my hands clasped in front of me, the sounds of sniffling and the moans of his mother suddenly faded as my focus moved to the coffin's gold handles and their maple-leaf design. I gasped.

My mother wrapped her arm around me and whispered, "It's okay, son." Then taking me by the hand, she led me down the other side of the church. I kept turning my head back, though, unable to get the golden leaves out of my mind.

"I hate funerals," Drew said, yanking his tie off and throwing it to the ground as we walked back to the house.

"Why, Drew Edwards, you pick that up right this minute," our mother said.

"Yes ma'am." His reply was as wilted as the shriveled piece of cloth he'd just flung away.

"When we get home, I want you boys to remember one thing."

Whenever Mom told us to remember one thing, it was often followed by another thing, usually something with consequences.

"I want you to remember to behave or else you'll find yourselves in your rooms until dinner."

I followed Drew into his room, and he immediately dropped face-first onto the lumpy mattress. "This has been the worst week ever," came his muffled voice.

"Drew, sit up a minute. There's something I need to tell you."

"I don't feel like talking any more today."

"This is important. Would you please sit up?"

He rolled over. "What is it?"

"Remember when you caught us in the showroom, and I said there was something I wanted to tell you?"

"Yeah."

"Well, I have to tell you now. You're not going to believe me, but I have to tell you."

"You guys shouldn't have been messin' around in there. It's not a—"

"I know, but just listen. The reason the coffins were all out of place is because Mary Lib had us bunch them together so she could take our picture in them."

He rolled his eyes.

"When we took the last picture, I fell asleep."

"In the coffin?"

"Yeah, or I kind of fell asleep. I-I'm not sure what I did but it was like I did."

"You're not making a lick of sense."

"What happened is I got in the coffin and was closing the lid when it shut on me. Next thing I know, Mary Lib's opening it up."

"Wow," he responded as flat as the paper-thin rug next to the bed. "That's a doozy of a story."

"No, that's not it. It's what happened when I was *in the coffin*. It's what I saw." I leaned toward him. "I saw things that happened today back then!"

"Today? Back then? What's that supposed to mean? Cody, you're making even less sense now."

"What I meant to say is that when I was in the coffin

and asleep, or whatever I was, I saw things that actually happened today. I saw you moving the feather and finding Peeps' lens and I saw Irvin-Dell's coffin. I saw the gold maple-leaf handles. They were just flashes of images, but they were there as clear as clear can be. Any minute now Mom's gonna come in to tell us *The Wizard of Oz* is on TV tonight and, if we want, we can invite friends over to watch it."

Drew reared his head back as if I'd just dangled a dead rat in front of his face. "You're crazy."

"I'm telling you. I saw this stuff."

He grabbed a pillow and buried his face in it.

"Listen to me, Drew. I'm—"

"Go away," he said, blindly pointing toward the door.

I jumped to the floor and ran to my room, returning with a small notepad. "This'll show you," I said, wrenching the pillow from his face.

"What're you doing, you little fart?"

I held up the pad in front of him. "This proves it."

"Proves what?"

"Just read it."

His drawn-out sigh gave me little hope he wanted anything to do with my request when suddenly he snatched it from me. After pretending to examine it, he tossed it back at me. "Done. Now go away."

"You didn't even read it." I pushed it back to him. "Would you really, really read it this time, pleeease?" Drew's stubbornness usually won the day, but something in my plea struck a chord. With a huff, he grabbed it back and gave it a halfhearted look-over. "All I see is a bunch of random words that…" His voice trailed off as his brows slowly arched upward along with a slow, curious tilt of his head.

"I see the one that says, 'Drew finds a sparrow's feather and finds Peeps' lens under it,' and the one that says, 'White coffin, gold handles with maple leaves.'" He stared back to the page, glanced up at me, then back to the page as he continued reading. "'Woman crying in church.'" He paused at the next sentences, his eyes growing larger with each word. "'Drew—throws—tie—on—ground.'"

Just then came a knock at the door and Mom stuck her head inside. "Dinner will be ready in an hour in case you want to go outside and play." She smiled. "How're you boys doing?"

"Fine," I replied.

"Drew? What about you, honey?"

"I-I'm fine."

"Gonny just told me PaPa will be home next week sometime. How about that?"

Typically, news of our grandfather's coming home would've had him dancing, but the record of my visions prevented his focus from going anywhere else.

"Are you sure you're okay?"

"Really, I'm fine."

"Let me know if you're not, okay?"

"I will," he replied.

The moment the door shut, all Drew's attention fell back onto the page. A few seconds later Mom poked her head back inside.

"I forgot to tell you. *The Wizard of Oz* is on TV tonight. If you guys want to invite any of the gang over, you can. Just let me know so I can have enough popcorn ready."

While she spoke, Drew's eyes remained fixed on the notebook as he unknowingly mouthed each word on the page. After she'd left and closed the door again, he said, "When did you write all this?"

"The day we took the pictures in the coffin. I wrote down the images I saw when I was inside. That's what I wanted to tell you. I saw all this stuff on that day and now—"

"And now it's all happened…" His voice faded as he finished my sentence. "Over a week later all these—these visions or whatever they are—you saw?"

"I'll swear on a stack of Bibles, Drew. I saw 'em all clear as a bell. Well, except for the one that hasn't happened yet."

"Which one's that?"

"Turn the page. I didn't know how to describe it, so I just drew what I saw. It was moving fast and was real blurry."

Drew rotated the notepad one way, then the other. "Looks like a triangle flying through the sky. Is it one of those UFOs?"

"I don't know. Could be, I guess. All I remember is it was red, and moving so fast it was a blur."

Drew flipped the page back, fixating again on my list of visions. He swung his head back and forth. "None of this is possible. Nobody can see the future."

"I know, but it happened. I promise. Get me that stack of Bibles. I'll swear right here and now on all of 'em."

"How come you wrote this stuff down?"

"I wrote it because I had to!"

His eyes darted to the door. "Would you simmer down?"

"I can't simmer down. It's all making me crazy. I don't know what happened, but it did." I felt my eyes welling with tears. "I-I'm sorry but what I saw was real. I had to write it down like Mom taught us."

"Alright, alright. Just don't cry. Listen, we need to do more research."

"What do you mean?" I said, thrusting my finger at the notepad. "That's the research."

"No, little brother, that's what's called your conclusions. My science teacher says to get to conclusions you have to do research to figure out how you got 'em."

"So?"

"So, we need to go to where it happened and see if we can recreate it."

"You mean do it again?"

"Yeah, but this time we won't need anybody else. It'll just be you and me."

The spark in my brother's eyes told me his sense of adventure was dragging him out of the doldrums back to his old self. His eyes wandered through the room as he thought. "Okay," he said zeroing back on me. "We have an hour before dinner. That gives us plenty of time to run to the coffin factory and set things up. I'll ask Mr. Merriweather for some random favor—no, better yet, we'll say we just wanted to see Happy. While we're there, I'll jimmy Happy's door so it doesn't lock."

"You can do that?"

"Yeah, Mr. Merriweather showed me how when Happy started locking himself out. I just have to plug the strike plate with a piece of wood."

"What?"

"Don't worry about it. You just concentrate on conjuring up more images."

"But why do you need to keep Happy's door open?"

"Because we'll be going back later tonight when the factory's closed."

"Why can't we just ask Mr. Merriweather if we can hop in the coffins really quick?"

Drew looked at me as if I had two heads. "Those coffins are like pieces of art for him. He'd never let us do that. Besides, he's told me more than once how sacred they are."

"Can't we just ask? I'm not sure about going back at night."

"You gettin' scared?"

"N-no, it's just that, well, yeah, I guess a little."

"Cody, how many hours have you spent over there since I started working there?"

"A lot."

"And you like it, right? No ghosts or goblins or anything, right?"

"Yeah, but you never know what goes on there at night."

He smiled. "Sure you do. It's the same place, with or without lights."

"Cackles told me, 'You gotta be careful—the gates of hell can pop up anywhere, anytime.'"

"I also remember Cackles saying if you carried an acorn on you all the time, you'd never grow old."

I laughed. "Yeah, I think old man Kunkle's been carrying one for years. His must be busted."

Drew slapped my shoulder. "So you ready?"

"Sure! Let's go see Happy."

Chapter 8

Instead of going through the coffin factory's front door, Drew led me to the back.

"Why're we going this way?" I asked.

"I don't want to take a chance of running into the new owner so we're going through Happy's door."

After squeezing through the tiny entrance, we were standing in Mr. Merriweather's office.

"What do we do now?"

"We just wait until he comes in," Drew said, jamming a small wooden cube into the little door's frame opposite its lock. He swung it open then shut. "Perfect."

Several minutes later Mr. Merriweather came in, his head down, his black book under his arm.

"Hello sir!" Drew exclaimed with such over-the-top enthusiasm that it sent the old man staggering back into the door. He dropped his ledger.

"My heavens! You gave me a start."

"I'm sorry, sir. I didn't mean to scare you."

"No, no. That's just me not paying attention. Come here, my dear boy. Give me a hug."

Drew stepped into his outstretched arms.

"And you, Mr. Cody," he said with a smile I didn't think could get any bigger. "I've missed you too, and Happy's been especially eager to see you."

"Where is he?" I asked.

"I'm afraid you just missed him. I had to take him to the vet this afternoon and leave him overnight. They want to run some tests on him."

"Is something wrong?" I asked.

"Oh no. It's just a routine thing they do every few years with these types of simians."

"That means monkey," Drew said proudly as he picked up the book.

Mr. Merriweather clapped his hands together. "I'm so glad you dropped by. I have the best news. The new owner, Mr. Rosen, wants his son to learn part of the business, but he's not happy about it."

"Why's that good?" Drew asked.

"Rosen wants me to teach his boy the coffin-making side of things, but I told him if I was going to have to keep it going while managing the onboarding of the lumber business, I wouldn't have time." He pulled his glasses from his face, the sparkle in his eyes prompting a smile out of us even though neither knew why. "So, I went ahead and let the cat out of the bag and told him about you."

"You told him I worked here?"

His smile stretched wider.

"But I thought that would get you in trouble."

"Here's the thing. I can sense when a man's willing to make concessions. I also know a shifty character when I see one, and based on what I've heard and seen so far, Rosen is just that. He's the type of man that will make a deal with the devil if it gets him what he wants."

"I still don't follow."

"I told him you could teach his son."

"You did what?"

"I knew he really wanted him to learn the ropes, so I told him you were his best bet."

"You'd really trust me to do that?" Drew said.

"My boy, in all the years I've been doing this, I've never seen anybody pick up on it as fast as you. And you can come to me for what you don't know, and I'll tell you. No need to let anybody know you had to ask either." He stepped back, looking for my brother's response. "One thing though. It'll only be until he learns it all. But from what I've seen, that'll be a while. And once Rosen sees what a good job you do, he'll want to hire you on full-time, especially if he can pay you under the table. And if we do this right, he might just decide to keep the coffin business going."

"But I only want to work for you."

"That's the best part. You will."

"Then I'll do it! Of course, I'll do it!"

I'd never seen my brother dance, but the jittery-bounce thing he was doing was close.

"What about me, sir? Can I still come over and play with Happy?"

"Let me see how things go first. Can you be patient a little while?"

I bit down on my lower lip to keep it from sticking too far out. "Yes sir, I can wait—I guess."

"When do I start again? Soon, I hope," Drew said.

"Is this Friday after school soon enough?" he beamed.

"That's tomorrow!"

"I know!"

"Of course. Yes, tomorrow's fine!"

"Perfect. I'll introduce you to Slate then."

"Is that Mr. Rosen's son?"

"His name's actually Slater, but he likes to be called Slate." He cleared his throat. "One other thing you need to know. He's a year older than you, so he might take a high-and-mighty attitude. He's already a little snot, but this might make your job a little more difficult. Have you seen him at school yet?"

"No. I usually don't hang out with the older kids."

After scrounging through his desk drawer, Mr. Merriweather tossed Drew a quarter-sized leather ring with two keys on it. "The long silver one is to the black door on the side of the building and the tiny bronze one is to Happy's door." He smiled. "This time you'll be able to lock up if I leave early."

"Good gosh, don't drool all over 'em," I said, ragging Drew for his extended ogling of his new possession.

He swatted my arm. "Hush up," he said, chuckling at himself, realizing his absurd fascination with them. "Thank you. I promise not to let you down."

"I'm just glad to have you back, my boy. Things haven't been the same without you."

"I know," Drew said, his voice dropping. "It's been doubly bad with Irvin-Dell dying."

"I know." Mr. Merriweather's tone fell, matching Drew's. "I can't imagine how his parents are taking it."

"So you heard?"

"His uncle came in looking for a coffin for him. He told us some of what happened but not everything. The poor man couldn't make it through the details without getting choked up. I still can't believe they didn't even stop."

"What do you mean?"

"It was a hit-and-run. A car came around the corner and apparently sideswiped Irvin-Dell. And it barely missed hitting the little boy he was with. The driver just kept going."

I could feel my blood beginning to thump through my veins. "The police will get 'em," I said. "They'll throw 'em in jail for good. Just watch. They'll get 'em."

Mr. Merriweather scratched his sideburns. "Unless they find another witness, I don't think they will. The other little boy couldn't offer any real details. He was so shaken up all he could tell the police was the car had horns."

"Horns?" I said. "Like devil horns?"

He shrugged. "I don't know about the devil, but that's all he had to say."

"He was probably…" Drew paused. "What's the word they use in the army when they come back from battles?"

"I believe the term's *shell-shocked*. And you're probably right." He turned to the clock on the wall. "Well, how about that?" he said, taking the conversation down a brighter path. "It's quitting time. Drew, you've got your keys now so feel free to try them out tonight if you want. I'll see you boys later."

Drew stood beaming. "How 'bout them apples?"

"Boy, he sure thinks a lot of you. He's gotta be the nicest man I've ever met." I suddenly found myself bouncing as the thought entered my brain. "We won't have to come back tonight to do that research. We can do it right now!"

"I'm sorry, Cody, but I don't think I can do it now, not after he stuck his neck out on a limb like that for me."

"But you said you wanted to!"

"I know, but…well, it just wouldn't be right."

Desperate for him to see I hadn't imagined everything, I went straight to my trump card. "Drew, I'm your brother.

And you promised. You can't renege on a promise to family—not to me."

"It's not fair. You know how much pride he has in his work. He'd be heartbroken if he knew I went behind his back and defiled any of the coffins."

"Defiled?"

"It's when—never mind. I just can't do it. Plus, I'm starting to think—"

"You don't believe me now, do you?"

"I didn't say that. I'm just starting to think it could be your imagination and that somehow—"

"Oh, come on! I wouldn't make this stuff up."

"I just said I didn't think that. I said it could've been your imagination."

"It's the same thing. You gotta do this for me. You gotta see it was for real. Please, Drew! We can take off our shoes and I promise we won't mess anything up or do any defiling. Pleeease!"

My brother hemmed and hawed as he sometimes did over major decisions, but a minute later he slowly started to come around. "If we did this, you'd have to wear all clean clothes and take off your shoes *and* socks. Not a speck of dirt can be left on anything."

"I promise. Spick-and-span, head to toe. I'll be clean as clean can be."

He skewed his lips. "And if we do it, we're still going to wait until tonight. We gotta make sure there's no chance of anybody catching us."

"That's good with me. We've got the key, so it'll be easy-peasy."

"Okay, we'll do it. Right after Gonny goes to bed, we'll sneak out and come over."

"Now we're talkin'! I promise you'll see I wasn't makin' it up."

By the time the clock in the hall chimed nine times that evening, Gonny was already in bed. The sound of the kitchen fan whirring its nightly tune provided cover for our footsteps as we tiptoed through the house. Slowly we squeezed past the back screen door, making sure not to let it slam. The walk across the back lawn to Maudie's house started at a run, gradually slowing to a crawl the closer we came to the factory. A half-moon loomed over the factory's metal roof, transforming the building from the daytime wonderland it had become back into the sinister tomb we originally thought it to be.

"Sure is a lot different at night," I said.

"You okay?" Drew asked, fumbling between his keys and a flashlight he'd brought.

"I just wish we could've done this earlier."

The door swung in. "Well, we're here now so let's get with it."

During the day the factory was nonstop noise and motion, a controlled chaos of productivity. At night it was silent and deathly calm, an image more befitting the products being manufactured. Cackles' voice echoed in my ears, "You gotta be careful, the gates of hell can pop up anywhere, anytime"— my mind adding that the devil already knew our plans and was waiting in the showroom ready to pull us into eternal damnation. Another thought jarred my brain.

I yanked at Drew's sleeve. "What if the coffins *are* the gates to hell?"

"Shhhh, you gotta be quiet," he said, ignoring my logic.

"Is that as bright as your flashlight will go?"

"It's bright enough. Now come on."

"Wh-What was that!"

"For Pete's sake," Drew groaned. "Are you gonna have a conniption every time we step on a squeaky floorboard?"

"Sorry, I-I just didn't realize how spooky this place was at night."

Drew handed me the flashlight. "You can hold this if it makes you feel better."

A moment later we were in the showroom.

"Okay, this is your deal," he said. "Tell me what you want me to do."

Without the flashlight shining directly on them, all the coffins looked pretty much the same in the dark, just hollowed-out, rectangular blocks of wood with lids.

I swiped the beam of light across the line of coffins closest to the entrance, landing on two of the fanciest on the end. "Let's do those two."

"Remember to take off your shoes," he said.

Forgoing the undoing of laces, we pushed them off and jumped inside.

"Now what?" he said.

"Just lie down and close your eyes."

"That's it? No chants or anything?"

"No, just lie down. And don't forget to close your eyes."

"They've been closed, now what?"

I sighed. "Just wait."

"Are you sure we're—"

"Just be quiet, will ya!"

As our chatter fell away, the sound of the wind persisted. With the occasional gust came the clunking of a

far-off shipping-bay door and the rattling of the metal roof.
A minute turned to two, then three.

"I'm not falling asleep, Cody. Are you sure we're doing
this right?"

"Shoot, I forgot. We have to close the lids."

"We'll suffocate."

"That's the only way it'll work."

"I know what to do," Drew said. "There should be a
small pillow in there with you. Place it on the edge of the
coffin and let the lid rest on it."

I pulled my coffin's lid down, the pillow allowing a gap
of several inches. As I closed my eyes, the dark grew from
black to pitch-black. My chest tightened and my fingers
curled into fists and then uncurled. I was suddenly dripping
sweat. I heard myself swallow as the sounds of the wind,
the clunky bay door, and the shaky roof faded away. The
only thing growing louder was the throbbing beats of my
heart in my ears. With each beat my anxiety rose. Unable
to take it anymore, I threw open the lid, gasping.

"I-I can't stay in this thing anymore. I'm sorry. I wanna
go home!" I turned to Drew's coffin where I found him
already sitting up. He was holding a finger to his mouth.
"Shhhh. Listen."

"What?" I whispered.

He shook his head and narrowed his eyes at me.

"What is it?" I mouthed.

He pointed to the bottom of the door.

There in the darkness, a crevice of light quivered underneath it, snaking its way into the room.

"What do we do?" I mouthed again.

Grabbing his coffin's lid, he motioned me to pull
mine down.

I shook my head in protest, an objection I instantly abandoned at the sound of voices from the other side of the door.

Chapter 9

For an eternity I lay in my coffin as stiff as the corpse that would one day occupy it. I held my breath, waiting for someone or something to enter the room. Over the pounding of my heart, I heard the murmurings of two men talking, their voices rising and falling between fits of laughter. When they did speak, their words were too muffled and slurred to make out. There were bangs and clangs of objects being jostled about, tossed to the floor or thrown against walls. They were the sounds of destruction mixed with joyful revelry.

But then came a silence that broke into gentle moans of distress, transforming into mournful wails accompanied by a consoling voice, a voice cut short by the only word I could make out—*NO!* A second later came the sound of breaking glass and a loud yelp. Next came a garbled slurring of what sounded like cursing alternating with someone howling, followed by crying. I waited, holding my breath, knowing that at any moment the door would burst open and whatever was happening outside would spill into our hiding place. But the moment never came as the voices drifted off into another part of the factory.

I peeked my head out of the coffin. "Are they gone?"

"Don't come out. Let's wait a minute."

I ducked back inside, closed my eyes, and prayed for the night to be over. I began counting, "One Mississippi, two Mississippi, three Mississippi…" On the forty-third *Mississippi*, I leaped out. "I've had enough. I'm going!"

Drew's nod was all I needed to send me rushing to the door.

"Wait, you gotta be quiet. They could still be around."

"Well, good for 'em if they can catch me." I bolted out the closest exit I could find, only stopping when I reached the street.

"I can't believe you just left me like that," Drew said, puffing his way up to me.

"I told you I was ready to go. Who were those guys?"

"I don't know. I couldn't make out anything they were saying."

"Sounded like somebody got hurt."

"Whoever they were, they weren't supposed to be there. I'll find out more tomorrow from Mr. Merriweather. So did you forget anything?"

"No."

His disapproving smirk found its way to my feet. "Where're your tennis shoes?"

Before I looked, I knew from the chill between my toes I had left my Converse high-tops next to the coffin. "Well, I'm not going back. Not tonight I'm not—no way, no how!"

"Don't worry about it. I'll get them tomorrow."

With our adrenaline running high, we sat up well past midnight, piecing our adventure together one detail at a time, dissecting it into tiny nuggets of time that we knew we would retell hundreds of times throughout our lives.

"When we go back, can we do it in the daytime?" I asked.

Drew yawned. "We'll talk about it later. I'm too bushed."

I bounced on the mattress. "But I can't sleep."

"Well, I can."

"Come on." I urged. "When can we try again?"

"Go to bed," he said, turning off the lights on his way out of my room. "We can talk about it later."

The next morning Drew was off to school before I had a chance to pester him anymore about when we would be going back to the factory for a proper round of "research," as he called it. I also missed out on talking to him after school. Somehow he snuck off to the factory without my seeing him. It wasn't until after dinner that I found out he'd been avoiding me, which was also when I found out how upset a brother could get with his sibling.

"What's wrong?" I said, tracking him out into the orchard. "You didn't say a word during dinner."

He pulled out my tennis shoes from behind his back. "This is what's wrong."

"What?"

"Your high-tops almost got me fired on my first day back. Mr. Merriweather found them in the showroom first thing this morning. He also found tables turned over, broken chairs, a broken glass vase, and a finished bottle of whiskey." He dangled the shoes in front of my nose, the veins in his forehead bulging. "And these—these Converse of yours…"

"Did you tell him about hearing those voices and that they were the ones who busted up everything?"

"Are you kidding me? I couldn't tell him we snuck in and took a spin in his coffins. He'd have me out on my ear. Jesus, Mother, and Mary, sometimes you amaze me, you know that?"

"But I didn't do anything. Are you blaming me?"

"It was *your* idea, wasn't it?"

"So now he thinks I broke all that stuff and drank that liquor?"

"Noooo, he doesn't think you drank anything. But my gut tells me he thinks you and some of the gang might've gotten my key and snuck in and did the damage because there were no signs of a break-in. It had to be someone with a key." He glared at me. "Because of you, he almost took my key back."

I didn't know whether to continue to argue, burst out the crocodile tears, or run to the factory and plead my case to Mr. Merriweather. Instead, I tucked my tail and begged for my brother's forgiveness. "I'm sorry, Drew. You're right, it was my fault. I'm sorry for forgetting my shoes and I'm sorry for talking you into going back." I dug my fingernails into my thigh. "And maybe all that stuff I wrote down was just my imagination. Maybe I am going crazy. Maybe I'd be better off in the funny farm alongside crazy Uncle Vance."

Drew's eyes softened. "No, you're not crazy—forgetful for sure, but not crazy."

"Is there anything I can do to make it right?"

"I tell you what, Mr. Merriweather wants me to come in tomorrow and begin teaching Slate because he didn't show up today like he was supposed to. Since it's Saturday, you can come along and explain to him why your shoes were in there and how there was no way you were at the factory."

"Yeah! That's it. I'll come up with one of those air-tight alibis."

Drew chortled. "Maybe all that detective-show stuff you're into will pay off. But whatever it is, it better be good."

The rest of the evening I sat in my room replaying

Perry Mason reruns in my head and scanning through my *Sherlock Holmes* books looking for tips on how to pull off a winning criminal defense. By midnight I was fast asleep with a smile on my face and a *Dick Tracy* comic spread across my chest.

Around seven thirty the next morning, Detective Tracy's head was receiving a good poking from Drew. "Time to get up," he said, prodding my chest with his index finger.

I brushed my comic book aside. "Wh-What time is it?"

"You've got ten minutes to get ready. Grab a banana and meet me outside."

"But I haven't—"

"Don't make me leave you," he said, closing the door behind him.

Exactly ten minutes later I was outside chasing after my brother, catching up with him just as he was about to enter the coffin factory. "You left early," I wheezed.

"Maybe." He grinned. "You got your alibi ready?"

"Maybe."

He reached for the doorknob. "Smart aleck."

"Wait," I said, holding him back. "You've gotta do me a favor and play along on this. Pretend you didn't give me my shoes yet."

"Why?"

"You'll see. Just do it."

When we walked in, a pair of furry arms wrapped around my neck from behind.

"Happy!" I said, reaching over my back to give him a hug.

"He must have heard you boys talking outside," Mr. Merriweather said from across the room.

"You couldn't hear us, could you?"

"No. Why?"

"Is Slate here yet?" Drew said, changing the subject.

"I think I heard him on the other side of the factory as you were coming in. Let's see how long it takes him to figure out how to get here," he chortled. "Cody, are you going to be here awhile? I wanted to speak with you."

I cleared my throat. "I'm sorry, sir, but I've got to go help my grandmother. She's feeling poorly and I was going to help her with her Saturday chores."

Drew rocked back at hearing my plans for something he'd never witnessed before.

"I just followed Drew in to see if you'd found my shoes I left in the showroom the other day. I took them off because I didn't want to get dirt on that expensive rug in there. I was looking for an earring Mary Lib said she thought she'd lost while admiring one of your coffins."

"And you forgot to put them back on?"

I pursed my lips. "I'm afraid I'm a barefooter by nature."

Drew's eyebrows rose as I continued laying out my syrupy-rich alibi.

"A barefooter?" Mr. Merriweather said.

"Yes sir. It's what Momma calls me because I prefer to be barefoot all the time. If I take my shoes off, I almost always forget to put 'em back on. Anyhow, I didn't get to come back for 'em because of my class's overnight field trip to Raleigh. We were gone all day. We even got to spend the night," I said, emphasizing *night* for good measure. "It was so much fun. You wouldn't believe all the stuff we did. First thing we did was—"

"Okay, little brother. We know it was fun. We can hear about it later. Besides," Drew said, dishing a hidden smirk at me, "Gonny's probably waiting for all that help you're gonna give her."

"Where are you?" A perturbed voice came from out in the factory.

"Stay here a minute, Cody. I'll introduce you to the new owner's son."

"That's okay, sir, I'll…" Before I could escape, he was out the door, returning a few seconds later. Trailing him, wearing a red Burlington Bulldogs baseball T-shirt, was the young G.I. Joe replica we'd encountered on the factory's front steps over a year before. He was slightly taller now with broader shoulders, and his crew cut had grown out a couple inches into the neatly cropped style of a teen idol. With him came a scowl for Drew and me along with an annoyed once-over of Mr. Merriweather's office.

"*This* is where you work?"

"This is it," he replied cheerfully. "Slate, these two gentlemen are—"

"Wow! There's the chimp I've heard about."

"That's right. You haven't met him yet. Allow me to introduce you to Happy, and these two young fellows are—"

"I've never seen a real live chimpanzee before."

"He's not a chimpanzee," I said. "He's a Panamanian white-faced capuchin."

Happy's hold around my neck tightened as the new boy stepped forward for a closer look.

"Hey there, little chim-chim," Slate said, reaching up to pet him. As his hand passed my ear, Happy hauled off and whacked the hand with a screeching hiss. The lightning-fast rejection sent Slate stumbling back into Mr. Merriweather.

"Why, you little long-tail rat—that hurt!"

Happy sat on my shoulder, bobbing up and down and giggling. In his hand was a piece of red-tainted gauze.

"Give that back," Slate demanded, swiping unsuccessfully at the piece of cloth as Happy continued jerking it away, giggling all the while.

"Okay, boy, time to give it up," I said, reaching over my shoulder.

The strand of cloth lightly fell into my palm, and I handed it to Slate with a warning. "You gotta let him get used to you."

Slate bowed his chest while gnashing his teeth at Happy. "Ain't no chimp the boss of me." Drew and I exchanged baffled glances, then watched as Slate wrapped the gauze around his other hand, covering what appeared to be a two-inch gash across the fold between his thumb and index finger. Tying it off, he leaned forward while still keeping his distance. His eyes passed through me to Happy. His lips crept upward. "We'll see who's boss," he snarled.

My face flushed red. "You need to just—"

"Get acquainted with the factory," Drew said, nipping my oncoming outburst in the bud. With a quick sidestep next to me, I could feel his hidden grip on my belt from behind. "Pardon us a minute," he said, hauling me to the door.

As Drew pulled me away, Happy dropped to the floor and bolted outside into his Happy Place, leaving Mr. Merriweather glaring at Slate who continued seething, his eyes fixed on Happy's escape route.

"I'll be right back, sir. I just need to speak with my brother before he leaves."

Outside Drew spun me around by the shoulders. "I know you wanted to punch that guy but that would have—"

"He was going to hit Happy!" I said, yanking free of his grasp.

"You don't know that. If you went for him, he could've hit *you*. Just simmer down and let me get a gauge on him. I bet his bark's bigger than his bite. Just go on home and let me handle this."

"The guy's a foot taller than you, Drew, and twenty pounds of muscle heavier."

He stared at me then slowly said, "Cody—go home. I'll see you around noon and don't worry. I promise he won't hurt Happy."

Chapter 10

For the rest of the morning, I paced around the backyard as our gang converged in the orchard for another Saturday of fun and games.

"Come on, Cody," Mary Lib called out, hanging upside down from a tree branch. "Let's get us a game of roller-bat."

"No thanks," I hollered back.

The swish of a hickory switch ran across my calves. "Don't make me give ya a whuppin', young man," Cackles laughed, running circles around me. "Come on, we wanna play roller-bat."

"Maybe later. You guys go on and play."

"What's eatin' at ya, Cody boy?"

"Nothin'. I just don't feel like it."

"Well, somethin' is 'cause you look like you're about to wet your britches."

"It's nothin'. I'm telling ya, it's—"

Drew's appearance from across Maudie's lawn left my response to Cackles hanging in the air. "I'll play in a while," I called back to her.

"What happened?" I asked, running up to him.

"Well…" he said, his eyes searching the sky, moving from

cloud to cloud and looking for the right words. "Hmmm, I'd say he's definitely difficult."

"Why? What'd he do? He didn't hurt Happy, did he?"

"No, Happy's safe. He stayed outside all day. It was like he was waiting for him to leave. I tell you one thing though—Mr. Merriweather's got some kind of patience. Everything that came out of Slate's mouth was rotten."

"Bad breath?"

"No, it's what he said. It was just all negative. He'd take something nice that Mr. Merriweather would say, like, 'Building coffins is more art than carpentry,' and then he'd say something like, 'I'm not sure how slapping six pieces of wood together to make a box is art.' And when Mr. Merriweather was finally able to introduce me to him, all he could do was grunt. Didn't shake my hand or anything. All he said was, 'Let's get on with it.'"

"You're his boss though, right?"

"No, I'm just teaching him the process."

"Of building a box." I grinned.

Drew sighed at my attempt at humor.

Seeing the need to switch gears, I asked, "When can we have a do-over with the coffins?"

"I've been thinking about that. If we go back, you need to be in the same one that you were in the first time. That way I can watch and see what happens."

"But not at night. Please not at night."

"No, we'll go tomorrow after church."

Within minutes of shaking the preacher's hand the next day, Drew and I were ditching our clip-on ties and racing off to the coffin factory.

"Shoot," Drew said, pulling his key from the factory door. "What?"

"The door's unlocked. Somebody's here." He eased his head inside. "Hellllooo, anybody here?"

Two taps of the old man's cane to the top of Drew's head sent him backing into me.

"Scared you, didn't I?" Mr. Merriweather chuckled. "Did you think I had forgotten to lock up?"

"Sorry, sir, I just didn't think you'd be here."

"Same question for you, my young apprentice." He tilted his head behind Drew. "What are the Edwards boys doing here on such a nice sunny day? Shouldn't you be in church?"

My heel hammered the steps, waiting for Drew to pull off a believable reply.

"I didn't finish cleaning the showroom, so I thought I'd knock it out. I heard we had a customer coming in early Monday morning and I didn't want the place looking shabby."

"I don't know about a Monday customer but, by all means, have at it. And tote that little vagabond along with you. I'm sure Happy will welcome the weekend visit."

Drew turned back to me with a wink and a smile. I'd begun to realize the man's mere presence always brightened his mood. "Come along, little vagabond!" he said.

Once inside, our paths split. I squeezed through Happy's door to his playground and Drew dashed off to the showroom to do his imaginary cleanup. A half hour later, the sound of them talking pulled me back in. Hoping to hear Mr. Merriweather say he'd be leaving shortly, I instead found my brother quizzing him about the white coffin.

"I haven't seen it around. Did it get moved?" Drew asked.

"I thought you knew. That's the one your friend Irvin-Dell was buried in."

Drew and I froze in unison.

"I-I didn't know. I guess I haven't been paying much attention to which ones get sold."

"I don't think I ever told you how that part of the business works." His arthritic hands struggled to pull the black book from the shelf behind his desk. It was the length of his forearm and several inches thick, and he plopped it down with a thud. "This ledger contains every coffin we've ever sold, or at least every one sold since I've been here. In fact, I'm the one who set up the system for recording their sales."

Several seconds of flipping blank pages finally brought him to one filled with lines of names, numbers, and dates all penned in meticulous cursive lettering. His knobby index finger slid down, stopping on the first column of the last entry. "Janice Zimmerman…just three days shy of her ninety-fourth birthday." He tapped her name. "Each row contains everything about the sale. The first column is the name of the person the coffin was intended for, second column is the price it was sold for, next is the date of the purchase, followed by the person who bought it along with their address and telephone number. The last series of numbers and letters is the coffin code. Pretty simple."

Drew leaned closer to the page. "The code is the numbers and letters I see etched on the bottom-right corner of all the coffins, isn't it?"

"That's right."

"I don't see Irvin-Dell's entry…"

"Here you go," Mr. Merriweather said, pointing ten rows down. "Mathew I. Dellsworth."

"We only knew him as Irvin-Dell."

Mr. Merriweather's tone turned as curious as our intent

on locating the white coffin. "Why are you boys so interested in it?"

Rather than wait for my brother to come up with another excuse, I dove in. "Drew told me about the maple leaves on the handles and how nice they were, so I asked if he'd show me because I think I want to be a sculptor one day. To be honest, it was just an excuse to come see Happy."

Mr. Merriweather smiled. "Why, Cody, sculptor or not, you can come and see Happy anytime you want." He looked at Drew. "But when it comes to the coffins, once we make them and they're on display or even lying around the factory, they're not to be moved unless I tell you to move them. And no horseplaying with them. Understood?"

"Yes sir," Drew said.

"Good. Now why don't you boys run along. I'll be here another hour or so working on the books, then I'm off to see that new picture show playing downtown."

The moment we left the factory, Drew's head became a swivel.

"Why are you shaking your head like that? Are you giving up already just because he said not to move the coffins? He didn't say anything about getting inside 'em."

"You know that's what he meant." He continued shaking his head. "Dang it, I really don't want to go against his wishes, but this is too much to ignore. Your visions—Irvin-Dell's coffin—the connection's too great."

"That's right. It's too great," I said.

"They have to be tied together."

"Absolutely. They have to be."

"Would you quit agreeing with everything I say?"

"Sorry, I was just wanting to—"

"I know what you're doing, so please stop. Can't you tell I'm with you on this?"

"Just wanting to make sure. So should we tell Mr. Merriweather?"

"We can't. There's a chance it's all a coincidence and all this is just some sort of trick of the brain. If we could have recreated it with you in Irvin-Dell's coffin, that would have said it all."

"So what do we do? We can't dig him up."

"No, but we can have a redo using other coffins."

"Now *that's* the brother I know!" I stepped back. "Are you sure?"

"Yeah. We'll just come back in a couple hours. Unless you'd rather do it at night."

"Oh, no! I'm good with coming back sooner."

Chapter 11

For the next two hours I altered our Sunday game of neighborhood tag by racing in and out of the house, checking the clock. When enough time expired, I tracked Drew down in the orchard. "It's time."

Cackles snuck up behind me and whacked me on the shoulder. "You're it!"

"Sorry. Me and Drew gotta go to the factory."

"Can I come?"

Peeps poked his head through the muscadine vines. "How about me?"

"What about me?" Reubin said, dropping from a pecan tree.

Mary Lib stumbled out of a bush, but before she could make her own request, Drew held up his hand. He announced our departure was work related and Mr. Merriweather didn't want anyone else in the factory but us.

A minute later we were back in front of the single black door. "You think we can tell the gang what's going on?" I said.

Drew looked back toward the orchard. "Seriously? You wanna tell Cackles?"

"I guess you're right. She'd squawk in a minute."

Drew pushed the door open. "Well, maybe Mary Lib." He eased inside. "Come on, let's get going."

The factory was a peaceful place during non-workdays. It was wide open spaces with a silence accented by the occasional cooing from a family of mourning doves who had claimed the upper rafters as home.

Halfway across the factory floor, Drew stopped. "What's that?"

"What's what?"

"I thought I heard voices."

The squeaky hinges of one of the tooling-room doors opening turned Drew and me around. Out came Slate, his red Bulldogs T-shirt covered in sawdust.

"What're you guys doing here?" he asked.

I hid my groan behind pressed lips. *Not another delay*, I thought.

"I left my watch in the showroom when I was cleaning up," Drew said.

"That's right, Merriweather said you were here just before we came in."

"You're with somebody?"

"Yeah. Me and Ozzy."

"Who's Ozzy?"

"I am. Who're you?" The voice was thick and direct.

"This is Ozzy," Slate said, moving to the side to reveal a barrel-chested boy. His forehead was broad with a protruding brow that hung over the bridge of his nose under a blonde buzz cut that came to a point. The tank top he wore stretched across a meaty frame; like Slate's T-shirt, it was covered in sawdust. Dangling from his side was a knee-length green canvas sheath with a fist-sized wooden handle sticking out.

"Is that a sword?" I asked.

"Ain't a sword," he said, whipping it out. "It's a machete."

"How come you're wearing it like a sword? You guys playing pirates?"

The boy's fleshy nostrils flared. "You makin' fun?" He crept toward me, angling his head as if about to sniff me like some prey. Drew moved to my side as Ozzy leaned down. "I wear it in case I have to make a point."

"That's enough," Slate said. "You're going to give somebody a heart attack with that thing."

Ozzy stepped back with a snort. "Who're these guys anyway?"

"Drew works for Merriweather and that's his little brother, Corey."

"It's Cody, not Corey," I said, ignoring the shivers Ozzy sent up my spine.

"Do you know how to use the lathe machine?" Slate asked Drew.

"Not yet. Mr. Merriweather said he'd teach me in a few months though. How come?"

"We're trying to make a bat."

"A baseball bat?" I asked.

"Of course a baseball bat," Ozzy said. "Geez!"

"But why?" Drew asked again.

Slate released a sigh that seemed to come more from boredom than frustration. "We're on the team and we were wanting to make a special bat from some black walnut I found in the raw materials room."

"Did you ask Mr. Merriweather if you could have it?"

Ozzy laughed. "You think he needs permission for a piece of wood when he owns the factory?"

"I don't own anything," Slate said. "My father owns it."

From across the room a door slammed shut, sending the doves flushing from their nest. "That's right," Mr. Rosen shouted as he marched toward us. "*You* don't own anything."

Slate grumbled under his breath. "Is it time for practice already?"

His father passed him by to give Ozzy a slap on the back. "How's it going, big fella?"

"It's going, sir."

"You gunning to make all-county again this year?"

"You know I am."

My stomach churned, watching the pointy-haired gorilla kiss up to Slate's father.

He turned to Slate. "Did you make the bat?"

"No sir."

"You've had over two hours. How hard can it be to carve a bat out of a stick of wood? Well, forget it now. You guys need to get to the field."

"Oh, alright." Slate headed to the door, putting one lazy foot in front of the other. His father's palm found the back of his head with a whop.

"Get a move on, boy. If anybody needs practice, it's you. Now double-time it before my palm becomes a fist." He turned back to Drew. "Whatever mess they made, clean it up, then lock up. You understand?"

"Yes sir."

I felt my lip curling into a snarl as we watched them heading out the building. "Mean runs deep in that family."

"Come on," Drew said. "Let's see how much damage they did."

"Can't we do the coffins first?"

Drew stood at the door to the tool room. "Go ahead

and pick out your coffin. It's just a few piles of sawdust to sweep up. I'll be there in a minute."

I already knew choosing my coffin was going to be easy. If I was going to do this thing, I was going to do it in style.

When I got to the showroom, I headed straight to the top-of-the-line model. With gold leafing and platinum handles, it was the best on the showroom floor. Whatever visions were to come would surely be good.

As Drew had instructed, I took off my shoes and climbed in. Unlike Irvin-Dell's cramped quarters, this one was spacious with fluffy silk lining stuffed with goose down. I closed my eyes, comparing the fabric's cool softness to the stiff sheets of the lumpy bed I had at home. I let out a long, relaxed breath.

"Wake up!"

"Dad blame it, Drew!" I said, grabbing at the coffin's edges. "You're as bad as those meatheads."

"Sorry, brother, I couldn't resist. Are you ready?"

I took a quick look around the room, thankful for the warm rays of light flooding in. "I'm ready."

"Are you sure you're not going to freak out when I pull the lid down?"

"You're not gonna close it all the way, are you?"

"I found out you won't suffocate. You'd have to be in there for five hours."

I let this sink in. "Ummm, well okay." I suddenly began missing the idea of having a sliver of light keeping me company inside the coffin.

"Don't worry, I'm right here. If you start to panic, bang on the lid, or heck, just push it open."

I forced a laugh. "Alright, let's do it." I slowly drew the lid to me. When all went dark, I closed my eyes. If I had them shut, my mind would think I was ready to sleep. I needed to sleep anyway, to see the visions. And I needed to control my breathing. I needed anything that would help me get through what I'd pestered Drew into doing for me. I had to be strong, and I needed him to believe me. I squeezed my eyes tighter as I willed the visions to come.

Several minutes passed and nothing. Five minutes passed and still nothing. After ten minutes, things began to change. I was becoming comfortable without the light. My breathing was slow and even. I was actually comfortable. A peaceful easiness had me on the verge of whatever had brought on the visions from before. But after another ten minutes I was still on the verge with nothing happening.

"Are you okay?" came Drew's muffled voice.

"Yeah, I'm good."

"Anything happen yet?"

"Not yet."

Several minutes later the coffin's lid swung up.

"What's the deal—I wasn't finished," I said, shielding my eyes.

"You've been in there over twenty minutes. If something was going to happen, it would've already done it. Besides, Happy's been making a ruckus for the last ten minutes and it's driving me bonkers."

"Oh, alright," I said, climbing slowly out of the coffin. "I'll go see what's going on with him." I stopped at the door. "Are *you* still going to try?"

"Sure, but if nothing happens within fifteen minutes, I'm calling it quits. Now go check on Happy and hurry back. I don't want to risk anybody coming in on us."

I returned a few minutes later, cradling Happy in my arms. "Where are you?" I said, scanning an empty room. "I brought Happy so he—"

"Over here," Drew said, popping his head up from a lavender-colored coffin at the end of the line.

"This is your pick? Kinda girly, don't you think?"

"I never realized how soft they are," he said, lying back down. "I can't believe you didn't fall asleep in yours."

"Sorry about bringing Happy, but he gave me that look of his and I couldn't say no."

"Just make sure to keep him quiet." He took a deep breath as he grabbed the lid's corner.

"Good luck," I said as he disappeared inside.

As soon as it shut, Happy began slapping my forearms in a manic scramble to free himself.

"Happy, behave." Before I could pull him back, he leaped out of my arms onto Drew's coffin. He paused for a giggle then spun around several times. Before I knew it, he was back in my arms, his head bobbing away as he continued his little laugh.

In one single motion the lid flew open and Drew bolted upright. His eyes bulged. "How long have I been gone?" He stared at me. "How long?"

"Just seconds," I said.

His eyes jetted from one corner of the room to the next before turning back to me. He looked inside the coffin as if witnessing something rising out of it.

"What was it? What did you see? You saw something. Visions, you saw visions."

His mouth hung open, the words hesitating to come out until finally he said, "I—believe—I—did."

"I knew it. I knew it. I knew it."

"How long did you say I was gone?"

"I told you. It was just a second. When the coffin closed, Happy sprang on top of it and then you popped up like a jack-in-the-box. Tell me what you saw."

"I'm not a hundred percent but I'm pretty sure it was the library. I do know I saw Miss Riddles."

"The librarian?"

"Yeah. She was sitting at a desk, rocking back and forth. She was pale and sweaty." His expression went blank. "What time is it?"

I leaned toward the door, straining to see the giant wall clock hanging at the opposite side of the factory. "It's almost a quarter to five."

He leaped from the coffin and stuffed his feet into his shoes. "I gotta go."

"Go where? You want me to come?"

His keys smacked me in the chest.

"Aren't you going to tell me more about what you saw?" I yelled after him.

"I will when I get back home. Just make sure to lock up."

Chapter 12

For the next hour I lay on my bed as the sounds of my friends playing out in the orchard filtered through the open window. Their laughter would have drawn me outside on any other day, but instead all I could do was wait for the sound of the screen door slamming shut, signaling my brother's return. As the excitement of the day's adventure finally caught up to me, I fell asleep.

"Cody. Wake up."

"Wha…"

"What're you sleeping for?" Drew said. "It's not even dinnertime."

I rubbed my eyes. "Why'd you take off like that and what took you so long?"

"I had to get something."

"Like what?"

"Evidence. Maybe *proof*'s a better word."

"Proof of what?"

"Proof that I really did have visions. Brother—you weren't imagining it."

His revelation jolted me upright. "I told you."

"I don't know how it happened or why, but it did."

"What vision made you believe?"

"This one." He laid a crumpled rectangular tan card on my lap.

I turned the object in my hand, flipping it over and inspecting it from every angle. "It's an old library card."

"It's actually not that old. The owner just doesn't take care of her stuff like she should."

I rubbed my eyes again, adjusting my vision to read the name of the owner of the card. "Mary Libowskenstein. You found Mary Lib's card." I wanted to share my brother's excitement but failed to make sense of why he'd be so jazzed about an ordinary library card. "I'm sure she'll be glad to get it back, but why are you so excited about it?"

"Because it's proof. It's part of the vision I didn't tell you about. Remember how you saw me throwing my tie after Irvin-Dell's funeral and how you saw Mom come in to tell us about *The Wizard of Oz* being on TV that night? I had the same kind of vision about the library. Clear as a bell, I could see Mary Lib in the science-fiction stacks at the library. She was reading a book about séances in one hand and had the card in the other. I guess she got tired of holding it, so she stuffed it in between the pages. A couple minutes later she put the book back in the rack, forgetting to take the card. I ran off like I did because I wanted to get to the library before they closed so I could find it. And sure enough, it was right there in that book."

"Holy cow!"

"Holy cow's right."

"Come on, let's go give it to her."

"We'll have to wait. I went straight to her house from the library, but her mom said she's at a sleepover with her cousin across town. She's going to school with her tomor-row, so she won't be back until the afternoon."

A knock came at the door. "Boys," Gonny said from the other side, "it's dinnertime."

"We'll be there in a minute," Drew replied. "I've got to work tomorrow so why don't you come with me, and we'll go from there."

"I can't wait to see how freaked out she's going to be."

When school let out the next day, I met Drew on our front porch. "Did you find Mary Lib?"

"I stopped by her house, but her mom said she might not be back until this evening. I left a message that if she got back before five to come to the factory. You still wanna come along?"

"Course I do. I didn't load up my Pez dispenser for nothin'."

"Good. After you give Happy his treats, I've got a job for you."

"How much you payin'?"

"You wish. While I'm working, I want you to sneak over to the showroom and get the code off the bottom of the coffin I was in yesterday."

"What for?"

"It's part of our research. You'll see soon enough."

"What about the one on my coffin?"

"Don't need it."

The moment Happy saw us coming into Mr. Merriweather's office, he climbed onto his desk, clapping his hands.

"I do believe my boy is fonder of you than he is of me," he said. "That or he just knows you come bearing Pez or pecans."

"Watch this. I bet I can make him turn around." I pulled my Mickey Mouse dispenser from my pocket, triggering Happy to launch into spin cycle. "Told ya."

"Well, I'll be," he said.

Drew smiled. "How'd you know what he'd do?"

"It's just something he does now when he sees Mickey come out."

The sound of slow, sarcastic clapping preceded Slate into the office. He held his head low and wore a Bulldogs baseball cap pulled down to the bridge of his nose. "Looks like you and the furball are ready for the circus."

I struggled for a comeback, but Drew cut me short when he asked, "What happened to you?"

"Nothing happened," he said, turning away.

I finally found a snappy reply but surrendered it when I realized what Drew was talking about. Slate's right eye was a painful-looking purple shiner.

"My God, what happened?" Mr. Merriweather asked.

Slate stepped back toward the corner. "I told you, it's nothing."

"No, you said nothing happened, but something happened alright." I pointed to his eye. "It happened to your face."

Drew dug his knuckle into my shoulder. "Would you shut up?"

Mr. Merriweather stooped down to examine his injury. "Son, did you—"

"I got hit with a baseball yesterday in practice. Now would you leave it be?"

"You didn't need to come in today. If you're not feeling well, you can—"

"No! I'm here and I'm working."

"But don't you—"

"I said no. I came in to work and that's exactly what I'm going to do. I'm not leaving. Now tell me where you want me to start."

"Why don't we wait for your friend Ozzy to get here and then you and he can take care of moving the maples and walnuts that are out on the loading dock to the raw room."

Out the corner of my eye, I saw Drew grimace. "Is he working here now?"

"He's not working anywhere," Slate blurted. "I know my dad told you he wanted you to give him a job, but he changed his mind."

"Why?" Mr. Merriweather asked.

Slate turned his gaze to the floor. "I don't know. I guess he needed a fishing buddy or somebody to play catch with."

"I don't get it," I said. "Why would he need a fishing—"

"Cody, don't." Drew stopped me with a shake of his head. "Sir, how about I help Slate move that lumber today?"

"I don't need your help, Edwards. I can do it myself."

"No, I think that's a good idea. You boys go fetch two hand trucks and I'll be back there in a minute to tell you which stacks need moving."

"I told you. I—don't—need—help!"

Mr. Merriweather put a hand on Slate's shoulder. "I'm sorry. That wood needs to be in production sooner than later so I'm afraid you do."

Slate swung his head, conceding his position with muted grumbling.

As they were leaving, Drew brushed past me. "The code," he whispered. "Don't forget the code."

As soon as I was alone, I put Happy in his cage then grabbed a pen and paper and raced off to the showroom.

Drew returned an hour and a half later, dripping with sweat. "Did you get it?"

I held out the piece of paper to him.

He squinted. "What kind of chicken scratch is this? Is that an eight or the letter B?"

"The letter B. The code's BL2024. Where's Mr. Merriweather?"

"Talking to Slate." He pulled the coffin ledger from the shelf, plopped it on the desk then flipped it to the last page. "Hmm, it's not here."

"So what's that mean?"

"It means it hasn't been sold," Mr. Merriweather said, entering the office.

I jumped at his voice. "How do you do that?"

"Do what?"

"Sneak up like that."

He chuckled. "It's the only advantage to being old and slow. No one hears you coming." He turned to Drew. "Are you still confused?"

"No sir, I was just curious to see how many coffins we've been selling."

"We haven't sold any for several days. That is, until this morning." He picked up the pen and let it hover over the last open line on the page. "I need to show this to you again. There's one part I left out." He pulled a palm-sized notepad from his pocket and began transferring the information on the page to the ledger in slow, artful swoops and swipes. "There," he said admiring his entry.

"How come the last column's blank?"

"That's what I forgot to tell you." He stooped over the ledger and began the final entry, explaining each letter and number of the coffin's code as he wrote. "*B* is for basic. If it was our most expensive coffin, it would be a *T*, which stands for top-of-the-line. Our next level is *S*, which means standard. We only have three types. Easy enough, right?"

"Yes sir," Drew said.

"Good. Now L is for the color. In this case, lavender." He paused. "With me so far?"

Drew nodded, his eyes locked to every stroke of Mr. Merriweather's pen.

"And the final four numbers, *2024*, are simply the next series of numbers for that line of coffin. There you have it."

Drew stood frozen. I nudged his arm, bringing him back into the moment.

"Do you know anything about the person the coffin's for?" he said.

"Only that she died suddenly. Seems it was from a burst appendix late last night."

"Anything else?"

"I believe she was a librarian." He studied Drew. "Are you okay?"

"Yes sir. I-I'm fine."

"Good. I need you to wheel her coffin to the loading dock. The funeral home will be here in a half hour to pick it up."

"Okay," was the best my brother could muster.

Chapter 13

It wasn't until we crossed the street, back into Maudie's yard, that either Drew or I could speak. When we did, it was a jumble of words all coming out at once with neither of us hearing what the other said. A minute later we were out of breath, and with no more adjectives to describe what we'd learned from the ledger entry, we stood staring at each other.

"What do you think's happening?" Drew finally said.

"I think those coffins are magical and the factory is the gates to heaven or hell like we thought. Maybe God's using them to tell us something."

"Having visions isn't a part of heaven or hell."

"You must be sleeping in church, big brother, 'cause the Bible's chock-full of 'em. And coffins are part of dying and dying's a part of what comes before heaven and hell."

"Why do you think *you* didn't have another vision?" he asked.

"I don't know. I guess not all of them are magical or God didn't have anything to tell me right then. What do you think?"

Drew scratched his chin. "I don't know the *why*, but I have a feeling about the *how*. The one thing I do know is we gotta have more information. And there's only one person to provide it."

"Mary Lib?"

"Yep." He patted me on the back. "Come on. We've got an hour before dinner."

Drew left me in the dust in our sprint to Mary Lib's house. By the time I got there, she was already on the front porch, chatting up how much fun she had at her sleepover.

"Hey, Cody. I was just telling your brother how awesome my cousin is. You guys would love her, especially you, Drew. She's into séance too."

"Is she interested in them as much as you are?" he said with a sly glance my way.

"Well, I guess. I don't know, maybe."

"Does she go to the library to read up on 'em?"

"I don't know."

"Does she use her library card as a bookmark?"

"What kind of questions are these? Are you making fun of me?"

My cheeks puffed up as I held my laughter back.

Drew's smile grew as he pulled out her library card. "You been missing something?"

"My card! I've been looking all over for it. Where'd you find it?"

"At the library in the science-fiction section."

"Are you following me?"

"No. And to be more exact, you left it in a book on séances and other paranormal stuff."

"You *are* following me. I'm going to tell your mom, Drew Edwards. That's a sick thing to do."

"Cross my heart, I'm not following you."

"You're lying."

I swung my head side to side. "He's not lying, Mary Lib."

"This is one of your pranks, isn't it? You talked to the librarian or somebody who was there."

"It's not a prank and I didn't talk to anybody."

"You know what? I think I'll go down there and talk to the librarian to see if she remembers you being there when I was. Yeah, that'll prove it."

"I'm afraid you won't get anything from her."

"How do you know that?"

"Come over here," he said, leading her to a porch swing. "You're going to need to sit for this."

For the next twenty minutes my brother laid out everything about our visions and everything that had brought us to this point, including the librarian's death, her coffin, the code, and the ledger. Without a word she listened, her eyes widening as he spoke, then narrowing as if spotting a crack in his story. When he finished, the corners of her mouth curled, holding for a second before bursting into laughter. "You guys are too much. I swear, Drew, you should write this stuff down and sell it to the newspapers."

"Darn it, Mary Lib. This is—not—a—joke!"

Rarely did Drew get upset, which was why I was sure she suddenly softened.

"You're really telling the truth, aren't you?"

"Yes," we said in unison.

Her gaze fell downward then back up. "Okay then."

"You believe us?" Drew said.

"This is so crazy, but yes, I guess I do."

"Good, because we need your help."

"What kind of help?"

"Do you remember what happened on the day you took the pictures of everybody in the showroom?"

"Pretty much. Why?"

"Can you explain what happened from the time Cody entered the coffin to when he got out?"

"He was only in five or six seconds. When the lid came down, Happy jumped on it for a couple seconds then jumped off, then Cody came out. That's all there was to it."

"When Happy was on top of the coffin, what'd he do?"

She smiled. "A little dance. It was so cute."

"What kind of dance?"

"Now that I recall, it wasn't really a dance. It was more like him bouncing from one foot to the other then he whacked the lid like it was a drum. Maybe smacked or patted is a better description. Then that was it. He was back on the floor."

"What're you thinking?" I asked Drew.

"I think we're getting closer."

"To what?" Mary Lib said.

"To our furry little friend." He turned to her. "What're you doing tonight?"

"Why? Are you asking me on a date?"

My eyes flew from her sheepish grin to my brother's blushing cheeks.

"I, um…I'm just wondering if you might be up for an adventure at the coffin factory. No, no, what I meant was—"

Mary Lib chortled. "Relax, Mr. Edwards, consider that payback for that cliff-hanging intro you started out with."

"She's good," I said, poking him in the ribs.

"So what do you say? Can you sneak out tonight for a trip to the factory? If what I'm thinking is right, we can confirm my hypothesis."

"No, I got it," I said. "If we can recreate what Happy

did on the coffins when we had the visions, then that'll prove how it's done."

Drew and Mary Lib laughed at whatever inside joke they shared at my expense.

"Yeah, that's perfect, Cody," she said. "That's exactly what we can do."

"Only one thing," I added. "I think we should do it tomorrow afternoon right after work while it's still light out."

"No can do," Mary Lib said. "I'm back at my cousin's for her mom's birthday party."

Drew tilted his head my way. "Cody?"

"Oh, alright," I conceded.

"Great. Mary Lib, meet us behind Maudie's back porch at eight and we'll all go together."

Although the factory continued to give me the heebie-jeebies at night, having two people along made it less spooky. The only thing now was what was going on with the coffins. All those tales about ghosts and our neighborhood chatter about the place being the gates to heaven and hell were all the more possible in my mind. Visions of things from dead people's coffins were anything but normal, so when Drew asked me to go get Happy by myself while he and Mary Lib headed off to the showroom, I gave him a big fat no. "How about *you* go get him and me and Mary Lib will meet you there?"

"Alright. Go ahead and pick a coffin though. You're going first."

A few minutes later Drew came in with Happy swinging from his shoulders. Upon seeing me, he jumped into the silver coffin I'd chosen. "I'm sorry, little fella," I said, lifting him off my chest, "but you're gonna have to go back with Drew."

"I'll take him," Mary Lib said, pulling him from me.

Drew stepped beside me. "Okay, buddy, I'm going to close the lid now."

No sooner had he shut the lid than I heard Happy leap onto it. I even heard the pattering of his feet as he spun around before vaulting back into Mary Lib's arms. A second later I pushed skyward with both hands, sending the lid flying open. I shot up, clinging to the edge of the coffin, gasping like it was the edge of a pool I'd come close to drowning in.

"You saw something again, didn't you?" Drew said.

I answered with a dozen swift nods.

"Here," Mary Lib said, thrusting a pen and tiny notepad at me. "Write it down before you forget."

She and Drew stood motionless, watching me scratch out the visions I'd seen. I closed my eyes after my last entry. "How long was I in?"

"Five or six seconds," she said. "Just like last time."

"And everything was the same as before?" Drew asked.

"Exactly."

"Okay, let's keep this going," he said, climbing up into the coffin next to me.

"Don't you want to hear what Cody saw?"

"Not now. We can go over everything when we leave. I want to see if we can repeat it again." He grabbed the lid then stopped, leaned over the edge, and patted a golden horseshoe that had been fashioned on the side. "This one's good luck," he said with a smile.

As Drew's lid fell shut, Happy once again sprang onto it. This time he stopped. Holding his hand above his head, he hesitated before smacking his palm flat on top of the coffin, following it with a giggle and another whack before jumping back into my arms.

Instead of my thunderbolt exit, Drew's was the equivalent of waking from an afternoon nap. The lid slowly rose. The only evidence of his experience was a growing smile and his request for Mary Lib's pen and pad. And unlike my unruly chicken scratch, his was controlled and fluid. A moment later he handed it to me. "Get the codes from the bottom."

Mary Lib held out his sneakers to him as he climbed to the floor. "I can't believe this is happening."

"Me neither," he muttered.

"Got 'em," I said, handing the notepad back to him.

"Great. Now let's go check the ledger."

Within minutes I had Happy back in his cage and was in Mr. Merriweather's office helping to search for the black book that would shine light on whose coffins we'd just lain in.

"Is this it?" Mary Lib said, pulling out the giant book and flipping through its pages.

"You found it," Drew said.

"No wonder this thing's so thick, the dates in it go back to 1914!"

"That's when Mr. Merriweather came to work here. He's the one who started the system. See the last column? That's where the coffin codes are entered. That's what we're looking for. Skip to the last page. I wanna check to see whose coffins we were in." A few seconds later he was running his finger down the last column of entries. "Shoot. They're not here."

"What do you mean they're not there?" I said.

"The codes haven't been entered yet."

"So what do we do?"

He sighed. "We just wait until they are."

"In other words," Mary Lib said, "we have to wait until they die."

"And then?" I said.

She held up the notepad. "We match the visions to the unfortunate souls."

"Can you stay out a little longer?" Drew asked.

"I'm not going anywhere until I hear what you guys saw."

"Come on," he said, "we're going to the dungeon."

Chapter 14

"Do you guys think your grandparents will hear us down here?" Mary Lib said as we approached the back of the house.

"PaPa's on a trip and Gonny sleeps like a log. We still need to be quiet though. Cody, grab the flashlight from the peach crate beside the steps there." The room's musty scent hit us full force as Drew slowly pulled the door open. He handed Mary Lib the notepad. "You'll read what we saw and if something's not clear, we'll elaborate."

I shined the flashlight on the pad. "Is this okay?"

She nodded. "Okay, this one's yours, Drew. First thing you wrote was *big pasture far away*. Under that you wrote *giant tree*, then *lots of cowboys*. You circled the word *lots*. After that you wrote *black hats*, then the word *crying*."

"It was women who were crying, not the guys in cowboy hats," he said.

"I can't make out this next one. Does it say *dog* or *hog*?"

"Dog. There was one sitting next to a little boy. Now read the last one. I guarantee this one will blow your mind."

"Oh wow," she said, staring down into the book. "This is too—"

"What? What is it?" I said.

"It says *horseshoe on coffin*. Drew, that's the coffin you were in."

"I know!"

Mary Lib held her palm to her forehead. "This is too weird. I think you were witnessing this person's funeral."

"Just like when I saw Irvin-Dell's," I said. "Was there anything else?"

"That was all."

"Are you ready to hear Cody's?" she said.

"Absolutely."

She twisted her head, her face contorting into a mask of frustration. "Cody, I don't think I can make any of this out."

"I'm sorry. I was so nervous. But it's okay, there were only three things. They're kind of boring compared to Drew's, but I remember them. The first thing I saw was a long, dark hallway. I think it might have been a hotel because it was lined with the same doors up and down. It was quiet then suddenly there was this nasty noise, like Gonny's teapot whistling except super annoying. The last thing I saw was some sort of glowing green line."

"Was there anything special about it?" Drew asked.

"Not really. It just sat there like a big green clothesline strung across the night sky. It did jiggle once, like it hiccupped, then went straight again."

"That's it?" she said.

"Yeah, I told you they were boring."

"How come you were so spooked? You nearly threw the coffin lid off its hinges getting out."

"I'm just freaked out that I'm seeing stuff that has to do with dead people. Why don't you ask Captain Cool why he doesn't?"

She smiled at my brother. "I think the captain's just wired differently than us."

"I don't know about that," Drew said, "but I do know we're gonna have to be wired for patience. It could be a while before these coffins get sold. Until then we can't confirm any of this. And whatever you do, don't say a word to anybody."

Drew was right. Weeks went by and the coffins remained on the showroom floor. Drew's and Mary Lib's patience held fast while mine began to wither with the summer heat that arrived.

One day I asked Drew, "How come we can't do another round of coffin-jumping?"

"What's that?"

"It's the name I came up with for when we use the coffins to see visions."

"Hmm, I kinda like that. But no more coffin-jumping until we see what happens with the last ones."

"I sure wish these people would hurry up and die so we could—"

"Cody! Think about what you just said. For land's sake, you can't be wishing somebody dead."

"I-I'm sorry, I just—"

"I know, but you can't be saying that out loud. If anything, we should be hoping they don't get sold for a long time."

"You're right. I'm sorry." My chin dropped to my chest as a wave of guilt rushed over me. "I'm going to hell, I know it."

"No, you're not. To be honest, I've thought the same thing and I'm pretty sure Mary Lib has too. It's definitely a moral conundrum."

"What kinda word is that?"

"It's when someone's in a situation where they want to do the right thing, but there's a reason they do or say something different. Like when you tell Peeps he looks good in glasses when you know the lenses make him look like he's from outer space."

"I'm still sorry I said it."

"I know you are. The important thing about stuff like this is just doing what you know is right for someone else, even if you have to fib a little."

"Yeah, I guess you're right."

Drew's voice lightened when he said, "I actually saw a conundrum just yesterday when Mr. Rosen was talking to Mr. Merriweather."

"What happened?"

"Mr. Rosen came in screaming about the lack of parking around the factory and how bad it was hurting business. He said that since the lumber business was increasing, customers were having to park two blocks away. That's when Mr. Merriweather said why not have them park in the back where the loading docks are."

"Oh, oh! I know what the conundrum is."

He smiled at me. "Okay, smarty, what is it?"

"The customers can park in the back, but if they do, it'll jam up the trucks going in or out."

"Not bad. That's definitely a conundrum of sorts."

"Did Mr. Rosen like his idea?"

"Nope. In fact, he yelled at him, saying it was stupid. He said customers would think we didn't know how to run a business. But that's not the moral conundrum I was talking about. After all the yelling, Mr. Rosen said the smart thing would be to just buy one of the houses on our block and turn it into a parking lot."

"I don't get it. Where's the conundrum?"

"It's when he asked Mr. Merriweather what he thought about the idea. The conundrum is that Mr. Merriweather knew the idea made sense, but he doesn't want to see any of the neighborhood turned into a parking lot."

"So what did he say?"

"Luckily, he didn't have to say anything because Slate came in, complaining about his elbow hurting. That's when Mr. Rosen went off on him about how he needed to stop throwing sidearm and learn how to throw overhand like the pros."

"Is he a pitcher?"

"Yeah, supposedly a pretty good one too."

"So why was he yelling at him?"

"I don't know. He's always yelling at him for something. To be honest, I don't think I've ever heard him say anything nice to him."

"Not a hug or anything?"

"Nothing." Drew stared downward, his thoughts moving elsewhere. "He's nothing like Dad was," he said softly.

The following day Drew came home for lunch, bursting with excitement. "Where's Cody?" he said, panting from his obvious sprint from the factory.

"What's got you all hopped up, young man?" Gonny asked as she lathered three swipes of pimento cheese onto a piece of bread. "Remember to chew."

"I heard you come in," I said, sliding into the kitchen like a surfer in slick socks. "What's up?"

"Cody, that's enough with the kitchen skating. Now sit down and eat your lunch."

As I pulled my chair up to the table, Drew grabbed my sleeve while cramming half his sandwich into his mouth. "They sold it," he said, spitting chunks of pimento cheese across the table.

"Drew Edwards, I told you to chew not spew. Now have some manners and eat like the gentleman you're supposed to be."

"I'm sorry, Gonny. I gotta get back to the factory."

I leaned toward Drew. "Are you talking about what I think you're talking about?"

He nodded, still working to finish the remaining sandwich. With one final gulp and a quick swig of juice, he whispered, "I saw your coffin being loaded into a van as I was coming out the building just now."

I bolted out of my chair. "Alright! Let's go."

"Oh no, mister," Gonny said, "whatever shenanigans you're planning, it'll have to be done without you. I'm spring-cleaning this afternoon and I need your help."

"Aww, do I have to? Besides it's not spring, it's summer now."

"Call it whatever type of cleaning you want but you're going to help. Just because it's summer break doesn't mean you get to lollygag through it. Your brother's working nine to five every day during his recess, so I reckon you can pull your weight every now and then."

"Sorry, Drew," I sighed.

"Don't worry, I'll tell you everything this evening."

"You hear that," she said, "he'll tell you everything. Now go put some shoes on and fetch the mop and bucket."

A couple hours into my chores, Mary Lib came to my rescue when she stopped by and asked permission to steal me away for a game of roller-bat. To my surprise, Gonny's heart had softened, and I was released into the backyard with a pat on the head and a request not to leave the yard because she would soon have boxes needing to be moved to the root cellar.

Seeing us approaching, the gang began bopping around, chanting my name, "Co—dy, Co—dy…"

"Wait, I need to tell you something," I said, grabbing her arm and pulling her to a standstill. "They sold one of the coffins."

"Which one?"

"Mine."

"And?"

"And that's all I know. Drew only saw it being loaded. He's getting the info this afternoon."

"Well, what're we waiting for? Let's go over there now."

"You heard Gonny. I gotta wait. If she were to need those boxes moved and I wasn't here, I'd be off on a death march for sure."

Mary Lib eyed the bush at the corner of the house. "I'd just about take that switching in exchange for that coffin info."

"Come on, let's play. Drew will be off soon enough."

When the sounds of the factory's buzz saws subsided, Mary Lib's and my attention went straight across the street.

Peeps peered over the rims of his glasses in the direction of our interest. "How come you guys keep looking at the coffin building?"

"No reason," Mary Lib said.

"None at all," I added, picking up the bat for my turn at home plate.

Just then Drew appeared from around the corner of Maudie's house.

I dropped the bat. "I'm done!"

"Me too!" Mary Lib shouted, following on my heels.

A minute later we were bent over, panting, in front of Drew. "Did—Did you get it?"

"It was sold to a doctor named Russell Cadwaller who bought it for his father."

"What else?" Mary Lib said.

"It just so happens that Dr. Cadwaller is a dentist, a dentist for none other than Mr. Merriweather."

"Go on."

"This won't sound remarkable, but it proves Cody's visions were real. You see, Cadwaller's father was eighty-four and livin' in a nursing home. He had a stroke a week ago and, for the last few days, was on life support. The young Cadwaller told him how much he hated seeing his father hooked up to all the tubes and wires. But the worst thing he said was how traumatic it was for him and his family to watch as he passed away. He said watching the monitor's green pulse line go flat will always be with him."

I bobbed my head. "That long hall I saw that looked like a hotel was actually a nursing home. I'm sure of it. Our aunt Betty's in one and when I think about it, they look just like those at a Holiday Inn."

"And his pulse on the monitor," Mary Lib added, "that had to be the green line you saw. The little hiccup you mentioned was probably his last heartbeat." She turned to Drew. "Why are you shaking your head? You know that's what it is."

"No, I agree completely. I'm just blown away by it."

"What're we going to do with all this?" she asked.

"It's like having a superpower," I said.

"Not unless you know how to use it," Drew said.

I held up my hands. "But we do. If Happy jumps on a coffin we're laying in, then we see visions."

"True," he said, scratching his head, "but we still don't know why some are in the future and some are in the past. We just gotta wait for my coffin to be recorded in the ledger." He gave me a sideways glare. "And don't you dare say what you're thinking. We just have to be patient."

My heart fluttered. "No, it's not that. I just thought of something. Something huge."

"Care to share?"

The idea was on the tip of my tongue, but I swallowed it, resisting the urge to blurt it out, knowing I had to wait until the right time. "No, I'm with you. We wait."

Chapter 15

The month of June came and went and Drew's coffin remained unsold. Rather than letting it eat at me, I took the time to develop my plan for using our coffin-jumping superpowers. Besides, I also had Maudie's July Fourth barbecue extravaganza to occupy my time. Coming in a close second to Christmas, this was the World Series of feasting and fun. In just three days, every uncle, aunt, and cousin would be there along with the entire neighborhood gang. Starting at noon, a spread of every imaginable dish along with cakes, pies, and cookies was ours to scarf down, to be followed by dozens of games and contests, including the all-important softball game. Parents even joined in, creating fierce competition among us kids. It was my brother who threw the only cold water on my excitement when he told me he'd invited Slate to the party.

"Are you kidding me?"

"Nope."

"Why on earth would you invite that goon? He's been nothing but a pain in the butt ever since he started working at the factory."

"Yeah, but you don't see what I see every day."

"He didn't say he'd come, did he?"

"No."

"Good. Maybe he won't. I'm tellin' ya, I don't like the guy and I definitely hate that slab-of-meat friend of his."

Drew sighed.

"What is it?"

"Starting on the fifth, Ozzy's coming to work for us."

"Ah, come on," I groaned. "Why?"

"Mr. Rosen seems to really like him. Plus, he said because the lumber side of the business is picking up, he needs the extra help."

"He needs slave labor is what he needs. I'm gonna have to come to work with you the rest of the summer just to keep Happy safe."

"That's up to you. You better stock up on Pez and pecans though."

By noon on the day of the party, half of Maudie's yard was jammed with a dozen cars, the other half lined with rows of folding tables butted up to one another. Each was packed with dishes of country ham, biscuits, snap beans, corn on the cob, mashed potatoes and boatloads of gravy, along with two tables of desserts. On the table, loaded in trough-sized metal bins, were chunks of pork pulled straight off the pig that lay roasting in a giant cooker manned by PaPa and Drew.

"Look at him," I said, motioning Reubin and Cackles toward my brother. "That boy is deep into hog heaven."

Cackles snorted.

Reubin licked his lips. "I'm getting me some of that right now."

"Hold up, you can't go hittin' up the table of deliciousness yet. You gotta wait until Maudie gives the blessing."

Several minutes later my aunt Beula wheeled her out beside the cooker where she delivered grace.

"Happy Fourth of July!" bellowed PaPa.

"Come and get it," Drew hollered. "Remember, ladies first."

In an instant, the yard was a buzz of activity as we maneuvered in and out of the tables, piling food onto our paper plates to the brink of collapsing. The gang and I sat crossed-legged on the grass, stuffing our faces and joking how we would soon be demolishing my uncles in marbles and how they didn't stand a chance in the softball game.

Peeps wiped his glasses while staring across the yard toward the coffin factory.

"Whatcha gawking at?" Mary Lib said, twisting around in the direction he was looking. "Well, I'll be…it's Slate Rosen."

I jolted up from my barbecue. "Who'd you say?"

"It's Slate Rosen. He's at the corner of the house. How come he's not comin' over?"

My plate slid off my knee. "Because he's not supposed to be here."

"Looks like Drew's gonna tell him to leave," Peeps said.

I narrowed my eyes as I watched him run up to Slate.

Mary Lib waved. "Hey, Drew, over here!"

I jerked her hand down. "Stop it."

"What's the matter? I just wanted him to know where we're at."

"He knows exactly where we are. Come on, let's go set up the field."

"I'm not finished," Reubin slurred through cake-filled cheeks.

"Well bring it with you."

"Oh, how nice," Mary Lib said. "He's introducing Slate to your grandad."

I grimaced at the sight of PaPa patting him on the back. My only consolation was watching Slate pull away from him. "Enough. Grab your plate, Reubin, and let's go. Cackles, come on, and Peeps, quit your eyeballing. You comin', Mary Lib?"

"Why's he look so skittish?"

"Don't know and don't care. Now let's go, guys. We need to get some practice in before we take on my uncles. Reubin and Mary Lib, you guys can bat, and Cackles and me will field your hits."

Through four rounds of batting, I dropped almost every ball that came my way.

"You got a plank in your eye today, Cody boy," Cackles quipped.

"Mind your own glove. I don't see you catchin' many."

"If you'd keep your eye on the ball and not on what your brother and Slate are up to, you might do better."

"Just hush, would ya?"

Uncle Dean trotted up behind home plate. "You guys ready to get clobbered?"

"Bring it on, old man," Cackles laughed.

"Come on, fellas!" my uncle shouted toward the pig cooker where all the men stood huddled around Slate and Drew. A moment later three more of my uncles, along with Drew, came trotting up toward our makeshift softball field.

"Where's Slate?" Mary Lib asked.

"He didn't seem like he wanted to play. I think he thought he was intruding or something, so I didn't press him."

"So he's just gonna leave?"

I breathed easy. "He doesn't wanna play, so let him go."

"Go ahead and pick teams," Mary Lib said, running back toward Maudie's.

"You quittin'?" I yelled.

"No, I'll be back in just a minute."

After several rounds of haggling about how the teams should be split, my uncle Dean brushed his hands together and declared the talent to be all even with five players on each team. "Drew, since Mary Lib's on your team, you guys can bat first. Just put her at the end of the batting order. If she's not back when her turn comes, just skip her."

Drew slapped me on the back. "Why don't you lead us off, little brother?"

"Sure thing, coach," I said, picking up the bat, my chest puffed up at taking the prized position.

As I approached the plate, Mary Lib came clomping onto the field. "Sorry about that, guys," she said, dragging Slate up to home plate. "Can we squeeze him in?"

I glared at her treachery. "No way! The teams have already been picked. He'll have to sit out."

"Are you kidding?" Uncle Dean said. "We can't deny Slate Rosen, the Bulldogs' ace pitcher, and make him sit on the sidelines. Of course he can play."

Slate looked around nervously, then began to walk away. "That's okay. I probably need to be getting home anyway."

"No way," Mary Lib said. "I didn't drag you all the way over here just for you to turn and leave."

"But I don't really—"

"She's right," Drew added. "You can take my place. I gotta get back to help PaPa clean the cooker anyway."

"Perfect," my uncle said. "He'll take your place and, as our guest of honor, he can bat first."

I threw the bat down. "Great, yeah, go ahead and take the plate. Make yourself at home."

Uncle Dean grabbed the softball and ran to the six-inch pile of dirt we'd fashioned into the pitcher's mound. "Okay, batter up, Mr. Rosen."

As Slate stood taking warm-up swings, Mary Lib pulled me to the side. "What's eating you?"

"Nothin'. Not a thing."

"Well, you're acting like a—"

Crack! The sound of Slate's bat crashing into my uncle's first pitch turned us toward the far side of the pecan orchard. Stunned, we all stood motionless, watching the ball sail over the trees all the way out into Mrs. Clegg's garden. Peeps and Reubin arched their heads up at the ball's line of flight as if watching an imaginary rocket's smoke trail.

Uncle Dean's jaw dropped. "I've never seen such a—"

"Home run!" Cackles crowed. "You see that, Cody Edwards? That's how it's done."

"Whatever," I muttered.

Mary Lib pulled at my sleeve. "That's what I mean. He's on our team and you're like *whatever*."

Slate started with a slow unenthusiastic jog to first base as everybody but me cheered him on. By the time he'd passed second base, my blood was boiling. Why would God grant a bully such a great skill?

As he was rounding third, a thunderous voice shook everyone on the field. "Stop that!"

Slate froze just a few feet past third base.

Out from beside the switch bush came Mr. Rosen, stomping across the infield, denying his son his victory lap by blocking his path. He planted a fist into his hips. "To the car! Now!"

Slate slung his head down without objection and proceeded to walk back in the direction from where his father had come. Unfortunately, Mr. Rosen did not follow. No one moved, not even my uncles, as we prepared for the scolding we all knew was about to spew.

"My boy's a baseball player, not some sissy softballer. Hitting oversized mushy balls hurts his swing. I don't know who invited him to play but—"

"I did, sir," Drew said, running up.

Rosen's eyes tightened into tiny slits. "You trying to ruin my boy's chances at all-county, Edwards?"

"No sir. Why would I do that? I-I didn't know softball could mess up a player's swing. All I did was invite him to our picnic. I just thought that—"

Mr. Rosen's head twitched, his glare moving from Drew back toward Maudie's house. "How many cars are over there?" he said, his voice shifting from irate to curious.

"Excuse me?" Drew said.

"That's your aunt's house?"

"No sir, it's my great-grandmother Maudie's."

"How old is she?"

"I'm not sure."

"How's her health?"

"She had a stroke years ago that put her in a wheelchair but she's good now."

In an instant whatever spell had come over him broke, and he was leaving the field in the same huff he'd been in when he came onto it. "Don't be inviting my son to play any more softball," he said over his shoulder. "Ever."

All eyes turned to Drew.

I took it upon myself to break the awkward silence with the one observation I couldn't hold in. "I've said it before and I'll say it again, mean just runs in that family."

"Would you shut up?" Drew yelled.

Mary Lib echoed my brother's remark with a simple raised eyebrow.

"What? I'm not saying anything that's not true."

Without a word Drew marched back to the pig cooker.

"You know it's true, Mary Lib. He's as mean as ole Bullet."

"Why, Cody Edwards—you've got some nerve to say that about my dog."

"I-I didn't mean that. What I meant—"

"I know exactly what you meant," she said, spinning on her heels and storming off the field.

"You know he wants to kill Happy, don't you?" I called after her.

I turned to find my uncles and the rest of the gang standing dumbfounded by our conflict at home plate.

"Well, he did," I said, holding out my hands. "I'm telling you, given the chance he'll kill Happy."

Reubin walked up but stopped a cautious distance from me like I was some rabid creature. "I-I think Peeps and me are gonna play some marbles."

Cackles stood biting her lip before following them. "I got winners."

Uncle Dean forced a smile as he put his hand on my shoulder. "Maybe we'll try again later."

There, on the empty field, I was more alone than I'd ever

been in my life. Apologies swirled in my head, wanting to come out, but I was at a loss for where to start.

Chapter 16

For the next hour, I sat on a stump in the far corner of the orchard, licking my wounds and staring into the dirt. Why was I the bad guy? Sure, I showed my rear end, but if everyone knew Slate, they'd know why. What was Drew seeing that I wasn't?

Just then, something bounced off my head.

"You done sulking?"

I looked up to find Mary Lib tossing a pecan from hand to hand. "You know you need a whole handful of these whacked across that self-centered noggin of yours."

"I reckon I do."

She squatted next to me.

"Here, you can have the stump," I said, hopping up.

"Oh no you don't. You can't go being all chivalrous on me now. I'm still mad at you for bad-mouthing Bullet." She smirked. "Even though he is rather cantankerous."

"I really am sorry about that. I was just so mad."

"Mad at Slate for stealing the show?"

I sighed. "I guess."

"Cody, I don't know him. All I've heard from you is how cold and distant he is and—"

"And how he doesn't like Happy and never calls me by my right name. It's like he's messing with me or somethin'."

"Maybe it's his way of playing with you, like how Cackles is always calling Peeps 'Four Eyes.'"

"I doubt it. Even if he is, it's not polite and I don't like it."

"You know what I think? I think you're more upset that Drew invited him."

My silence was enough to tell her she was right.

"You know Drew loves you, don't you?"

My skin flushed. The word *love* unnerved me. Brothers didn't use that type of word for each other. *Love* was reserved for parents and grandparents.

"He was just trying to be nice. It's what Drew does best."

"I don't understand why. It's not like Slate does anything nice for him."

"You don't always have to be nice to someone just because they're nice to you. But you're wrong about Slate not doing anything nice. He asked Drew if he wanted to come to his ball game tomorrow."

"That's just it. He only asked *him*. He's trying to take my place."

"Oh, now we're getting somewhere. You really *are* jealous. You think Slate's replacing you somehow. Well, get that out of your head because he also invited all of us too."

"Really?"

"Yes. And if it makes you feel any better, the reason he came to the picnic in the first place was because Drew said if he did, he'd do some of his chores at the factory tomorrow so he could leave early."

I suddenly felt lighter.

"So are you in for the game?"

"Yeah, I'm in." I wasn't going to be the odd man out

and spend the afternoon by myself like the loser I'd shown myself to be today. I would go and force myself to have a good time. I was still leery of Slate's motives, but I'd use his gesture to redeem my status as the good guy.

The next morning Drew got off to the factory without me having a chance to apologize for my attitude at the picnic. Luckily the gang's short-term memory kicked in and we played throughout the day with no mention of it. Even Cackles was mute on the matter. Apparently, Drew's memory had lapsed as well because when he ran out of the factory at the end of the day, he was all smiles.

"Did ya have a good day at work?" I said, testing the waters.

"I had a fantastic day. I'll tell you and Mary Lib all about it at the game. Where is she, by the way?"

"Her and Reubin are down at Mrs. Clegg's. She's letting them ride old Julius."

"Go get 'em and then round up the rest and head on up to the field. The game starts in fifteen minutes."

"Aren't you coming?"

"Yeah, I just need to talk to Gonny a minute and grab a sandwich. I'll meet you there." He pulled two dollars from his pocket. "This'll get everybody in."

The five-minute walk to our school's baseball field took Reubin, Cackles, and Peeps less than a minute as they sprinted the entire way, leaving Mary Lib and me to mosey along at our own pace.

"Everything good with you and Drew?" she asked.

"I think so. He said he's got something to tell us."

Mary Lib nodded toward the stadium's entrance. "Look at our bunch of crazies. You'd think they've never been out of the house."

Reubin was running circles around Peeps while Cackles bounced between them like a drunken sailor.

"We'd better get up there before they call the wacko wagon to pick 'em up."

"They won't let us in," Cackles said, running up to us. "We don't have any—"

"Money?" I said, handing over Drew's two dollars to the young girl staffing a table next to the gate. "Five please."

"What about Drew?" Mary Lib said.

"I'll wait for him here. You take the loonies in, and we'll be there shortly."

A few minutes later Drew and I were inside the gates, weaving in and out of the crowd as the man over the loud-speaker went through each team's roster, every name reverberating through the stadium. After passing through a short corridor, we were standing in the home team's seating section just as the umpire yelled, "Play ball!"

Mary Lib waved from the second row of seats directly behind the Bulldogs' dugout. "Over here!"

"Wow, she snagged us some good seats," Drew said.

"Yeah, I think…Oh no."

"What is it?"

I motioned him to Cackles. "See anybody you know?"

Drew rolled his eyes. "Of all the seats, she has to sit directly behind Rosen's dad."

After scouring the stadium unsuccessfully for other seating options, we made our way to the two open seats next to Mary Lib.

"I got dibs on the end," I said.

Drew looked down the row at Mr. Rosen. "Of course you do."

"You guys got here just in time," Mary Lib said. "Slate's about to throw the first pitch."

Cackles jumped around. "Wahoooo! Go, Slate, go!"

"Strike that boy O—U—T, out!" Peeps followed.

"Batter, batter, batter swiiing…batterrrr!" Reubin yelled.

Mary Lib patted his knee. "You gotta wait until Slate's about to pitch to do that one."

"Gotcha." Reubin smiled.

Mary Lib turned to us. "Either of you want to switch seats? You'll be closer to the plate."

"Nope," Drew replied immediately.

"Not a chance," I added.

"Chickens," she said with a playful scowl.

"Here he goes, ladies and gentlemen," Cackles announced as Slate twisted his torso back while pulling the ball past his hip. "There's the windup." She paused, waiting for the release. "And there's the pitch."

"Steeeerike!" the umpire yelled.

The crowd erupted. Cackles, Peeps, and Reubin leaped to their feet, hugging and screaming as if the game had just been won. Slate's father managed a slight nod. Another strike followed, then a ball wide and outside and then another strike smack-dab down the middle. The umpire stretched his arm then jerked his hand back to his side. "Outta there!"

The crowd's cheering went up again, with our end of the row and Cackles' screeching being heard above all others.

Mary Lib turned to Drew and me. "Did you guys realize how good he was?"

Drew shrugged. "I'd been told. But I never imagined this."

I declined to answer. Instead, I sat on my hands, eyeing Mr. Rosen and the brown bag he'd pulled from under his seat.

Two more batters came to the plate. Both ended up going back to their dugout, dragging their bats behind them.

Cackles, Peeps, and Reubin celebrated with increasing intensity.

Slate led the Bulldogs off the field for their time at bat. As they entered the dugout, Ozzy spied Mary Lib and blew her a kiss.

"Yuck. What was that for?" Cackles said.

Mary Lib turned to Drew, ignoring both the kiss and question. "Your brother said you had something to tell us."

"You bet I do," he said, tapping me on the shoulder.

Still focused on Mr. Rosen, I didn't respond.

"Cody, listen up. I'm gonna tell you guys what it was I had to tell you."

"Oh yeah," I said, straightening in my seat.

"Get closer. I don't want anybody to hear this."

He turned to Mary Lib then back to me. "The other coffin's been sold."

"The one *you* were in?" I said.

"Yeah."

"When?

"Just before noon. That's why I didn't have lunch. I was getting all the scoop from Mr. Merriweather." He paused, looking around.

"Come on," I said, "nobody can hear you above all this ruckus."

"A woman named Patricia Dalton bought it for her husband. They own a big cattle farm over in Mebane. Seems he was a horse lover whose horse evidently didn't love him as much."

I reared back, "Say what?"

"Two days ago, while he was grooming him, the horse kicked him in the head. Killed him dead on the spot."

Mary Lib covered her heart. "Poor Mrs. Dalton."

"Poor *Mr.* Dalton," I added.

"Do you guys see what this means? All the visions I had are on point with what I'm sure will take place at the funeral. The big pasture under a giant oak tree is going to be where he's buried and there're sure to be lots of cowboys there and since it's a funeral, they'll probably be wearing black hats."

"How can you be certain without being there?" Mary Lib said.

"I can't, and I'm not about to crash a funeral to find out, but I'm here to tell ya it all makes sense."

"It does to me too," I said.

Mary Lib nodded. "What about the dog you said you saw?"

Drew smiled. "Mr. Merriweather mentioned her, saying how her husband's Labrador was already in mourning, so I'm sure they'll have him at the funeral."

Mary Lib and I continued bobbing our heads.

"But the thing that locks it down solid is the vision of the horseshoe on the side of the coffin."

"Which is what yours had on it. It's just like me seeing the gold leaf handles on Irvin-Dell's."

His smile widened. "Exactly."

"Edwards!" came a thundering voice from above us.

We all turned at once in Cackles' direction. Towering above her was Mr. Rosen, his face beet red. "Control your people or else I'll have them frone out," he said, swaying. "I can't hear myself fink." He thrust his hand holding the brown paper bag in Cackles' face. "Especially with this one's squawking in my ear."

"But, sir, they're just—"

"I swear, boy, if I have to—"

"Sit down, ya drunk," a man called out from behind us.

"You're the one that needs to be thrown out," came another, and a chant began.

"Throw him out! Throw him out!"

By that time, half the stadium was more occupied with the disturbance playing out on our row than the action on the field. Even the Bulldogs' dugout had turned toward Mr. Rosen's staggering rant. The only player who didn't was Slate. He sat staring out to centerfield.

"Come on, guys," Drew said, waving Cackles in. "I just saw a row of seats come available closer to home plate."

As we migrated to our new location, I looked back toward the Bulldogs' dugout. Slate had shrunk down almost out of sight. His father, however, remained the center of attention as an assistant coach and groundskeeper escorted him from the stadium.

Chapter 17

With his father gone, Slate played the rest of the game in a quiet rage that resulted in a lopsided nine-to-one victory for the Bulldogs. Cackles, Peeps, and Reubin rushed the field, using up the rest of their manic energy celebrating with the team and jubilant fans. Cackles sprinted around the bases with Peeps and Reubin running after her, laughing and stumbling all the way to home base.

Drew made his own dash to the exit.

"Don't you want to wait for the others?" Mary Lib yelled after him.

"They'll be fine. Besides, I want to finish what we were talking about earlier. Come on."

When we arrived at her house, he led us to the koi pond in her backyard. "Nobody will see us back here."

Mary Lib and I sat on the pond's stony edge while he paced in front of us. Times like this were what I enjoyed most about being Drew Edwards' brother. Whether it was preparing for a make-believe séance or telling the run-of-the-mill ghost story, the boy knew how to set a stage.

A moment later he stopped, patted his fingers together,

and with the patience of a church pastor said, "I know how the coffin-jumps work now."

"How?" I said.

"Whatever coffin we're in is meant *for* the person that ends up being buried in it."

"We kinda knew that already," Mary Lib said.

Undeterred, he continued, "And the catalyst, the thing that makes it work—is Happy."

"Again, something we knew."

"Right. But—what is it *he does* that creates the visions?"

"He jumps on them," I blurted.

"Of course, but *what* exactly does he do that produces visions of either before the person dies or the day of their funeral?"

"He just bounces around like he always does."

"Wait…" Mary Lib said. "He does do more than that! He does something different for each type of vision."

Drew clasped his hands as he watched the cogs of her mind begin to turn in the direction he was hoping.

She slowly stood. "When you guys saw visions of the funerals, he was on top, smacking the lid with his hand."

Drew was gleaming now. He prodded her on. "And when we saw visions before they died—"

"He spun around!" she shouted. "That's exactly what he did! Happy spins time backward!"

He grinned at me. "Do you think you can teach him how to spin and tap on command?"

"The spinning's no problem. Remember, I just show him my Pez dispenser for that."

"What about smacking the lid? Can you get him to do that?"

"Probably, it would just take…" Suddenly thoughts of

training Happy came to a screeching halt. In their place rushed the plan I'd been bouncing around in my head since our adventure with the coffins.

"What's wrong? Don't you think you can do it?" he said.

"It's not that. I know I can."

"Awesome. If you're able to get our little buddy patting lids, do you know what that means?"

I wanted to scream it out. The thought was too big for anything less, but I had to be in control. I collected myself, took a breath and delivered my words in a concrete monotone. "We can change the world." My hand, having a mind of its own, grabbed him by the sleeve. The calm I'd somehow summoned vanished. "We can change everything. We can save lives. We can save—him!"

Drew pulled back, inspecting me for the source of the intensity I felt surging through me. "Who're you talking about saving?"

"President Kennedy!"

Time stretched out as my brother and Mary Lib exchanged concerned glances. "Buddy, I think there're things we can do with this but—"

"Listen to me. I've been thinking about this ever since the last jump but didn't want to say anything because I knew you'd think I was crazy. And you kept harping about doing the research. Well, we've done all that. And now we know what to do."

"Go on, Cody," Mary Lib said. "Tell us how we can save a man who's been dead for almost two years."

Drew took my place on the pond's edge. "Okay, little brother, we're listening."

I wiped my mouth. "It's actually pretty simple. We take a trip to Washington, D.C. and ask to speak to the person in charge of the funeral or whoever was in charge or maybe his wife." I swiped my sleeve across my forehead. "I'm not sure, maybe the vice president. Could be the new president. Yeah, maybe it's—"

Drew held out an opened hand, moving it downward. "Just relax. Take a deep breath."

"Okay…so whoever's in charge of that sort of thing, we explain to them how the coffin-jumping works."

Mary Lib angled her head at me. "I'm pretty sure they don't have a position for that kind of thing."

"I know, but whoever was in charge of burying him or digging him up is who we'll need."

Both reared back at the same time.

"You want to *dig him up*?" Mary Lib said.

"How else can we save him?"

Drew shook his head. "I know where you're going and it's insane."

"What's he talking about?" Mary Lib said.

"Changing time. He's talking about a coffin-jump with President Kennedy's casket."

Her lips parted but nothing came out.

I wrung my hands together. "All we have to do is dig him up—take him out for just a minute—pop inside—have Happy do his spin thing—and then—"

"*We* dig him up?" Drew said.

"No, not us. It'll be Washington people."

"And then what?"

"We warn him or do something that keeps him from going down that street in the limousine. Maybe it's telling the police about Lee Harvey being in that building or maybe just going up and distracting him while the president drives by." My head started to pound. "I haven't exactly figured all that out but whoever does the jump will have to use the time they're in the coffin to do whatever's needed to prevent him from being shot."

"And there it is," Drew said.

"Why're you saying it like that? You think it's stupid, don't you?"

"No. I think it makes sense. But it's got two holes."

"What?"

"First of all, who in their right mind would believe a story like that? Especially those Washington brainiacs. I guarantee everyone who hears it will try to put us away. But the main reason it won't work is that we've only seen visions. We don't know if we even can interact. All I did was see stuff. I never said or did anything but look—did you?"

"No, I was too afraid."

"Same here. It was like I had shell shock. I also don't remember if anyone saw me either."

"Now that you mention it, I kinda felt like a ghost." My heart sank as my plan took one hit after another. "I really didn't think it all the way through."

Mary Lib consoled me with a smile. "It did have some logic. And it would definitely be the patriotic thing to do."

Drew pointed at me, his mouth pinched tight, holding back whatever was running through his mind until finally he let loose. "But you still may have something. Your plan has holes but that doesn't mean they can't be plugged. We just have to figure out how to do it. And like you said, Mary Lib, it would be the patriotic thing to do."

I couldn't help bouncing. "Of course it would. We'd be heroes."

"Easy on the hero thing," Drew said. "This would be for mankind, not us."

"So what's our next step?"

"More research. And we have to tell Mr. Merriweather."

"I thought you didn't want to upset him by messing with his coffins."

"I still don't, but this has gotten way too big." He placed his hand on my shoulder. "You're coming with me to work tomorrow. Happy needs to start his lessons."

Armed with my Pez dispenser and pockets full of pecans, Drew and I went to the factory an hour before it opened to begin teaching Happy how to send us forward or back in time. Ten minutes after letting him out for a quick play session, he swung through his little door, bouncing around the office.

"Ready to get schooled, little fella?" I said, reaching to shut his door.

"You can leave it open," Drew said. "Mr. Merriweather likes it as cool as possible in here."

"I'm gonna teach him to smack first since he's got the spinning down."

"You might want to keep working on that to make sure he does it on command."

"Good idea, we'll get that right first." I reached into my pocket and pulled out my Pez dispenser. Like a furry little tornado, he began turning. "Not yet," I said, shielding my eyes from his tail as it whipped across my face.

"See what I mean?" Drew said. "You gotta give him a command first."

I put him on the floor and took his tiny hand. "Now watch." I slowly pulled the Pez dispenser back out. At the first sight of Mickey Mouse's head, he spun loose of my grasp and twirled around, chattering and giggling all the while.

"Remember," Drew said, "you can't let him start doing it on his own."

"I know, I know. Geez you're worse than Cackles and her roller-bat rules." I tossed the dispenser to him. "Here, you be me and I'll be him." I picked Happy up and sat him in a chair. "Now pay attention."

Drew stifled a laugh. "What do you want me to do?"

"Pop out a Pez candy and give it to me. But wait until I'm on top of the desk."

Drew shook his head, muttering something. The fact he was already questioning my teaching skills was annoying. "If you've got a better way, go at it."

"Oh no. You go ahead and hop on the desk, which I assume is playing the role of the coffin in today's performance."

I climbed up. "Yes, it's the coffin and no, you're *not* funny." I squatted, making myself small, hoping Happy would see himself in the same position. "Throw me the Pez."

Drew snickered. "Here you go, good boy."

Snagging the tiny treat, I mimicked Happy by frantically licking it while spinning. Several turns into my demonstration, I noticed him twirling along with me in his chair. Exhausted, I stopped, took a long breath, and threw my hands over my face. "Noooo, Happy."

Drew laughed and I peeked through my fingers to see my little friend perched up with his hands over his face. The corners of my mouth quivered. Seeing him also peeking was too much and I launched into a full-out belly laugh with Drew joining in. The tapping of Mr. Merriweather's cane on the plank floors brought it all to a halt.

"What in the world is going on?" he said from the doorway.

"M-Mr. Merriweather, what are you doing here?" I stammered.

"Last I checked, I work here."

"You're early."

"I wanted to see if the new guy had the gumption to come in before hours. You know, a little test to see if he's got a work ethic. I'm surprised, but he did. I sent him out to the docks to move those hardware crates out of the way before the morning lumber delivery arrives."

"So he's got some experience?"

"Not a bit."

"That's okay. We can teach him," Drew said. "What's his name?"

Mr. Merriweather avoided eye contact, choosing the ceiling as his focus. "Ozzy."

"Ozzy? Like Slate's friend Ozzy?"

He nodded. "I'm afraid so."

"But Slate said his father didn't want him to work here."

"He changed his mind. He wants him to learn the business alongside his son."

"Great," I said, climbing down from the desk. "Now that makes two jerks working here."

"Cody! Watch your tongue, young man."

"I'm sorry, sir. I'm just…well, I just don't cotton to those two."

He looked back toward the door then turned to me. "I'm of a like mind, but we have to do what we have to do."

"That's okay, sir," Drew said. "We'll make it work."

Mr. Merriweather patted Drew on the shoulder. "Somehow I knew you'd say that." He rolled his eyes back to me. "So now you can tell me what prompted you to scale my desk."

"I don't understand, sir."

"He wants to know why you were on it," Drew said.

I stared at my brother, waiting for him to rescue me. He said we needed to be up front with Mr. Merriweather and explain everything we'd experienced with the coffins, but I never thought I'd be the one presenting it. "I was just teaching Happy a trick. I wanted to see if I could get him to go in circles."

"On my desk?"

A bead of sweat rolled down the side of my face. "Uh, yeah. I-I was…"

Drew stepped in front of me. "Sir, there's something we need to tell you."

I closed my eyes and breathed a sigh of relief as Drew took the wheel.

"It's big. I hope you won't be mad at us. We don't know if it's magic, voodoo, or what, but this has possibilities that could impact all of us, the entire country—actually, the whole world. I'm afraid we had to use some of the coffins though to find it out."

Mr. Merriweather took a step back. With the end of his cane, he pushed the door shut. "No more hemming and hawing. Spit it out."

From beginning to end, I stood biting my lip, watching him as my brother described what we had done with his coffins, the visions we'd seen, and how we figured out that his pet monkey was the linchpin to everything. Through it all he stood rigid, one hand clutching the corner of his desk, the other squeezing his cane, twisting it back and forth, grinding the tip into the plank floor.

"So that's what we were doing when you came in. We were teaching Happy how to either spin or tap the coffin lid on command."

He dropped his cane and leaned on the desk, his hand over his heart.

"Sir, are you alright?"

"I—I need to sit."

Drew dragged a chair across the room and together we helped ease him into it. For a moment we stood silently watching as he buried his face into trembling hands. Just as I started to launch into how we wanted to save President Kennedy, he held up his hand. "Did either of you say or do anything while you were witnessing these visions?"

"No sir," Drew said, "we were too scared."

"Do you believe us?" I asked.

The hollow silence of the empty factory hung in the air.

He dropped his hand to his side. "Yes. I believe you."

"Really?" Drew said. "You don't think we're making it up or hallucinating?"

"I believe you because I know everything about the coffins." His gaze fell on me, then back to Drew. "And I know there are consequences if you're not careful. So hear me loud and clear." His voice rose with each word. "You will *not* go near another coffin for any other reason than to work on it. You'll forget all of this. Do I make myself clear?"

"But sir, we can save—"

"Nothing!" he said, slapping his palm on the desk. "You'll do as I say or you'll never set foot in this factory again." He grabbed his cane and hobbled out the door, slamming it behind him.

Drew and I stood staring at one another. Just as I found my voice, I noticed something lurking outside Happy's door—the silhouette of a person's leg. "Who's out there?"

"Who're you shouting at?" Drew asked.

"I think I saw somebody," I said pushing past him. I stuck my head outside but Happy's playground was empty.

Chapter 18

Mr. Merriweather's scolding was enough to send Drew into an emotional tailspin that left him moping about the factory for the rest of the day. For our transgressions I was sent home while he was tasked with shoving wood in and out of a planer, a monstrous machine with an ear-piercing saw that turned rough boards into smooth ones. By the time he got home that evening, he was covered in sawdust, half-deaf, and guilt-ridden for his perceived betrayal.

"What's wrong with you boys tonight?" Gonny said over dinner.

"Nothing," Drew replied, hypnotized by his untouched bowl of tomato soup.

"Well, something's up because your brother here didn't leave his bedroom all day. Did you two have a squabble?"

"No ma'am," I said.

"Drew, is he telling the truth?"

"Yes ma'am. We're fine." He swirled his spoon through his soup then stopped. "Gonny, if there's something you knew would be good for a lot of people but there was one person who said not to do it, would you go ahead with it?"

I inched to the edge of my chair, awaiting her response.

"If it's going to benefit people and it's not illegal, then yes."

I shot Drew a glance. "Heck yeah. If you can help others, then you should do it."

"But," she added with a tilt of the head, "you should find out why that person is opposed to it. You never know, there could be a good reason why they're against it."

The rest of the evening and into the wee hours Drew and I went back and forth on why our plan had been shot down.

"How does he know what the coffins can do?" I asked.

"Beats me. Only thing I can figure is that he's had Happy all these years, so somewhere along the line he must've been in one and Happy did his thing."

"How old's Happy anyway?"

"I don't know. Mr. Merriweather's never said. We'll ask tomorrow, but the first thing we need to do is ask for forgiveness."

The next morning, after breakfast and a quick practice round of apologies, we tucked our tails and headed to the factory ten minutes early. When we got there, the side door was already open, and instead of the lone sound of the rafter birds flittering about, we heard the moaning of a man, followed by a muffled lullaby. Rising above it all was Happy's unmistakable chatter that sounded somehow more distressed.

"Where's it coming from?" I asked.

"Sounds like it's up front. Come on."

Halfway across the factory floor Drew took off in a sprint. "That's Mr. Merriweather. He's in the showroom."

A few steps behind, I barreled into his back when he

broke his mad dash with a sudden stop in the doorway. "Oh no. What happened?" he said.

"What is it?" I said, craning my head around him.

"Something's wrong with Happy."

I pushed him to the side. Mr. Merriweather sat in a chair, cradling Happy in his arms, rocking him back and forth while stroking his head. Balled up against his chest, Happy clung to him, shivering. In his tiny hands he held a crimson-stained rag wrapped around the end of his tail.

I rushed to him and fell to my knees. "Oh, Happy…" I wanted to say more or do something to ease his pain, but nothing came. All I could do was rub his back while Mr. Merriweather continued rocking.

"Did he get it caught in a machine?" Drew said.

Mr. Merriweather glared down at the floor beside the coffin next to them. In a small puddle of blood was a six-inch piece of Happy's tail. "Whatever it was, it happened in here," he said, his eyes moving up to the coffin's lid.

Drew pushed it open, revealing its white satin interior. In the corner's edge was a small red patch. "He must have gotten in here last night and the lid fell on his tail."

Happy suddenly shrunk into a tighter ball and pulled wildly at Mr. Merriweather's shirt. His mournful whimpering transformed into a shrill hissing.

"What happened here?" Ozzy said, strutting into the room with Slate following.

"Happy had an accident," I said.

Slate hung by the door while Ozzy stood gawking at Happy. "Had a little trim, did he?"

Drew spun toward him with his chest bowed out. Fortunately, Mr. Merriweather diverted the potential encounter before any fists were thrown. "I want everyone to get to work. I'm going to take Happy to the vet. Drew, you're in charge."

"He's just a snot-nose kid," Ozzy sneered.

"And today he's your boss," Slate said, walking out the door. "I'll be on the dock waiting for the morning delivery."

"Oh, alright," Ozzy groaned. "I'm coming."

"No," Drew said. "I need you on the planer today."

Later that afternoon I went to the factory to see if Happy was back from the vet. Unable to find Mr. Merriweather or Drew, I started back outside when a hand reached out of a storeroom, grabbed me by the collar and threw me inside. My head banged against the wall as Ozzy's sweaty, saw-dust-covered forearm wedged under my chin and pinned me against it.

"You think it's funny your stupid brother put me to work on that devil's machine, don't you?" He rammed his shoulder into me. With his face inches from mine, he growled, "Well, I'm here to wipe that silly grin off your face. You're going to do something for me and if you don't, there's gonna be hell to pay."

"Wh-What do you want?"

"I need you to show me how to work those coffins."

"What do you mean?"

"You're going to show me how you create those visions, like the ones you saw before the people died." He laughed. "That was me outside the chimp's door yesterday. I heard everything."

"And what if I don't?"

The flash of metal took my breath as Ozzy removed his forearm, replacing it with the cutting edge of his machete against my neck. "Instead of your little buddy's tail lying on the floor, it'll be his head." He threw up the palm of his other hand to reveal two gaping holes in the pad of his thumb. "And if he decides to take another chunk of me like he did last night, I'll use this blade to take one from you."

"B-but, I'm not a hundred percent sure we can do it. Happy's not really trained yet."

"You got him to do it those other times so we're moving forward and we're doing it tonight."

"What if he doesn't come back from the vet or if they've got him drugged up and all he wants to do is sleep or if—"

"Shut up! We're doing this tonight, so be here exactly at ten. I'll leave the side door open. And Edwards, don't even think about saying anything to Merriweather, your brother, or anybody. You come alone—you hear me? Alone or I swear I'll do more than just cut off that rat's head."

For the rest of the day, I holed up in my room with a massive headache as I struggled to come up with a way to renege on Ozzy's demand. Drew came in after work to tell me Happy was back and even though he'd received fifteen stitches, he was doing okay.

"Remember what you asked Gonny the other night?" I said. "The question about should you do something to help others even if there was someone who said you shouldn't."

"Yeah."

"What if someone asked you to do something you knew was wrong, but if you didn't do it people could get hurt?"

"Why're you asking?"

"Come on," I pleaded, "what would you do?"

"I suppose I'd do what I knew was wrong. I couldn't just let people get hurt."

I sighed. Why did he have to say that? He was the smart one. Couldn't he have come up with something clever enough to free me of the task ahead? But I knew he was right.

"Seriously, why're you asking?"

"Oh, I, uh, I was watching a gangster movie earlier and there was a scene where a mob guy was trying to force a man to do something like that."

The moment he left the room, I smushed my face into a pillow, praying that when I lifted it, a new day would have arrived and my encounter with Ozzy would have been nothing but a dream. Two minutes later I rolled over and watched the clock's minute hand creep along until I heard Gonny's door shut and the TV click off. Drew had honored the house rules that everyone would be in bed by nine thirty. Fifteen minutes later I snuck out of the house, hoping for once to be caught. Unfortunately, we'd perfected it to an art, and I was on my way to meet someone I hated in a place that scared me to tears at night.

Just as Ozzy had said, the side entrance was open.

"I thought you woulda backed out." His voice came from out of the dark.

I pressed back against the door, and it slammed shut.

"Quiet," he said, whipping out a flashlight and shining it in my face. "You wanna wake up the whole neighborhood?"

"S-sorry. I just get spooked in here at night."

"Did you come alone?" He reached down and tapped the handle to his ever-present machete strapped to his belt.

"Y-yeah."

"Would you knock off the stutter? You're giving me the willies too. Now let's grab the monkey and get to work."

"He's not going to do anything if he sees you."

"Why?"

"He's scared of you."

"How do you know?"

I held back an eye roll. He really couldn't be that dumb. "You cut off his tail. And by the way he was hissing at you today, I'm sure he won't want to get near you."

His fingers found his machete's handle again. "Well, you're gonna have to figure a way to—"

"Wait, I got it. Go to the showroom, get in whatever coffin you want and pull the lid down. I'll bring him in and see if I can get him on top."

"And I'll see the past—right? It has to be the past."

"I told you, I'm not sure what he'll do. I haven't had enough time to teach him."

He lifted his flashlight as if about to club me. "Alright then. Here," he said, handing it to me. "I'll be waiting. Now hurry up."

Just as I thought, when I went to get Happy, I found him laid out and snoring like a miniature drunk. Even with my flashlight directly on him, he wouldn't rouse. I gently picked him up. "Come on, buddy," I whispered. "I need your help." He wrapped his arms around my neck then laid his head on my shoulder and slept all the way to the showroom.

Through the darkness I found the only coffin with the lid down. A second later it creaked open and Ozzy peeked out.

"Pull it back down," I said.

"What's wrong with him?"

"He's probably still drugged up from the vet's. I'm not sure this is going to work."

"Well, smack him or something."

"Just shut the lid." I reached into my pocket and pulled out my Pez dispenser. "Happy, look what I brought."

I popped out a candy. Like smelling salts, I waved it under his nose. His nostrils flared, taking in the sweet aroma. Mickey Mouse's Pez was the antidote to whatever the vet had given him. His eyes popped open and suddenly he was clapping his hands in anticipation of receiving his treat. Instead of handing it to him, I placed it on the coffin lid. Out of my arms he leaped, snatching it up, then turning in circles while nibbling away on it. A moment later, he was back in my arms, chattering for another. At the same time, the coffin lid flew open.

Upon seeing Ozzy, Happy began scratching at my chest as if trying to claw his way through me. "I gotta get him back to his cage," I yelled, rushing him out the door.

After several minutes of soothing and another Pez, Happy was back inside his cage, settled, and starting to nod off again.

When I arrived back at the showroom, Ozzy was standing next to the coffin, staring down into it.

"Did you see anything?"

"Yeah," he said flatly, then pointed to the door. "You can go."

It suddenly dawned on me that if I was going to risk helping this goon, I should have the right to know what happened. Besides, it was more research that could help our plans to save the president. "Come on. I want to know."

"I said no. Now go!"

His hand on his machete was enough persuasion to send me running outside. I wasn't about to spend eternity wandering the halls, helping Grandel's ghost pick out his long-overdue coffin upgrade.

Chapter 19

A week passed during which I spent most of the time with my chin to my chest, pretending nothing was wrong. I played marbles with Reubin, chased Cackles and Peeps through the orchard in games of tag, and took on Mary Lib in Scrabble, but I stayed clear of the coffin factory.

"How come you haven't been to see Happy?" Mary Lib asked.

I shrugged. "Just giving things a break."

"What things? Cody, you've been over there almost every day since Drew started working. Something's up."

"Nothing's up. I just don't want to spend my entire summer in a dusty old coffin factory is all." What I really wanted to say was I didn't want to chance another encounter with the machete-wielding Ozzy.

"Does it have something to do with Mr. Merriweather nixing all coffin-related activities?"

She'd given me my out. "Yeah, that's it. I'm just bummed we can't do the plan."

"Don't let that get you down. We just need to let things simmer."

"I guess you're right."

"You should also keep going over there to get things back to normal. It'll help Drew out too."

"How's that?"

"If Mr. Merriweather's still upset," she said, "it could fester and then he could take it out on Drew and fire him."

"I never thought about it that way."

"Well, what're you waiting on? It's only three o'clock."

"You want me to go now?"

"The longer you wait the more time he'll have to stew. You don't want the pot boiling over, do ya?"

"I guess you're right."

She flicked her fingers toward the factory. "Go on then. No time like the present."

I started toward the factory.

"Now get that chin up. You're going to see your best friend and brother. It's not like you're being thrown into the lion's den."

As I stood on the sidewalk across the road from the coffin factory, I noticed Rosen's Cadillac sitting at the corner. His driver, the large man in the black suit, was standing at the rear of the car, hands crossed. Seeing me, he waved me over. I looked behind me, hoping he was gesturing to someone else.

"Me?" I mouthed.

He nodded.

The day was already hot. As I walked to the car, it became sweltering.

"Mr. Rosen would like to speak with you," he said, opening the back door.

I eyed the dark entrance. I was about to be whacked. I'd seen every gangster movie that had come to town, and this was how they did it. They asked you into the backseat of a car, blew your brains out, then buried you in the desert.

"Please," the man said. His pleasant tone gave me little comfort. Half the gangsters used it. I turned my right foot in the opposite direction. Just as I was about to run, Mr. Rosen's voice rang out. "Cody, my dear boy!"

I looked up. Coming off Maudie's back porch, he strode up to me and placed his hand on my shoulder. "I was wondering if we might have a quick chat."

"S-sure," I said.

There was no shoving or kicking me inside the car. A simple motion of his eyes propelled me in. As I scooted across the seat, he followed, shutting the door after him. The man in the black suit remained outside.

"So, how have you been?"

"Good."

"School going okay?"

"We're on summer break."

"Yes. Of course. How could I forget? How's everything else? How's your mother and father?"

"Mom's fine."

"And your dad?"

"He's dead."

I waited for his apology. All I got was awkward silence.

He clasped his hands together. "I have a favor to ask. I understand you have a rather special ability. A very, very unique ability."

"Sir?"

"Ozzy has informed me that…" He suddenly broke out laughing then began again, starting and stopping as he stifled more laughter. "Ozzy came to me with this ridiculous story. A story about how you could send people into the past."

I felt the sweat beading up on my forehead.

"He said you used Merriweather's monkey to perform some sort of magic." He stopped and stared at me, his case of giggles vanished. "I'm a businessman who operates in reality, but I have to know—is this true? Can you indeed perform this trick?"

The leather seat squeaked as I shifted my weight. Another awkward moment came and went as I struggled for a response.

His tone went flat. "Call me crazy, but I believe you can. I believe it because all the things Ozzy said he saw when he was in that coffin match up with the man who's going to be buried in it at the end of this week." He smiled as he leaned toward me. "And he told me everything about what he heard standing outside that little door in Merriweather's office." His smile crooked into a snarl. "No need to answer my questions about whether you can do it or not, I'll just come to the point. I want you to do it again."

"But sir, like I told him, I don't know if I can get Happy to do it again, especially since he hates Ozzy. And the—"

"Quiet!" He closed his eyes and took a deep breath. "I understand about Ozzy, which is why you'll do the trick with Slate first."

"Sir, this isn't a trick."

"Trick, magic, voodoo, or whatever it is I don't care. All I care about is that you do it and they see the past."

"But why?"

"That's none of your business." His voice grew louder. "Besides, these are my coffins until they're sold so I have the right to do with them as I please." He glared at me. "If you want to keep the coffin side of the business going and continue to give your brother and the old man a place to work, then you'll do what I ask. As for your monkey friend, I believe Ozzy has already told you what might happen to him. So—I'll ask nicely. Are you going to do this for me?"

His options gave me no room for any rebuttal. I hung my head. "Yes sir."

"Excellent." He slapped my shoulder, leaving his hand on it for a few uncomfortable seconds then moving it down just above my elbow. "One more thing." His grip tightened. "Remember what Ozzy said about talking to others about this?" He dug his nails into the soft underside of my arm and I flinched. "Not a word to anyone—understood?"

I gritted my teeth. "Yes sir."

"Good." He released my arm. "We'll expect to see you in the factory at ten tonight. The side door will be open again. Meet us in the showroom."

"What if I can't get out of the house?"

"You haven't had a problem with that yet, so you won't tonight either." He raised an eyebrow. "Now get going. And Edwards, we *will* see you tonight."

Leaving the car, I noticed Maudie sitting on her back porch. She waved me over to her.

"You wanted to see me?"

Her eyes moved past me to the Cadillac. "What were you and Mr. Rosen talking about?"

"Just factory stuff."

"What kind of factory stuff?"

"You know, things like how the place runs, what I thought about it. That kind of stuff."

"Really? He wanted to know how to run his factory from a little boy who doesn't even work there?"

"Oh no, it was more about what I thought of the

showroom. Like did I think it was comfortable and friendly, stuff like that."

"Did he ask about me?"

"No ma'am, just the factory. He came to see you, didn't he?"

"Yes," she said, continuing to look past me to his car.

"What were you guys talking about?" I asked, keeping her aim away from me.

"A problem he has."

"What kind of problem?"

She clasped her hands together. "Good, he's leaving."

I turned to see his car pulling away from the curb.

"Never did like those fancy Cadillacs," she said.

"How come?"

"Something about the design, especially the new ones with those pointy taillights." She paused. "Makes the back-end look…sinister or something."

I stared along with her as it faded out of sight. She was right—something about it sent a chill up my spine. Maybe it was the man inside, maybe it was the fact that those taillights had a wicked angle to them, or maybe it was that in less than six hours I'd have to be doing something for a man I despised. I was suddenly lost in the moment. Ozzy's demand had multiplied by bringing Slate's father into the picture.

"Cody," came a faint voice. "Cody, do you hear me?" Maudie's soft touch to my forearm pulled me from my thoughts.

I blinked. "Yes ma'am."

"Before you go drifting off again, can you tell Gonny I'd like to speak to her when she gets a chance?"

"Yes ma'am, I'll go now." Without giving her an opportunity for any more inquiries, I broke away.

A minute later the kitchen screen door was slamming shut behind me.

"For heaven's sake," Gonny said, taking a break from the pile of dough her hands were buried in. "How many times do I have to tell you boys not to let that door slam like that?"

"Sorry, Gonny," I said, panting, "I'll be in my room."

"Don't you want to go outside? Cackles and Reubin are out picking up pecans for a pie I'm making. Anything left over you can take to Happy."

"I-I can't. I need to work on something in my room."

"Okay, just don't complain when your slice isn't as big as Drew's."

"That's okay, I'm not that hungry."

She stopped again. "You okay? This is pecan pie we're talking about. And I know it's warm out, but you're sweating like I just asked you to take a trip to the switch bush."

"I'm okay, I just…" My mind went blank.

"You're just what?"

"Oh yeah, I remember now. Maudie wants to talk to you when you can."

"About what?" she said as I backpedaled to my room.

"I don't know. She just wants to talk to you." I shut the door. With my back pressed against it, I slid to the floor and threw my hands over my face. Mentally drained and burning up, I curled into a ball on the cool hardwood floor and fell asleep. Two hours later a knock jarred me awake. Through the crack underneath the door, I could see the bottom half of Drew's converse sneakers.

"What're you doing in there? It's supper time."

I wiped the crusted drool from my mouth. "I'm coming."

A minute later I staggered into the dining room, groggy and stiff from the hard-earned time on my bedroom floor.

"Where's Gonny?"

"She's already eaten. I told her I'd wait for you." He gave me a sideways look. "What's up with you?"

I turned my ear toward the kitchen where Gonny was already working on another meal for tomorrow. I leaned forward and whispered, "I can't take it anymore. I have to tell you something."

"Is it something about the coffins?"

I glanced back at the kitchen. "Yes."

"Hurry up and eat," he said, scarfing down his meal.

Ten minutes later we were back in my room, sitting on the bed. "So, what's going on?" he said.

I began clawing the bedcover into my fists. "I can't believe this is happening. This whole coffin thing's getting out of hand." My eyes welled with tears.

"It's okay," he said. "Everything's going to be alright. Just take it slow and tell me what's happening."

"I'm in a bad spot. I-I don't know if I should even tell you."

"Don't worry, just go ahead with it."

I wiped my eyes. "Remember the other day when I asked what if someone wanted you to do something you knew was wrong, but if you didn't do it people could get hurt?"

"Yeah."

"Well, Slate's father has asked me to do something and if I don't, people could get hurt—you, Mr. Merriweather, and even Happy."

Drew sat stone-faced. "Okay, tell me everything."

Chapter 20

For the next twenty minutes I unloaded everything on my brother, from Ozzy's time in the coffin to Mr. Rosen's demands, even Maudie's questioning me. "What should I do?" I began to sob. "If I don't do it, he'll—"

"He won't do anything."

"How do you know?"

"Because you'll do what he asks. There's nothing else you *can* do."

"But isn't it wrong?"

"Was it wrong for us to do it?" he asked.

"I don't know. We didn't take advantage of anything we saw."

"That's right. In fact, your idea to save the president was a good thing."

I ran my sleeve over my eyes. "Yeah, all I wanted was to do good. What do you think Rosen's trying to do? I don't see him wanting to save anybody."

"I don't either." Drew scratched his chin. "There's a reason though and I'd bet anything it's to benefit himself."

"So you think I should go through with it?"

"Like I said, it's all you can do. We can't call the

cops—it's his factory. And he's right, since he owns it, he can do whatever he wants in there. The other thing is there's no law about people seeing visions. The only thing that'll get you is a straitjacket."

"I'm still afraid though."

"Don't worry. I'm going with you."

"You can't. He said not to tell anybody."

"It'll be alright. I'll go early and hide in the coat closet. I'll be right there, and I won't be alone."

"You thinkin' about bringin' Mary Lib?"

"No, PaPa's shotgun."

At eight o'clock that evening, while Gonny was at Maudie's having the talk she requested, Drew snuck into her room and pulled our grandfather's twelve-gauge out from under the bed while I guarded the back door.

"What time are you going to the factory?" I asked as we ran back to his room.

"Nine," he said, wrapping a blanket around the gun. "I gotta get there before they come."

A few minutes later we heard Gonny coming through the back door. "Boys, where are you?"

Drew stashed the gun under the bed. "We're in here."

The door cracked open, and she poked her head inside. She wore a thin, forced smile.

"Did you need us for something?" Drew asked.

"No, just checking. You boys get to sleep on time tonight. Don't forget, nine thirty."

As soon as the door closed, I was in Drew's face. "She knows. I'm telling ya, she knows."

"No, she doesn't."

"Then why'd she say that?"

"It's just what she does sometimes."

"I don't remember her ever just checking in on us like that."

"Well, she has. You just don't remember because you're scared right now."

"You bet I'm scared, especially now with you having a gun. You don't know how to use that thing. You don't even like guns. And I hate 'em. And I'm hating this more and more. Can't we just stay here? Please, Drew. This is a bad, bad idea."

"Are you finished?" he calmly asked.

"I'm telling you it's a bad idea."

"Listen, I don't like it any better than you, but if you don't get Happy on those coffins, I'm sure Rosen will make good with his threats. Let's just get through this. And if it makes you feel any better, I won't put any shells in the gun."

I sighed. "If you're gonna take it, you might as well load it. But do me a favor—please don't shoot anybody, okay?"

"I promise."

Just before nine I was in Drew's room, helping him stuff pillows under his bedcover to make it look like he was asleep in case Gonny came in. Stopping at the door, he turned to wish me good luck. "Remember, I'll be right there."

"Wait!" My feet took on a mind of their own and I suddenly found myself running to him. I threw my arms around him. "Thank you."

"Uh—okay," he said with a few quick pats to my back.

I pulled back. "Sorry about that."

He swiped his hand through my hair. "See ya later, squirt." With a quick smile he was out the door.

The following hour dragged on as every *what if* barreled through my mind. What if they found Drew in the closet? What if they had guns too? A man like Rosen surely carried one. And of course, what if I couldn't get Happy to spin? If Drew wasn't already there, I would have easily backed out. But just before ten, I mustered my courage, packed my bed with pillows, then snuck off to the factory.

With the side door once again open, I walked in to find a different scene than last time. Many of the lights were on, and unlike last time, the silent, sleeping factory echoed with a heated dispute.

"Hello," I yelled. "I'm here."

"Is that you, Edwards?" Rosen's voice came from a distance.

"Yes sir."

"We're in the showroom."

I paused for a moment, picking up that it was Slate and his father doing the arguing. As I drew closer, I could see Slate through the door. He was pacing back and forth, his hands waving the same way I'd seen one of his teammates do when thrown out at home plate.

I stopped in the doorway just in time to see Mr. Rosen slap him across the face. "You'll do this, or I swear by God I'll—" He raised his hand and held it above Slate who cowered next to one of the coffins. Just as he was about to hammer down on Slate, his eyes caught mine. "Where's the chimp?"

"Y-You said to come here." I glimpsed the coat closet out of the corner of my eye, hoping Drew was able to hear through the thick oak door.

Slate slowly stood. Raising his chin, he glared at his father then turned to me. The right side of his face displayed a growing red welt the size of his father's hand. "Go fetch Happy," he muttered.

I nearly tripped as I ran from the room. A few minutes later I returned with Happy to find Mr. Rosen standing alone in the middle of the room, a silver flask in his hand. He staggered between a dark mahogany coffin and a silver one. After a swig from his flask, he held it over the mahogany coffin. "Here lies Ozzy," he snickered, then swung the flask over the silver one, sloshing whiskey over the lid. "And here lies an ungrateful son."

Happy squeezed tight across my shoulders. "Who goes first?" I asked.

With his flask, he tapped the lid to Slate's coffin. "Before you do your voodoo, I wanna remind these dopes what they need to do."

"Sir, they don't have to do anything. They just need to lie there."

"On the contrary, monkey boy." His voice rose to a level that was sure to make it through the coffin lids. "Remember—stock prices, market conditions or anything that'll rise or fall in value. You got it?"

"Yes," came their muffled replies.

He rolled his bloodshot eyes toward me. "Now get the chimp moving."

"Yes sir." I pulled out my Pez dispenser. Immediately Happy began clapping. I unloaded one candy into my palm then placed it on top of Slate's coffin. Without any coaxing he climbed down my arm onto the lid, picked it up and spun three times. Back into my arms he landed, nibbling down the rest of his treat. "Good boy," I said, stroking his back.

"That's it?" Rosen shouted.

The coffin lid flew open, but Slate remained inside, gaping up at the ceiling.

Mr. Rosen slammed it back shut. "That wasn't enough time. Do it again."

"Wait." I nodded toward the coffin lid as it opened. Slate sprang up. His voice came slow and flat. "I think I have what you wanted."

"Well—spit it out."

"Craten Chemicals. The headline was *Craten Chemicals buys Hester Jones Pharma*," he said with a robotic delivery that matched his glazed expression.

Mr. Rosen took a quick hit from his bottle then wiped his mouth with his sleeve. "What about the date?"

"The twenty-first of this month."

"That's in two days." He leaned toward me. "You did say when the monkey spun around it showed the person inside things around the time the person began to die, right?"

"I-I think that's right, or it might send them back to an important day before they die. We really don't know."

"Whatever," he chuckled. "As long as this guy kicks the bucket day after tomorrow."

"Lady," Slate said. "It's a lady."

"Whoever it is, they just made me a mint."

The mahogany coffin's lid cracked open. "Guys, can we get on with it? It's burning up in here."

The sight of Ozzy peering out threw Happy into a rage. He leaped out of my arms and ran off into the factory, hissing and holding the end of his tail.

"Well, don't just stand there. Go get him!" Rosen shouted.

After taking fifteen minutes to find him and another ten to calm him, I was back in the showroom.

"What took so long?"

I bit my lip, holding back the response I wanted to unleash. Instead, I let my stare drill into him.

"Okay, already," he said, holding up his hands. "I get it. Your boy hates Ozzy but he's going to have to get over it. And this time I need you to make him go forward."

"What do you mean?"

"Make him do the thing that shows visions the day of the funeral. The ones Slate saw give me a couple days to work with, but I need to make sure this one's in the future."

"I don't think Happy can do that on command yet. I've been trying to teach him but he's not good at it."

"Well, we won't know until we try. So let's get going."

"I'm telling you I don't think this is going to work."

"Do it—now!"

Instead of bringing Mickey Mouse out again, I pulled out a pecan, placed it on the coffin, and tapped the lid. "Go on boy," I said, smacking the mahogany with my palm.

Happy's arms stayed wrapped around my neck.

"Go on, boy." I laid another pecan on the lid and got the same results.

Slate stepped up beside me. "What if you give him one of those Pez treats?"

"Those make him spin. He needs to tap the lid."

"Just give him the candy!" Mr. Rosen yelled.

"I don't think it'll help, but if you say so."

Happy remained disinterested when he saw the dispenser and only tightened his grip around my neck.

Mr. Rosen pried the dispenser from my hand. "Give me that thing."

"What're you doing?" I said, watching him rip off Mickey's head and pour all the candy onto the lid.

"That'll get him moving."

Happy stayed fixed.

"For God's sake," Mr. Rosen said, "I'll get him going." With that he yanked Happy from me, plopped him on the coffin then pounded the lid with his fist. "Now do it!"

I cringed as I waited for Happy to erupt. Instead, he sat in front of the Pez and pecans, staring down at them. Ever so slowly he turned his head to Rosen, his little nostrils flaring as his mouth widened, baring his fangs along with a shrieking hiss. Then, as if all his anger had disappeared, he reached down and picked up a single pecan. He sniffed it once then threw it to the floor. He picked up a Pez candy and threw it away too.

"Why's he not eating them?" Rosen said.

I shrugged.

Happy sniffed another Pez and tossed it aside. As if asking for permission to proceed, he slowly raised one hand above his head. "Come on, boy, tap it. You can do it."

With his furry hand hovering above him, he turned to me and giggled. But there was no tap or smack to come. He calmly lowered his hand and crossed his arms over his chest as he squatted. He then leaned forward, his back arching, the hairs standing on end. Squeezing his eyes into tiny slits, he let loose a loud grunt as he pushed out a trail of poop the length of his tail—plus another six inches for what had been chopped off.

Chapter 21

The grandfather clock down the hall was on its twelfth chime when Drew and I tiptoed back into the house. Knowing sleep wasn't possible, I went straight to his room, ready to chat it up until daybreak. There was just too much to unpack from the evening's events and I couldn't wait until morning. From successfully helping Slate coffin-jump to Happy doing his business on Ozzy's lid, we had to relive it, even at the risk of waking Gonny and getting a switching.

"I can't believe they left in such a huff after Happy gave Ozzy his little gift."

Drew's shoulders shook as he laughed. "I sure would like to have seen their faces."

"So what do you think it was that made Mr. Rosen so excited about Slate's vision?"

"That's easy. Money."

"He didn't mention anything about money."

"No but that's what it's all about. He wanted information he could turn around and use. In this case he's probably going to invest in the company Slate said had been bought. When the deal goes through, the money he invests will double or triple, maybe more. It's what's called economics. We started learning about it in school last year."

"Sounds like gambling."

"It kinda is. But if you know what's going to happen in advance, like he does now, then it's a sure thing."

"All he seems to care about is making money, big cars, and baseball."

"I feel sorry for Slate, don't you?"

I couldn't agree with the idea of being sorry for Rosen's son. To me they were still one in the same. For Drew's sake, I just nodded.

For the remaining few weeks of summer, I stayed away from the factory, only venturing in at night with Drew to see Happy. During the day, life on Maple Avenue went back to something I'd always railed against. It was normal to the point of being bland. There were still endless shenanigans with our crew, but there was nothing going on with the coffins and no Rosens or Ozzy threatening me or my family. They were simply the run-of-the-mill final days of summertime, and for once I was fine with that. It wasn't until the day before school began, when Mr. Rosen paid a visit to Maudie, that things took a turn.

The day started out with a clear-blue palette, not a patch of white in the sky, but by noon a wall of dark clouds rolled in, enveloping everything in a steely gray mist that hung down to the pavement. As Drew described it later that evening, it was so close to the color of Mr. Rosen's Cadillac that it almost prevented him from seeing it in front of Maudie's house.

"That's the second time this week it's been over there," I said. "What do you think he wants?"

"Drew shrugged. All I know is he's been almost chipper since that company in Slate's visions got bought. By the way, I overhead Slate telling Ozzy he also saw some of the Major League Baseball scores in his visions. All his information came from a newspaper he saw spread out over a kitchen table. One of the headlines was about the company buyout, which was next to a column of baseball scores. It seems his father was more interested in them than the buyout."

"Why? What good would knowing a baseball score… ohhhhh, wait a minute. I see what he—"

"You got it. He placed bets on those games using that info. I'd bank on it." He raised an eyebrow. "According to some of the guys at the factory, Mr. Rosen's got a pretty big gambling problem."

"Along with a drinking and attitude problem."

I waited for Drew to agree, but his mind was already onto something else. I knew my brother well enough to know when he had switched gears. He would skew his mouth while looking up and to his left. Never the right for some reason. The deeper the thought, the higher his gaze. This gaze was almost straight up.

"What're you thinking about?"

"Your idea."

"What idea's that?"

"President Kennedy."

"What about him?" I asked.

"I think we should do it."

"Wait. You think…" I paused, unsure of what I'd just heard. "You think we should actually go through with it?"

His eyes brightened. "Absolutely."

"But you said they'd throw us in jail or into an insane asylum."

"I never said anything about jail."

"So what changed your mind?"

"I've been watching the news with PaPa when he's been home, and things are getting bad in this country. More of our soldiers are being sent to Vietnam to help fight a war he doesn't think can be won. He said if Kennedy was still president, we probably wouldn't be sending them." His eyes moistened. "And a war will just take more dads from their sons, just like it did with—" His voice cracked. He tucked his chin to his chest, hiding his tears from me.

"I wish I could remember him," I softly said.

Even though Drew only had six years with our father, his love for him was there. I came into the world the day after my mom received the telegram telling her he'd been one of the last to be killed in the Korean War. During times like these I knew better than to rattle on. I would simply wait and let my brother work his way out of his sadness. Gonny's knock at the door helped him do that.

"Boys, are you in there?"

"Yes ma'am," I replied.

The door opened. "Good. I want to talk to you both." She took a moment to examine Drew. "Honey, is every-thing alright?"

He blinked. "Yes ma'am, I-I'm okay."

"How much do you know about Mr. Rosen?" she said, tilting her head first to me, then Drew.

"Only that he's the biggest, meanest, most hateful man that ever lived," I blurted.

"Drew, what about you?"

"Well, I don't know about all that, but he is kind of…"

"Evil," I chimed in.

"I think he's, um…"

"Drew, you don't have to mince words or be soft about it. Just tell me."

"Yes ma'am. Then I'd say he's certainly…well he's not exactly the nicest person I've ever known."

"You got that straight," I added.

"He can sometimes be moody," Drew said.

"How about all the time?" I added.

"Cody, would you stop it?" she said with a whack to my wrist. "What else, Drew? Has he ever been mean to you?"

Seeing my dam of grievances about to break, Drew gave me the keep-my-mouth-shut look. "Well, he's never actually been outright mean to me. He's been angry though."

"How angry?"

"I don't know, just angry."

"I want you to watch yourself around him. If he somehow puts you in danger, you'll have to quit working there. And, Cody, if you're at the factory and he starts to do something irrational, just leave. In fact, just try and steer clear of him altogether."

"Yes ma'am, you can count on that."

"What's going on?" Drew asked.

"I'm surprised you haven't heard about it at the factory," Gonny said.

"Heard what?"

"He wants to buy Maudie's house."

"So, that's why he's been over there those couple times," I said.

"Try four in the last week. He's determined to get it too. He's even offering twice what it's worth."

"Please don't let her sell it, Gonny. Having him live next to us will be…" I said.

"Go on, you can say it. It'll be hell. That we all agree on."

My appreciation for her being so colorful with my own thoughts had me smiling.

"But he won't be living there," Drew said. "No one will."

"Then why does he want it?" she asked.

"Because it's not the house he's after. It's the land. He needs a parking lot for the factory, and her place is exactly where he needs it. He can't grow the business without it."

"How'd you figure that out?"

"His economics class," I said.

"No. Mr. Merriweather told me."

"Did he also tell you how intimidating he could be? He's almost had Maudie in tears several times. She even threatened to put a restraining order on him to stop him from coming over."

I took a deep breath. "So she's not going to sell?"

"Absolutely not. Maudie told me years ago she'll die there before she'd ever move." She patted me on my knee. "Those were pretty much the same words she told him today, so I think the message may have finally sunk in. He'll just have to find his parking lot someplace else."

"I wish PaPa was here," Drew said.

"Me too," I added.

Gonny smiled softly. "I'm sorry, boys. I didn't mean to scare you."

"No, we're fine, Gonny," Drew said. "We know Mr. Rosen has some problems."

I stomped my foot. "Problems? Why can't you just come out and say he's evil and that his son is too?"

Gonny turned to him. "I told you that you didn't have to hold back. Were you?"

"No ma'am. Cody and I just see things differently. I'm

at the factory most of the day, so I see the stress he's under. That's where I think his anger's coming from."

My chest tightened. As I started to rip into another rant, he caught my attention in a way that told me I'd better swallow my thoughts before they became words.

"Hmmm, maybe so," she said. "You never really know somebody's true character until you've walked in their shoes." She looked at me on her way out. "You'd be wise to remember that, Cody. Nevertheless, you boys be careful around him."

I spun toward Drew. "Why'd you do me like that? Now she thinks he's just got some bad habits. Heck, in a few more minutes you would've made him out to be a Boy Scout." I braced myself for either a sock in the jaw or a tongue-lashing. Instead, I got a calm explanation.

"I'm sorry about that, but you gotta think it through. If we're going to save Kennedy, I'll have to keep working at the factory. We still need to do more test jumps." He put his hand on my shoulder. "And when we're ready, you're the key."

"Me?"

"You and Happy, that is. You're going to have to make rock-solid sure that when it comes time, he does his spin on command. Otherwise, it's off to the asylum for all of us."

Chapter 22

The new school year came with a bonus delivered by Drew on the third day. After he got home from the factory, he tracked me down out in the pecan orchard where I was in the midst of a tiresome game of tag with Cackles and Peeps. "Come here!" he yelled.

I trotted up to him. "What's up?"

"You ready to start coming back to the factory this week?"

"Not if you-know-who's around."

"Well, you-know-who won't be there," he said, grinning. "Neither Slate nor Ozzy are working at the factory this year. Mr. Merriweather told me the big man wants them to concentrate on baseball since the county tournament is coming up in October."

I bolted to my feet and spun around in circles. "I'm doing my Happy dance. Get it? It's Happy's dance." I fell to the ground, dizzy from my twirling.

Drew stood over me, shaking his head. "Good grief, would you get up?" He held out his hand and pulled me to him. "And they aren't gone. They're just not coming to the factory after school anymore."

I staggered to my feet. "And that's good enough for me."

The following day I rushed home from school, grabbed one of Gonny's prewrapped pimento-cheese sandwiches she always had waiting for us, and sprinted the entire way to the factory. Standing on the front steps, I tossed the wax paper and devoured it in four bites. Remembering Mr. Merriweather was a stickler for a clean factory, I went to pick up my trash. Just as I was about to snag it, a breeze flittered it away.

With my head low, I raced after it like a farmer chasing a chicken who knew it was about to become supper. Fifteen more feet and I was right on it when out of nowhere a hand reached down and snatched it from my grasp. In its place was a pair of shiny black boots. I reared back. Looking skyward, I followed the silhouette of a man in a dark, knee-length coat. With the sun positioned directly behind his enormous wide-brimmed hat, I couldn't see the top half of his face. All I could make out was he had hair to his shoulders and an equally lengthy mustache that curled up at the ends. On his chin rested a tiny triangular patch of black hair.

"Is this yours, young man?" he said, holding out the paper in the palm of his hand.

"Yes sir." Just as I was about to pluck it from his hand, he clamped it shut.

"Ooops!" he said, opening it back up, only this time nothing was there. In the same breath he reached behind my head with his other hand, then showing me his fist, stretched open his fingers to reveal the wrapping paper neatly folded into a tiny square.

"H-how'd you do that?"

He leaned down and whispered in my ear. "Magic."

I stared at the paper, analyzing how tightly it had been packed. It was even neater than Gonny could've done. "Seriously, mister, how'd you…" When I looked back up, he was gone. The only thing on the street was a black van parked toward the back of the building.

A minute later I was inside, running from room to room, searching for Drew, eager to tell him about my encounter with the mysterious man. Unable to find him, I headed back to see Happy. After an hour Drew hadn't appeared and I had no more pecans or Pez to feed Happy, so I headed for the side door. Maybe I could catch a game of roller-bat with the gang before it was time to go in for dinner. As I approached the exit, in came Drew.

"Where've you been? I met the neatest stranger…" A tiny, veiled shake of his head told me I didn't need to keep talking. Slate's appearance behind him confirmed why. "Oh shoot," I said.

"Let's go outside," Slate said, turning around.

I butted up against Drew's shoulder and whispered, "I thought he wasn't gonna be here." All I got back was a shrug.

Back outside Slate motioned us around the corner. "Come closer," he said, wringing his hands together.

For the first time I sensed something less than outright cockiness. Unless he was about to prank us, he was truly concerned about something. He looked around then turned to Drew. "You know about Cody doing that coffin-vision thing to help my father, don't you?"

Drew hesitated.

"Don't lie to me," he said.

Drew nodded.

"You're not going to say anything to your dad, are you?" I pleaded.

"No, but there's two things I have to ask you to do. They're not for me. They're for him. The first is he wants you to help with another one of those…"

"Coffin-jumps," Drew said.

"Yeah, he wants Cody to get Happy to send me back for one of those visions."

"Why? What's he going to do with what you see?" Drew said.

"Don't ask questions. You just need to do it."

"But we're still not sure what can happen with all this. We've gotta keep testing."

Slate used his forearm to wipe sweat from his forehead. Immediately my eyes caught that he wasn't wearing his leather wristband. Where it had been were now ugly red scars on the soft side of his arm close to the palm.

"Well," he began slowly, "if you need a guinea pig for your tests, consider me it, because we're going to have to do it."

"But—"

"No buts, you have to do this for me." His demand came more as a plea. "I-I mean you have to do this or else." His voice fell to a whisper. "You don't understand what he's capable of."

"What was the other thing he wanted?" I asked.

"He needs you and Drew to help get your great-grandmother to sell her house to him."

"I'm afraid she doesn't want to," Drew replied.

"Does she have a price? He's willing to pay more if that's it."

"It's not that. She just loves it there. She won't budge."

"For God's sake, she's gotta be in her eighties. She should be in a retirement home already. Don't you…" He dropped his thoughts with a heavy sigh. "I'm sorry. I shouldn't have said that." His eyes found the pavement. "I guess I am my father's son."

The pause that followed grew more awkward. "I gotta go." Without another word he was sprinting down the street toward his father's approaching Cadillac.

"Hurry, get inside," Drew said, pushing me to the door.

Once we were inside, he left the door cracked, peeping out to make sure Rosen's car wasn't stopping. A moment later he shut it and leaned against the wall, his head arched back. He let go a long, slow breath. "This is going to be tricky, little brother."

"Yeah, it's hard to stay out of somebody's way when they own the place. What're we gonna do about his demands?"

"I don't know. I've gotta think about it."

"Well, while you're noodling on it, you wanna hear about that stranger I met?"

"Why not?" he said, staring straight ahead.

"Aren't you interested?"

"Yeah, go ahead. I just can't help thinking about what Slate said."

"Okay, but stop for a minute and pay attention."

"Alright, I'm listening."

"So…right before I came in this afternoon, I was on the front porch eating a sandwich when the wrapping paper flew away. When I went to grab it, this man in a long, dark coat with a big floppy hat and long hair picked it up for me."

"Let me guess, he had a big curly mustache."

"Yeah. Have you met him already?"

"He was in Mr. Merriweather's office for over an hour."

"What were they talking about?"

"I don't know. I asked Mr. Merriweather if he was buying

a coffin, but he wouldn't say. He just brushed me off. One thing's for certain, Happy sure was excited to meet him. When they came out, he was hanging all over him. We even had to pry him off when he left. I think he even kissed him goodbye like he did with you."

"Did what?"

"Yeah, the little fella actually had his face smooshed up against the guy's cheek."

My eagerness to continue my story drifted away.

"Was there anything else, about this stranger?" Drew asked.

I shook my head. As absurd as it was, feeling jilted by Happy for a stranger left me hollow. "No, I'll see you at home later on."

"Before you go, there's one other thing Slate asked us to do."

I rolled my head back toward him. "What?"

"He wants us to come to his game tomorrow. He's pitching again and thinks we're good luck. Evidently, it's a pretty big one. And don't worry, I'm only getting three tickets—for you, me, and Mary Lib. I'm afraid we can't be cat-herding the rest of the gang like last time."

"Don't you think he's just buttering you up to help get to Maudie? Even I can see that."

"Maybe so, but I did enjoy the first game—well, everything except Mr. Rosen."

"I'll think about it," I said as I walked off.

"Don't let the Rosens get you down, brother. We'll figure everything out. Just remember our goal—Kennedy."

Chapter 23

At three forty-five that afternoon, Mary Lib and I met Drew at the entrance to the baseball field.

"How'd you get out of work this afternoon?" she asked him.

"Slate asked Mr. Merriweather to give me the afternoon off to see him play."

I groaned in my distrust of the whole thing, but kept my mouth shut. "Where're our seats?"

"Halfway up the stadium behind home plate and far enough from Mr. Rosen that we can enjoy the game."

For the first five innings, when we were up three to nothing and Slate was pitching a no-hitter, the game was incredible. The crowd was going wild with each pitch. Fastball after fastball, he sent batters back to their dugout. During the sixth inning, a thundercloud in the form of Mr. Rosen's drinking came rumbling in to spoil it all. Even from where we were, I could see the bottle halfway hidden in his brown paper bag.

"Are you guys seeing what I am?"

"Yeah, Slate's crushin' it," Drew said.

"And so is his dad. Look."

Drew and Mary Lib turned to where Mr. Rosen was sitting just behind the team's dugout. He was staggering back and forth. When the other team finally scored, he kicked the fence, forcing the team's manager to have a word with him. In the next inning they scored again, and he yelled at Slate to get his act together.

"Oh no, he's going to ruin it for him again," Mary Lib said.

She couldn't have been more right. In the eighth inning, the game became tied when Slate walked a player that turned into a score. The crowd went wild.

Above it all, Mr. Rosen could be heard raging as if he'd forgotten Slate was his son. "The pitcher's falling apart like a cheap watch," he bellowed. "Get the hook, bring in somebody with an arm."

In the ninth inning, tired and beaten down, Slate lost it completely, letting two batters score home runs. As the other team rushed home plate, celebrating the victorious batters, Slate stood on the mound, his head down.

"We gotta get to him before he does!" Mary Lib shouted.

"Who're you talking about?" I said.

"Mr. Rosen."

Drew held out his arm, barring her from moving. "You can't interfere between a father and a son."

"But he's gonna—"

Drew and I turned just in time to see Mr. Rosen throw his bottle at Slate, barely missing his head. He grabbed him by the sleeve like a rag doll and dragged him off the field as the rest of his teammates stood horrified.

"You're right, come on," Drew said.

In an instant we were pushing and shoving through the crowd. By the time we got to the parking lot, their car was swerving out the exit gate. All we could do was stand and watch it speed away.

The next day I woke up to my favorite aroma—bacon. No matter what, Gonny always fried up a ton every Saturday.

"Do me a favor," she said, neatly packing a lunch pail full of the savory delights. "Drew had to work early this morning and didn't get a chance to eat. I want you to take this to him." She slid two containers of the same next to my lunch pail. "And if you see Mr. Merriweather, give this other one to him. Tell him it's from Maudie."

"Don't you mean you?"

"No, just tell him it's from her."

I scarfed down all I could, then when she wasn't looking, I snagged three more pieces, wrapped them in a napkin and shoved them into my pants pocket. If Mr. Merriweather was going to get his own treat, then Happy should too. It would be fun to watch him with a new snack. Would he chomp it down or just nibble at it? Either way, I needed to do something to regain my best-friend status over the man with the oversized mustache.

As I meandered across the driveway and through Maudie's yard, my heart sank when I saw the one vehicle I was tired of seeing. Sitting across the street was a silver Cadillac. Either Rosen was in Maudie's house harassing her again, or he was in the factory with Slate, probably smacking him around. Gonny's advice to stay clear of the man echoed in my head, and after what I'd witnessed last night, I decided Drew and Mr. Merriweather would have to wait for their bacon. I tucked into the magnolia bush beside Maudie's house and waited for him to leave.

Fifteen minutes later, Mr. Merriweather shuffled out the front of the factory toward the Cadillac. Behind him was a middle-aged man with long, black hair and a curly mustache. It was my mystery man minus the floppy hat. I pried my way out of the bush and ran to the street. Seeing me coming, Mr. Merriweather waved me to them.

"Come to see Happy?" he said.

"Yes sir," I replied, unaware of my fixation on how far the mustache spanned past the mystery man's cheeks.

"Cody, I'd like to introduce you to Mr. Mars."

The man's sudden formality startled me. "Cederic Mars," he said with a slight nod and an outstretched hand.

I stared blankly at it.

Mr. Merriweather cleared his throat, drawing my attention to the man's offer of a handshake.

"Oh, oh yes, I'm sorry," I said, taking his hand. "My name's Cody Edwards."

"I know." He looked to Mr. Merriweather. "I had the pleasure of meeting the young Mr. Edwards the other day."

"Yeah, you picked up that piece of paper then made it disappear then made it come back. How'd you do that?"

He bent down in front of me. "I told you—magic."

"Seriously, how'd you do it?"

He tilted his head. "Looks like we have a skeptic, Avel." With a quick glance at his watch, he straightened back up as if at military attention. "I'm sorry but I'm afraid I must be on my way. Thank you, Mr. Merriweather. It's been a pleasure."

"Well, I'll be." I said, watching him pull away in his Cadillac. "It's not silver at all."

"What's not?"

"His car's gray." I stood staring at it where it waited for

the stoplight to change, its red taillight blinking. I started to turn back toward the factory but couldn't. I just stood as the taillight blinked red, over and over until it hit me. "Oh—my—God!" I dropped Drew's lunch pail, sending bacon tumbling onto the pavement. "Oh—my—God!"

"What? What is it?" Mr. Merriweather said.

It wasn't until the car finally turned and was out of sight that I blinked. I wanted to move but couldn't. I felt my arm being jostled.

"Tell me," Mr. Merriweather said. "Is something wrong?"

"N-nothing," I replied, dropping to my knees to scoop dirty strips of bacon back into the pail. "Here," I said handing it to him. "Give this to Drew. Oh, and this is for you." I tucked the Tupperware under his arm. "It's from Maudie."

"From Maudie—really?"

"Yes sir." I brushed my knees off. "I'm sorry, sir, but I gotta go." I took off down the street.

"Don't you want to see Happy?"

"I will later. Tell Drew I'll be by at lunch," I shouted over my shoulder.

Four blocks later and still running at full tilt, I turned the corner onto Main Street en route to the city library. Totally lost in my mission, I crashed into a little lady carrying an armful of books waist-high to her chin, sending her—along with *Huckleberry Finn, Moby Dick*, and a dozen other books—flopping onto the sidewalk.

"Would you watch where you're going?" she barked.

"I'm so sorry, ma'am." I started scrambling her books back into a pile. "Are you okay?"

"I'm fine, I guess," she said, brushing herself off, "but you need to slow down. You could kill somebody coming around a corner blind like that."

Her comment struck an odd chord, causing me to smile. Little did she know that's exactly why I'd come to the library.

"You think it's funny, running down a little old lady?" Her voice rose back up.

"No ma'am. I'm sorry, ma'am. I-I really am sorry. Is there anything I—"

"Just hand me that book out of the gutter."

I fished out *Moby Dick* and handed it to her. "If it's okay, I'll go now," I said, taking a step toward the library's entrance.

"Go. Nobody's keeping you from—"

It was rude, not waiting for her to finish, but my mission called for it. I bolted through the front door, clomping my way through the silence. Behind a long marble counter was a pretty young lady with chestnut hair and the softest blue eyes I'd ever seen. For a moment I was lost in them, suspending the reason I was there. Slowly the image of the lady she'd replaced, the one from Drew's visions, brought me back.

"Can I help you?" she said.

"I need to know where the visions are—I-I mean magazines are," I said, stumbling out my response. "Do you have a magazine section?"

"Of course. Just head to that last row of books, take a left and keep going. They're on the other side of the restrooms. You can't miss them."

"Thank you." I could feel myself blushing as I sidestepped back from the counter. "Thank you for your help. I appreciate it. You've been such a…" I groaned to myself. I was such a creep.

My embarrassment propelled me to the last row of books and back on track to the task at hand. Arriving at the magazine section, I was overwhelmed by the hundreds of publications stacked onto long rows of shelves that appeared to run half the length of a football field. After realizing they were arranged alphabetically, I ran to the beginning where I hit pay dirt. With a stack of twenty-plus magazines in my clutches, I snuck off to a dark corner where I began my research.

An hour later I trotted past the counter with no desire to connect again with the pretty young librarian. My only goal now was to get out as fast as I could without being caught.

Chapter 24

Unable to find Drew back at the coffin factory, I went to the front desk to ask Ms. Haverstash as to his whereabouts. "I can't find either him or Mr. Merriweather anywhere."

"Oh, they went fishing."

"Fishing?"

"Yep, fishing."

"They've never done that before. And in the middle of the day?"

"Well, that's where they're at."

"Then you can just tell Drew when he gets back that I went home." On my way out I turned back to Ms. Haverstash. "You know, I own a fishing pole too. You can tell that to Mr. Merriweather." I stepped outside. "I'm a good fisherman," I muttered.

Just before dinner that evening I heard the back door slam. "What in the world do we have here?" I heard Gonny exclaim.

I raced out of my room to find Drew standing proudly in the kitchen holding a stringer of five catfish.

"What do ya think, little brother? Caught 'em all on a store-bought jitterbug Mr. Merriweather bought for me."

"Nice," I said flatly. Five catfish deserved more of a response than that, but it was the best I could muster.

"Don't worry, you'll get to go next time," he said, swinging them up into the sink.

"Can you come into my room? I've got something I know you're gonna want to see."

"Not until you clean those things," Gonny said. "They'll have the whole house stinking to high tuna within the hour. Besides, we'll be wanting to have them for dinner tomorrow night. Both your mother and PaPa will be here."

"Awesome," Drew said. "Maybe you, me, and PaPa can go fishing. What do you think, Cody? We could go back to the same spot."

"Maybe," I said, holding back the urge to drag him back to my room to show him what a real day of fishing looked like.

Immediately after dinner, Drew pushed back from the table. "I'm going outside for a—"

"Oh no you don't," I said, grabbing him by the arm. "You need to see what I found this morning."

When I opened my bedroom door, Drew's jaw dropped. Spread across my bed, covering every inch of the cover, were ripped-out pages from magazines, every one of them showing pictures of cars—not different cars but one car. A Cadillac. And not just any Cadillac, a 1964 DeVille. And not just any shot from any angle. All of them were from the rear.

"Is this some sort of fetish?"

"Before you start thinking I'm crazy, just listen. For

some reason I've started to have these weird feelings about the taillights on this type of car."

"Where'd you get all these?"

"The library. I ripped them out of their automotive magazines."

"Cody," he said, shaking his head, "what's wrong with you?"

"Are you gonna listen or not?"

"Go ahead," he sighed, "but you know what you did was wrong, don't you?"

"I know, but I had to. You see, I've been having these thoughts, these flashbacks to the vision I had when I was in Irvin-Dell's casket. And what I keep seeing is that blurry red triangle that was flying through the air." I grabbed one of the pages and pointed to the picture of the car's left taillight. I traced around it with my finger. "Do you see the triangle?" I grabbed another page, jabbing my finger onto one of the taillights in the picture. I grabbed another one. "Look." I grabbed another page. "You see it…a red triangle." I scooped up three more pages and began leafing through them. "You see it? Another triangle, and another—"

"Alright, alright, I get it. You're seeing red triangles, and yes, I agree that's what they are but why does this matter?"

"Because…the triangle we're seeing is the same one that little boy saw."

"What little boy?"

"The boy that was with Irvin-Dell the day he got hit by the car. What he saw were these taillights."

Drew scanned the bed.

"Look at all of 'em," I said. "What else do you see?"

"I see the trunk, the Cadillac logo, the tires and the taillights. So?"

"What about horns?"

"You can't see the horns, stupid. They're under the hood."

"No, I mean horns, like devil's horns."

"Oh, for Pete's sake. Now you're hallucinating."

"Drewww! Come on, open your mind." I handed him one of the pages. "Here, squint your eyes and just think about it. You know it's a car, but to a first grader…what else can you see?"

He narrowed his eyes, tilting his head from side to side. "Hmmm, yeah, I guess maybe you could say they look like horns. At least if you were a little kid, they might look that way. So where're you going with this?"

"All these pics are of 1964 Cadillac DeVilles."

"Right."

"And who's the only person we know that owns a 1964 Cadillac DeVille?"

"That would be…" his eyes widened. "Mr. Rosen."

"Exactly!"

Drew's eyes slowly moved up and to the left as I watched him churning through his thoughts before frantically gathering up the pages into a pile.

"So what do you think we should do?" I asked.

Without saying a word, he calmly straightened the stack, folded it in half and stuffed it in his pants pocket.

"What time do first graders go to bed?"

"I don't know. Maybe eight o'clock."

His eyes found the ceiling again. When they lowered, he was smiling. "Go get Mary Lib. Tell her we need her to come with us for a favor and tell her to bring her box of Girl Scout cookies along with all the paperwork that goes with it." He pulled out one of the pages and handed it to me. "Here. Show her this picture and go through everything exactly the way you explained it to me. I'll meet you in front of her house in a few minutes."

"Where're you going?"

"To talk to Gonny."

"Is your brother trying to prank me?" Mary Lib asked Drew as he trotted up to her front porch.

"Did he tell you everything?"

"Yeah, the red taillight, the whole triangle and horns thing—the whole kit and kaboodle. And it sounds completely crazy."

"Only one way to find out?"

"How's that?"

"We ask Timothy McLean."

"Who's that?"

"The kid who was with Irvin-Dell when he got hit. And according to Gonny, he only lives two blocks away down at the corner of Billings and Saint James Street."

"Why do you need my Girl Scout cookies?"

"We actually need you *and* your cookies." He looked at his watch. "We've only got about an hour before they put him to bed so we'd better go now."

"I don't understand."

"I'm a little lost now too," I said.

"Just come on. I'll tell you guys the plan on the way."

By the time we reached the corner of Billings and Saint James, Mary Lib and I were fully on board with what Drew wanted us to do.

"Now remember," he said, "we've got to get the little

guy off by himself. If his parents catch on, they're gonna yank him."

"Are you sure about this?" Mary Lib said, biting her nails. "They could call the cops on us for child abuse or something."

"Don't worry. Just stick to the script and we'll be okay."

Through the picket fence, up the steps to the McLean house, we marched with Drew leading the way. After two knocks a lady wearing an apron came to the front door.

"May I help you?" she said.

Mary Lib pushed past Drew. "Yes ma'am, my name's Mary Lib. I live down on Maple Avenue and we're with the Girl Scouts."

She eyeballed me and Drew with a curious grin.

"Oh no," Mary Lib chuckled nervously. "I mean, I'm the only Girl Scout. These are my friends. They're keeping me company."

"We're her bodyguards," I added for a touch of humor.

The lady smiled. "Well, we've never really been a cookie family, so I think—"

"Have you got any children, ma'am?"

"One, but I really don't—"

"Maybe he'd like some. Our first box is free."

"Tell her about the special," Drew said.

"That's right, your first box is free, but since you've never ordered before, you get the second one free too if you buy just one box."

"Hmmm, maybe I will get one."

Mary Lib bounced. "Great! Is your son nearby?"

"Yes, why?"

She pulled out her paperwork. "I have to fill out this form, but I also have a survey we ask any kids in the household to take. They don't do any writing or anything. They just taste several cookies and tell us the first thing that comes to their mind."

"Oh, how fun. I'm sure he'd enjoy that." She turned her head back into the house. "Timmy, can you come here?"

A minute later a little boy with a mop of blonde hair came bounding up beside her. "Whatcha want, Momma?" he said, clinging to her leg.

"We're going to buy some cookies from these nice children, and they want to ask you some questions."

The boy's head disappeared behind his mother's leg.

Mary Lib bent down to his level. "It's okay, Timmy. For every question we ask, you get a cookie. How's that sound?"

The boy's head reappeared. "I get a cookie?"

"That's right. In fact, you get *five* cookies."

"Now now, you'll get a bite from each and then we'll save the rest for later."

A nudge from Drew's elbow told me it was time for my performance. "Oooohhh," I said, crossing my arms over my stomach.

"Is it acting up again?" Drew said.

"Yeahhh," I groaned.

"Do you have a stomachache?" the lady asked.

I nodded while squinching my face tight. "I-I think I might throw up."

"Oh no! Come inside. I've got some Pepto-Bismol in the medicine cabinet. Timmy, stay here and answer the nice girl's questions. I'll take care of your friend. Follow me, young fellow."

For good measure I let out an extra moan. Drew rolled his eyes at me as I passed him on my way inside.

"Yuck," I said, walking out of the McLeans' yard twenty minutes later. "I hate the taste of that pink stuff."

"Here, have a cookie," Mary Lib said, sticking a snickerdoodle in front of me. "You earned it."

"So what happened?" I said, looking back at the house.

"Don't turn around," Drew said. "Just act normal." As soon as Timothy's house was out of sight, his pace went from a trot to a full-out sprint.

"Wait! I'm sick, remember?"

"Sick in the head," Mary Lib laughed.

Instead of going back to her front porch, Drew led us down into our root cellar. "You guys did great," he said, panting.

After finally catching my own breath, I asked, "What happened?"

"You tell him, Mary Lib."

"It was just like a detective show. I gave him a cookie. After he took a bite, I asked him what flavor he tasted. He immediately said, 'Peanut butter.' I took the cookie and gave him a gingersnap. 'Now tell me what this one tastes like,' I said. He took a bite then gave me the cutest grin and said, 'Sugar!' 'Good,' I said, taking the cookie. And then," she paused, "that's when I pulled out a picture of the Cadillac."

My heart began thumping. "And…"

"He just stared at it."

"Is that all?"

Her head swung slowly back and forth as she pulled out one of my magazine pages with the picture of the car. Holding it out in front of me, she rested her finger over the left taillight. "Timmy pointed here and then here," she said, moving her finger from the left taillight to the right one.

I swallowed. "Did you ask him anything?"

"Didn't have to. That's when he said, 'Those are the devil's.'"

"This next part's gonna blow your mind," Drew said.

"That's when Timmy turned to me and said—" she took a deep breath, "those are the horns of the devil that killed my friend."

"Oh my gosh! Ohhhh my gosh! Oh my…"

"That's not all. After he said that, I pulled out a picture of a blue Cadillac and asked him if this was the color of the car with the devil horns that hit Irvin-Dell and he said no. I showed him another one with a red Cadillac and asked the same thing. And he said no again." She reached into her pants and pulled out a page with a silver Cadillac. "But when he saw this one, he looked like he was about to cry." Her voice cracked. "'That's the devil's car that hit my friend,' he said."

"What happened next?"

"I didn't want him to start crying, so I passed all the pages to Drew, then turned back and handed him a cookie and asked him what he tasted. Two cookies later he was back to normal and that's when you and Mrs. McLean came back out."

Chapter 25

Drew and I sat on his bed into the wee hours discussing what to do with Timothy McLean's testimony.

"Can't we just go to the police and tell them to go talk to his parents?" I said.

"And say what? That we tricked a little boy into saying the devil ran over Irvin-Dell in a Cadillac? They'd throw us straight into juvenile detention. Cody, to tell you the truth, I don't know which way to go with all this."

"But we do know the Rosens are murderers."

"No, we don't. We know it was their car or at least a silver Cadillac." Drew threw his head back with a groan. "But who in their right mind will ever believe the reasoning behind it? It's hard enough for us to even comprehend it, let alone explain it to someone else. I swear," he said, pacing the floor, "I sometimes think I'm just dreaming all this."

"Well, you're not, so come on. You're the brains in the family. Keep thinkin'."

An hour ticked away while nothing came to either of us.

The next thing I knew, Gonny was calling us to the kitchen for breakfast.

"What time is it?" Drew said, rubbing his eyes.

"I don't know except we're probably about to miss school."

A groggy glimpse at the alarm clock shot him upright. "Shoot, it's ten after eight. I've got a test first thing this morning. I'm gonna have to skip breakfast." He started out of my room but stopped at the door. "Tell Gonny I had to run. Oh, and I know what we have to do."

"About Timothy?"

"Yeah, we're going to confront Slate about it."

"When?"

"Right after his practice this evening."

Instead of waiting for Drew to come home after work, I met him at the factory. Lighting into Slate Rosen was a long time coming, and now that we had the ammunition, I was ready to unload on him and reveal who he really was.

"I'm sorry, but I couldn't just sit around waiting. Let's go lower the boom."

"Would you look at yourself? You're like a bloodthirsty wolf. We're not going to lower any boom. We're going to calmly explain what happened with the McLean boy and then let him respond. The one good thing we have going for us is that he knows how the visions work."

"That's right, so there's no way he can say my vision wasn't real or that the little boy was lying. If he shows any sign that he's involved, we need to call the cops—immediately."

"All in good time. Facts first, then we decide. But I'm telling you, if you're going to pass judgment before we get there, then you need to stay home."

Drew was right. I'd become unhinged and in the midst of my anger forgot about what I had seen his father put him through. But that was between them. This was about murder and if he had anything to do with it, then he had to pay. But I'd be danged if I was going to stay home during his moment of reckoning, so I straightened up, put on a smile and toned down my attitude.

"Are you good now?"

"Yeah, I'm fine," I said through taut lips.

"Then let's go. They should be finishing practice right about now."

When we got to the stadium, Slate was nowhere to be found. Other than the groundskeeper spreading dirt across the pitcher's mound, the field was empty. "Sorry, but you boys can't play here this afternoon," he said. "We got a game tomorrow."

"We're just looking for the team," Drew said.

"Sorry, but they've been gone for almost an hour."

I kicked up a cloud of dust. "Shoot, he's probably skipped town already."

"No he's hasn't, you dufus," Drew said, nudging my arm. "He's right over there. At least I think that's him."

Sitting on the far side of the bleachers behind the opposing team's dugout was a boy in a Bulldogs practice uniform. His baseball cap was pushed low, hiding most of his face.

"Slate, is that you?" Drew called out.

The baseball hat rose.

"It's him alright."

Halfway to the dugout Drew gave me the order to let him do the talking, emphasizing that if I said anything out of line, he'd pound me later on. My brother's threats seldom materialized but when they did, I was never quick to forget the warning.

"What're you doing here?" Drew asked as we walked up.

Slate replied with only a sigh before turning his gaze somewhere in the outfield. "It's calm here," he muttered.

"Yeah, I can see what you mean." Drew directed a faint shrug my way.

"Is your dad comin' to pick you up?"

"Don't know."

"Well, there's something we need to discuss with you."

He looked at us with an indifference that seemed to say, "I know why you're here, so let's get on with it." I could smell it. He was ready to confess his sins.

"Do you remember the little boy who was killed in that hit-and-run last year?" Drew said.

Slate's face went blank. "What about him?"

"Sweet Jesus!" The groundskeeper cut off Drew's questioning before it could begin.

Slate catapulted up, looking past us toward a billowing cloud of black smoke rising into the sky. "That's a fire. And it's coming from the coffin factory."

Within seconds we were all racing down Maple Avenue, Slate more than thirty yards in front of us, when suddenly he stopped in front of our house. "It's not the factory!"

"Dear God, it's Maudie's!" Drew shouted.

Half her home was a raging inferno, fire and smoke pouring out almost every window and door. The other half had already begun to crumble. Circling the house were dozens of gaping-mouthed onlookers.

Over the roar of flames, Gonny's voice wailed, "She's in there! Someone, please help!"

Hanging onto Drew's sleeve, we wedged through the crowd to find Gonny running toward the blaze before Mrs. Libowskenstein pulled her back. Beside her, Mary Lib sat on the ground, sobbing, her head buried in her hands.

Dozens of men from the factory were rushing toward the blaze. They attempted to enter but the heat pushed them back every time.

"Please!" Gonny screamed. "My mother's still in there. For God's sake, somebody help!"

"Where's the fire department?" a man shouted. Just then we heard sirens coming from blocks away.

"It's going to be too late," she cried. "Someone's got to get her."

Drew wrenched my arm loose. "I'm going through the back porch!"

A man reached out at him. "Stop! It's too dangerous."

Without thinking, I took off after him.

"Grab them!" a man yelled after us, but we were already on the back steps.

Taking Drew's lead, I pulled off my shirt. Wrapping it over my nose and mouth, I started crawling behind him toward the door, smoke rolling out in waves and covering the entire porch in a thick, scorching haze.

"Stay low, Cody. Breathe through your nose."

Surprisingly the air coming up through the decking boards was fresh and almost cool. I slid my cheek over the wooden slabs, keeping an eye on Drew's legs to guide me in the right direction. When they suddenly stopped, I glanced up to find him standing in the smoke-filled opening. In front of him was the faint image of a man hunched over. He appeared to be leaning backward as if tugging at something.

"It's Mr. Merriweather!" Drew shouted.

Just then, the older man fell through the door next to us, his right sleeve on fire. Drew threw his shirt over it.

Mr. Merriweather stretched out his smoldering arm toward the door. "Maudie…" He squeezed out a rusty whisper before his head smacked the deck.

Drew jumped to his feet, crouched low then disappeared inside, reappearing a minute later carrying Maudie. Where his strength came from, I'd never know because I tried the same thing with Mr. Merriweather but couldn't budge him. The smoke had sapped all my energy. I could only stand over him, coughing uncontrollably. My head began to spin just before I collapsed beside him.

As I lay helpless, I watched his body float up into the deadly gray cloud looming above us, then he was gone. Moments later two arms reached down through the smoke, lifting me up and carrying me out onto a cool patch of grass far from the firestorm now engulfing the entire house.

Two fire trucks, five police cars, and an ambulance all arrived within minutes of one another. Bystanders frantically waved the ambulance down the driveway to where Maudie and Mr. Merriweather lay. As the firemen pounded the house with water, the emergency medical staff leaped from their vehicle carrying oxygen tanks, masks, and medical boxes. Two men followed behind pushing gurneys.

Gonny knelt beside Maudie, gripping her hand, rocking back and forth, repeating over and over, "Don't die, don't die…"

While Maudie lay motionless, Mr. Merriweather was curled up, coughing in spasms. "Here," one of the emergency people said, strapping a mask across his face, "try to breathe slowly."

A hand reached under my back and pulled me upright. "You too, young man," a woman said, holding a mask over my nose and mouth. I took three deep breaths. As the cool, clean air filled my lungs, I looked up to find Drew and Slate staring down in horror as a man in a blue-and-white uniform hovered over Maudie. He pressed down on her chest, stopped, then started again.

"Boys, you're going to have to move back," a policeman said, brushing them into the crowd.

Another policeman split through the horde of gawking bystanders, his arms stretched wide. "Get back! Everybody back—now!" Behind him, the two men pushing gurneys came rushing in.

"We've got a pulse!" shouted the man who'd been working on Maudie. Within seconds the medical team had her and Mr. Merriweather up and inside the ambulance. The siren blared as they went, tires screeching, back onto the street. Left in its dusty wake, Gonny, Drew, and I stood hugging each other as the crowd turned back to the house and watched the firemen soak the charred ruins of the once-beautiful home. The only remaining structure was the deck and the back door Mr. Merriweather had rushed through, risking his life for my great-grandmother.

Chapter 26

The following morning I woke to a household of sobbing, consoling voices, muffled prayers and my mother whispering outside my room, "Let the boys sleep."

"Mom!" I said, flinging the door open and running into her arms.

She squeezed me tight. "Oh, Cody," was all she could say. She pulled back, revealing her face stained with the tracks of her tears. "How's your brother?"

"Okay, I think. What about Maudie?"

Fresh tears began to form. "She's in the hospital."

"Is she okay?"

"Cody, she's old and…"

"We know she's old, Mom," Drew said, stepping out of his room, still in the smoke-filled clothes from the day before. "And we know how weak she is. But is she going to be okay?"

"Come here, son," she said, pulling him to her. With both of us in her embrace, she said. "I don't know. She's been through so much and all the smoke she's breathed in is…"

"She's a tough ole gal," came PaPa's voice.

Drew and I turned together to find our grandfather

standing behind us. With his arms outstretched, he wrapped all of us up in one giant bear hug.

"What about Mr. Merriweather?" Drew asked.

PaPa leaned back. "That's absolutely the finest man I've ever known."

Drew gasped. "What do you mean *known*? He's not dead, is he? Tell me, is he—"

"No, no. He's fine. He was released from the hospital early this morning. In fact, I drove him back to the factory. He's there right now taking care of Happy."

Just then the kitchen phone rang. A minute later we heard chairs scraping across the floor, doors slamming, and above it all Gonny's moans.

PaPa had started into the kitchen when he collided with our uncle Dean who grabbed him by the shoulders. "We have to get back to the hospital."

"What's wrong?"

My uncle paused. "They think she's about to pass."

Everyone rushed outside and began cramming into cars, leaving Drew and me standing in the driveway, waiting to be pulled along in the mayhem. Mom grabbed us by the sleeves. "You're going to have to stay here."

"But, Mom..." Drew began. "We have to—"

"No. You need to stay here." With that she slammed the door shut and the car sped away just as the ambulance had the day before.

Suddenly everything was quiet, except for the wind rustling through the trees and birds chirping. Drew and I stood scanning the blackened rubble where Maudie's house once stood, the view to the coffin factory now unobstructed. My lips quivered. Drew's arm around my shoulder softened the moment, but the tears still came. I buried my head in his chest and began to weep.

He lowered his head below my chin and looked up at me. "Do you want to go with me to see how Mr. Merriweather's doing?"

I wiped my eyes. "Yes," I said softly. "But can we go by the street? I'd rather not go through Maudie's yard."

"Of course."

He led me out to the sidewalk like a wounded pup. Just as we were about to make our turn, he looked back toward our house. "What's Slate doing here?"

I turned to see him running toward us. "Would you please make him go back home?" I pleaded.

"Hey, guys," he said, trotting up to us.

If there was ever a time to rage on somebody, this was it. Too drained to do anything, though, I held back and said nothing, letting my glare do the work.

"I came by to see how your grandmother was."

"She's not so good. Everybody's at the hospital right now. They think she's…" Drew said, unable to finish what neither of us wanted to hear.

Slate hung his head, shifting his weight side to side, his obvious discomfort somehow giving me a sliver of pleasure.

"My grandfather told us Mr. Merriweather is at the factory, so we're going to see how he's doing," Drew said.

"You mind if I come along?"

I pinched Drew under his arm.

"Sure," he said, swatting my hand away.

By the time we reached the side door to the factory, I'd concluded that Slate's concern for Maudie and his need to see Mr. Merriweather were nothing more than playacting. Like his father, he had to be up to something. It wasn't until we entered the factory and found it empty that I realized I might have been wrong.

"Where's everybody at?" I asked.

"Yeah, it's a workday," Drew added. "All the guys should be here."

"My father decided to shut down for the day in light of yesterday's tragedy and that Mr. Merriweather almost died."

My jaw dropped. Surely, I'd heard wrong. "Let me get this straight," I began. "You mean to tell us—"

Drew shoved me to the side. "That's nice of your dad. Would you tell him thank you for us?"

Enough was enough. I'd reached my boiling point. Unable to take Drew's continued oversight of Rosen's true nature, his cruelty, and criminal activities, I exploded. "There's no way your father would ever close this factory if he didn't have a reason, some—some sort of reason where he'd get something out of it." My mind was a jumbled mess of angry thoughts that spewed without thinking them through. There was no way to turn them off. "He's a gambler who used the coffins to place bets, he harassed our grandmother for months, and—"

Drew grabbed my arm. "Stop it!"

"No! I'm not going to stop." I looked Slate in the eye and continued my rant. "Your father's nothing but evil. He's a con man, a drunkard, and he killed Irvin-Dell. We have proof!" I stood with my chest heaving. "And you! You're just as—"

Suddenly I was flying backward. Drew's hands spun me around and pinned me to the wall.

With his face inches from mine, he yelled, "I—said—STOP!"

What followed was a pressure cooker of silence with the anticipation that any second Slate would pull him off then beat me senseless. Instead, he stood in the corner staring into the floor. His hands had not balled into fists, there was no rage brewing, no heavy breathing, only a long sorrowful sigh, a sigh that morphed into a moan, a moan that turned into crying—none of which was coming from Slate, but from some distant part of the factory.

"Where's that sound?" Drew said, releasing me from his grip.

Slate turned his head to the ceiling. "I think it's coming from upstairs."

"Who'd be upstairs? Nobody goes up there." He paused. "There it is again. Wait…is that…"

"Mr. Merriweather!" I shouted.

"Come on," Drew said, running out onto the factory floor. When he got to the middle of the building, he looked up. In the back corner was a pile of crates that had toppled over, revealing a single door.

"I never knew that was up there, did you?" Slate said.

"No," Drew replied.

A mournful wailing followed.

"That's where he is, alright." Slate said. "He sounds like he's in pain!"

All at once we were clamoring up the stairs then racing down the long corridor to the back corner from where his cries had come. Drew kicked a box away from the door then slowly opened it halfway. With only a sliver of light coming in, all we could make out was the slumped figure of a man sitting in a rickety, old chair. His head was down.

In one hand he held a cane. The other was stretched out beside him.

Drew edged forward. "Sir, are you okay?"

Slate opened the door all the way, allowing a beam of light to pass inside, washing over Mr. Merriweather and his hand that rested on top of a dusty coffin.

"We heard you crying," Drew said.

His head swung slowly side to side, then stopped. "Is—Is she dead?"

"We don't know. But everybody's at the hospital. They all rushed out at the same time, leaving us behind."

His head fell farther. "She's gone, I can feel it."

"We really don't know," I said.

"My darling girl is gone."

Drew gave me a puzzled glance. "Sir?"

Mr. Merriweather turned to him, his eyes puffy, his face etched with more wrinkles brought on by the last twenty-four hours.

"Are you okay?" Drew asked.

An overwhelming sadness filled the room. Holding out his hands, he slowly raised them to his chest. "She was my sweetheart."

"Are you saying *Maudie* was your sweetheart?"

He nodded.

I drew a quick breath, feeling the impact of his statement. "You and our great-grandmother—you and she were what—a couple?"

He nodded again.

"Did our great-grandfather know about this?"

"No," he replied in a distant voice.

"This was before him?"

"Yes, of course."

"Were—Were you married?"

"No…" A tear rolled down his cheek. "But we were supposed to be."

Slate stepped forward. "Sir, whose coffin is this?"

"Hers."

Drew shared a look with Slate and me in a way that had us moving back toward the door.

"Boys," Mr. Merriweather said calmly, "there's nothing to be afraid of." He wiped his eyes. "This is from many years ago when she was very sick—from when we thought she was going to die."

"Die? When was that?"

"At the end of the war."

"What war?"

"The First World War. It's when she contracted typhoid fever. Back then it was almost always fatal."

At the same time, we all stepped back toward him, leaning closer.

"How come we never heard about this? That's a story I'm sure Gonny would've told at most family get-togethers."

"Yeah," I said, "Gonny's always going on and on about family stuff like that."

Slate moved beside the coffin and laid his hand on the lid. "So you're saying that years ago she was actually going to be buried in this exact one?"

"She actually picked it out herself."

"Why's it still here?"

"I couldn't bring myself to sell it."

The air suddenly sucked from my lungs. I threw out a hand toward him, at the same time pointing to the coffin with my other one. "You—You…"

"What is it?" Drew said.

"We can save her!" I blurted. "We know how. If it's her coffin, then we can save her. We wanted to tell you before but—"

He dropped his cane. "What've you done?" His chest rose and fell faster and faster. "Tell me, boy, what have you done?"

"I-I haven't done anything," I stammered.

"Then how do you know you can save someone with their coffin?"

Drew stepped up, wiping sweat from his brow. He cleared his throat then began slowly. "It's what Cody was going to tell you before about saving President Kennedy, but you didn't—well, it's uh…it's only a hunch but—"

"Just tell me!"

Drew wrung his hands nervously. "I know you didn't want us to do anything else with the coffins, but Cody was able to train Happy to spin on the lids when someone's inside. Since this causes the person to see visions in the past, we think they can use that time to do something to alter things or prevent things from happening. So if we can do this with Maudie's coffin, then we can warn her."

Mr. Merriweather's head rolled back and forth.

"We can make sure she's out of the house before the fire begins."

"No," he whispered.

"We could possibly even find out what caused the fire in the first place."

His voice rose, "No."

"We could actually—"

"No!" he shouted. "I said, no! For God's sake—no!"

The room went silent as we all stood watching Mr. Merriweather lift himself slowly out of his chair, his eyes flashing between us with something we never thought him capable of—true anger. "You boys have betrayed my trust in the most wicked way." He turned to Drew. "And it's you I trusted the most."

My heart broke for my brother in that moment as I watched him sink with every word of his rebuke.

Chapter 27

As Drew stood dejected, I stepped in, pushing for Mr. Merriweather's blessings to use Maudie's coffin. "Sir, if you
know about the visions, don't you want us to use them to
save her?"

He didn't reply.

"Cody's right," Drew said almost in a whisper. "We can
do this. We want her back. Don't you?"

"Of course."

"Then let's go." I started for the door when Drew grabbed
my sleeve.

"Wait, he hasn't actually said it's okay."

"It's gotta be okay. It's the right thing to do." I jerked
my arm free. "I'm going to get Happy."

"No! Do *not* go anywhere," Mr. Merriweather com-
manded. I turned back to find him shaking his head at me.
"Don't you budge."

"Sir, we can do this," Drew said.

"I don't want you to do anything."

"But why? Don't you believe we're able to?"

"It's not that. I know you can."

"Then why won't you let us?"

His eyes softened. "Because it's not safe."

"For Maudie?"

"No. For whoever seeks to alter her destiny. Boys, you don't know what you've stumbled upon. You've been lucky. Had you interacted with anyone or anything while in those coffins, it would've had devastating consequences for you."

I watched as his anger was replaced with concern for us. "I'm sorry, sir. We really just want to help."

"I know you do, Cody." He reached out, placing a feeble hand on my wrist. "I'm sorry too. It's just that this whole…"

"We call it coffin-jumping."

"Interesting name. We never knew what to call it."

"Sir, do others know about this?" I asked.

"It used to be only me and Thiago. Now it's just us four."

Before I could launch into how Ozzy and Mr. Rosen also knew, Drew waved me off with a hidden swipe of his hand and a quick question for Mr. Merriweather. "Who's Thiago?"

He sighed. "A dear friend of mine."

"Is he still alive?"

"He passed away a long time ago." His face suddenly brightened. "Thiago was like a father to me. He's the one who introduced me to Happy."

"I thought Happy was always yours."

"Oh no, initially he was Thiago's. I only came to know Happy when I was working on the Panama Canal."

"That's the river that runs through the country and connects the oceans," I said.

"When were you in Panama?" Drew asked.

"And tell us how you met Happy and learned about coffin-jumping," I added.

Drew nudged my arm. "Sir, I'd like to apologize. Here we are jumping all over the place with questions and throwing around our crazy notions when we should be thinking about Maudie."

"I understand."

I leaned forward. "Then you'll tell us how you met Happy and when you discovered how to see visions and about you and Maudie?"

"My gosh, little brother. Would you let up?"

"Really, it's fine," he said.

"Are you sure?"

"Yes. Since you know what Happy can do, you deserve the story. More importantly, it's something you have to hear." He paused, seeming to search for his beginning. After a slow breath he closed his eyes. As he opened them, a smile appeared on his face as if he was watching an invisible scene play out on the wall that only he could see. "It was 1910. I was eighteen and living in Panama, working on the canal. I'd only been there for about two weeks when I met a guy named Thiago who made coffins. If you've been paying attention in your history classes, you'll know that death was a big business with the canal. More than five thousand workers died during the ten or so years it was being built."

Drew pulled a bench from the corner and sat down while I remained standing, mesmerized by the staggering loss of life.

"Was Thiago rich?" I asked. "With all those people dying, he had to be making a lot of money."

"For Panama he was doing well enough. But it was his sideline job that was making him famous. You see, Thiago, or rather his pet monkey, Happy, knew how to conjure up visions of people's loved ones. The same type of visions you've described. So, when people lost someone, they'd come to him to help them reconnect, even if it was just seeing the images."

"Sir, is Happy magical?"

"I believe you've asked me that before, and I think I said he's more spiritual. To be honest, Cody, I don't know what he is other than a monkey with unique powers. Whether Thiago endowed him with this ability or he already had it, I never knew. But don't go thinking it was all dark and sinister. Thiago was a good man. He was loved by the people. And of course, they all loved Happy."

"So how'd you end up here?"

"I don't mean to be funny, but as work on the canal was wrapping up, his business died out. Tragedy also struck when his wife and little boy passed away. With nothing left for him in Panama, I persuaded him to come back to the States with me. As luck would have it, I saw a help-wanted ad for Mr. Fletcher's new coffin factory. We both applied and were hired on the spot. Thiago was made foreman, and I was his helper."

"What year was that?" Drew asked.

"It was 1915, the best year of my life." He turned his gaze to a distant memory. "That's the year I met Maudie." His cheeks rose, taking on a crimson glow. "If I said she was beautiful, I'd be lying. She was ravishing, with hair the color of raven's wings that fell to her waist when undone. And that smile—a smile that melted the coldest of hearts—and dimples that accented the sweetest, most infectious laugh that stole the heart of every man she met. But I was the lucky one. She chose to keep my heart."

"How old were you?"

"I was twenty-three and she was twenty. And after two years I proposed."

"And she accepted, right?"

"Of course." He raised a playful eyebrow. "How could she not? I was debonair, witty, and believe it or not, actually a rather handsome fellow." In an instant his face lost all expression, once again fading to someplace else, this time a place much darker. "In 1917 America entered the war, and with my father and his father's voices ringing in my ears, I knew I had to follow in their footsteps and enlist. But instead of being a sailor like them, I joined the army. Believing the war would only last a year or so, we decided to get married when I returned."

"That's right," Drew said. "We studied that in history class. We were in the war for just over a year and a half."

He closed his eyes as he continued recalling the past. "It was at the end of the first year when it all went wrong. I'd been lucky and had never been injured, but during that last month I received something worse. I got word from Thiago that Maudie had contracted typhoid. Fearing she would die, I bribed my captain to let me take leave. When I got home, Thiago picked me up at the bus station. The first thing he told me was that the doctors said she only had a matter of days. He even told me she'd picked out her coffin."

His story left my chest hollow. "This coffin here," I said.

He opened his eyes. "After he told me about her coffin, Thiago asked me what I wanted to do. I told him I didn't have a choice—I had to use it."

"You mean her coffin?" I asked.

"Yes. That's when I told him to go get Happy. During all the years I knew him, Thiago and I had never argued until then, but for the next hour we went at it tooth and nail. He begged me not to do it."

"Not do what?"

"Not to have Happy conjure visions of the past."

Drew gasped. "You weren't going back to just be a witness—you were going back to alter things!"

"That's right."

"But you told us earlier we shouldn't do that because there would be devastating consequences," Drew said.

"I know, but back then I was young and stupid, plus I'd never seen what could occur firsthand. Thiago had only told me that bad things could happen. He never said that they definitely would. And at that age I considered myself invincible, the same way you boys probably do right now."

"Did you guys keep fighting?" I asked.

"No. Seeing how determined I was, he eventually relented, letting me climb into Maudie's coffin while he had Happy spin on top. The visions came immediately, but rather than just being a phantom bystander, I engaged."

Drew and I inched to the edge of the bench. "What did you see?" I asked.

"The real question," Drew said, "is who or what did you interact with."

"What I saw was a young girl about the same age as Maudie. She was writing a letter, asking Maudie to come visit for the weekend. I can still remember the feeling. It— It was like I was a ghost. I could see her, but she couldn't see me. I could even walk with her, which is what I did. I followed her down a flight of stairs out of her house and to a mailbox where she deposited the letter."

"Why didn't you keep her from mailing it?"

"I did. As soon as she walked back into the house, I simply grabbed it from the box and stuffed it into my pocket. The next thing I knew, I was waking up."

"So what's the letter have to do with Maudie almost dying?"

"Everything. The first thing the doctors told me after telling me she had typhoid was that she'd contracted it from a trip she'd made to see her cousin in Raleigh. The poor girl had not only given it to Maudie but also her whole family, causing a brother to die."

"Maybe that's why Gonny never talked about it," I said.

Drew tilted his head upward, thinking out loud. "So because she didn't get the letter, she didn't go to Raleigh, which meant she never contracted the disease from her cousin."

"Then why aren't you with Maudie now?" I said. "Everything should've worked out for you."

He sighed. "Consequences. Remember, I said Thiago told me there would be consequences."

"But you're here and you're healthy," Drew said.

Mr. Merriweather slid his hand down his cane, then moved it to his leg to rub his knee. "This limp of mine didn't come from old age. I got it after waking up from the coffin."

"You got injured here in the factory?"

"Not even close. Instead of waking in the factory, I woke up in a little foxhole on the front lines in Germany. You see, because I stole the letter, Maudie never visited her cousin, which meant she never got sick, which meant I never got a message that brought me home. And that little foxhole was just that—little—not big enough to shield me from the bullet that blasted my knee apart. I guess you might say I was lucky though. The rest of my platoon were all killed. My reward was spending the rest of the war in a prison camp." His eyes became moist. "Maudie did end up getting a letter though…" A tear rolled down his cheek.

"A copy of a letter from the United States War Department stating I'd been killed in battle." His chin fell to his chest.

"Oh my gosh," Drew said. "Gonny's told us stories about how Maudie married our great-grandfather at the end of the war." Drew put his hand on Mr. Merriweather's shoulder. "I'm so sorry."

"There's no need to be sorry. To her I was dead. She had to move on."

"But…you sacrificed yourself for her."

"That was the consequence for altering her destiny. It takes away something that's an important part of your life. In this case it was my future with her." He paused. "It was hard on Thiago too."

"How's that, sir? Wouldn't he be like everyone else and not remember her being sick? Didn't he think you had been killed in action too?"

"Unfortunately, no. That's a consequence that also extends to anyone who knows about the coffin-jump as you call it. I, of course, remember what happened, but Thiago had the burden of knowing too, and because of it he never forgave himself for letting me go through with it."

"Sir?"

"Yes, Cody."

"I would've loved for you to have been our great-granddaddy."

He smiled. "Wouldn't that have been something?"

"What do you think, Slate?" Drew said, turning his head from one corner of the room to the next, only to find empty space. "Where'd he go?"

I ran to the door and scanned the factory floor below. "He's gone! The side door's wide open."

"What's wrong?" Mr. Merriweather asked.

"He's running away," I replied. "I'm going after him."

"Wait!" Mr. Merriweather said. "Before you go, there's something else you need to know about the coffins."

But it was too late. I was already racing down the steps, determined to find out why he'd snuck out, knowing it had something to do with Irvin-Dell.

Chapter 28

Figuring Drew would continue showing Slate grace, I left him behind, determined to find fault with him for sneaking out on us. Knowing he could pummel me, I enlisted Ruebin and Cackles to help me search.

"How come we're going after him?" Ruebin asked.

"It's a game," I said, "like the ultimate hide-and-seek. He's a fugitive and we've gotta catch him."

"You don't even like Slate," Cackles said.

"Oh no, we're all good. In fact, this is his idea. He said if we catch him, he'll buy us a round of burgers."

"Well, what're we waiting for? Let's ride."

For the rest of the day, my posse and I searched the town on our bikes. From the ballpark to the library and even his house, across town we rode. As the sun began to set, and with no clue as to his whereabouts, our chase began to fall apart.

"I'm tired," Ruebin said.

"Me too," Cackles added. "Slate can keep his burgers."

With no real argument against the mutiny, I trailed along behind them.

"Where've you been!" Drew yelled as I pulled into the driveway. "I've been looking high and low for you."

I threw my bike to the ground and stomped past him without a word.

"I asked where've you been!"

"Where you should've been—looking for your good buddy."

"Would you just stop?"

I turned abruptly, staring daggers at him.

His voice fell. "Mom was just here."

"And…"

"She came back from the hospital to get some of Maudie's things." His lips pressed tight. "Cody, she passed away an hour ago."

I stood frozen in place not knowing whether to cry, scream, or hit something. All I felt was a sudden emptiness. I blinked away the tears. "Have you told Mr. Merriweather?"

"I just got back from over there."

"Is he okay?"

"I think so."

"What're we going to do now? She's always been with us." I stared at the ruins of her house. "Ever since Irvin-Dell died, things have changed around here."

"You're right. And I've been blind to what to do about it until now."

"What do you mean?" I said, wiping away the tears I couldn't hold back any longer.

"I know how to make this right."

"How?"

"In a half hour it's going to be dark. Meet me in the back of the coffin factory."

"Why?"

"You'll see. And when you come, bring PaPa's shotgun. It's under his bed."

"Are you sure you want a gun? Maybe we should call the police." The resentment that had been building as he continued turning his cheek with the Rosens suddenly took a new direction for me. I wanted justice but not violence.

"There's no way the police can be a part of this. It's something only you and I can do. Now that I think about it, you can forget the gun."

I breathed a sigh of relief.

"But I do need you to stuff the pillows under our bedcovers."

"How come?"

"This might take a while and when the adults come home, they need to think we're asleep."

Creating pillow decoys was an easy task, one that had me behind the coffin factory in less than fifteen minutes. Ahead of schedule I sat on the loading docks, nervously spinning an empty Coke bottle on the cement landing. A single bulb buzzed above me, flickering on and off, creating an eerie strobe effect across the vacant gravel lot. Each flicker cast light on something that hadn't been there before, all appearing for a split second, then vanishing and then reappearing in some seemingly different spot.

I let the Coke bottle slowly come to a stop as I watched a black cat scamper out of a far-off garbage bin. Three more flickers and he was suddenly at my feet with his back arched, hissing. Another flicker and he was gone. I pulled up my collar, cursing Mr. Rosen for not keeping his pitiful security light operating correctly.

Just then a pair of headlights blinked on and off from where the cat had come. The crunching of gravel mingled with the buzzing light as a cargo van made its way toward me. I slowly backed into the shadows and crouched into a runner's stance. Just as I was about to bolt, the faint image of an arm appeared out of the driver's side window.

"Don't run! It's me!" The van pulled under the light. It flickered twice, and on the third, Drew's head popped out, his hand waving me in. "Come on," he said, trying to modify a shout into a whisper.

I lunged off the dock and ran to him. "What're you doing?"

"Get in."

"But what're you doing in this van?"

"Just get in. And be quiet, would ya?"

I hesitated then leaped in beside him, leaving the door open.

"Would you shut that?"

"Not until you tell me what's going on. Drew, you're not old enough to drive. And you don't even know how."

"You're right on the first, but wrong on the second. Mr. Merriweather's been teaching me. I've actually been all over town in this thing. Now shut the door."

"Not until you tell me what's going on."

He started a slow inhale then slammed the accelerator to the floorboard, sending me flying back into the seat and slamming the door shut at the same time.

"What the—" I yelled, grabbing the door handle as we swerved out into the street in the opposite direction of our house. "Okay, I'm here. You gonna tell me now?"

"Sorry about the kidnapping, brother, but I didn't think you'd come if you knew where we were going. I know how you are with the scary stuff."

"What? Are you kidding me? I'm not afraid of things like I was when I was a kid," I said, defending myself.

His skewed grin told me he didn't believe me. "I had to be sure. And you're still a kid."

"I don't call confronting the Rosens scary anyway—risky maybe, but not scary."

"You think we're going to Slate's house?"

"Yeah. When you said get the shotgun, I knew you wanted to finally confront them about Irvin-Dell. And I figured Slate running off like that was the straw that broke your camel's back. I'm just glad you've finally come to your senses. But I'm glad you decided against the gun. That was a little over-the-top. We just have to be—"

"Cody, we're not going to the Rosens."

"Wha…"

"We can't approach them about this. Not this way."

I slammed my hand onto the dashboard. "What's with you? You keep doing this over and over."

"What do you mean?"

"You're taking up for him—again! This is the umpteenth time you've pulled this. You act like you'd rather have him as a brother. Is that it?"

"What?"

I clenched my jaw. "You want Slate for a big brother, don't you? Yeah, I think that's it. You want him to be your brother and Mr. Rosen can take the place of Dad!"

Drew slammed the brakes and sent me crashing into the dash as the van screeched to a standstill. "Don't you ever—I repeat *ever*—say I want to replace Dad!" His eyes flashed red. "You hear me?" The veins in his neck protruded, pulsing in angry waves. I could feel the heat of his stare as it burned through me.

I turned my head and squinted as I prepared to receive the impact from the back of his hand across my face. A long minute came and went without a blow. His hands remained clamped down on the steering wheel. "Aren't you gonna hit me?"

"I should," he said through clenched teeth.

I closed my eyes, angling my chin up to him. "Go on. Slug me." As I waited, I opened a fraction of one eye. He was still locked down on the wheel. "You're not going to hit me?"

"Of course not, you bozo." He paused then began speaking to me the same way Mom did when I'd gone off the rails without my knowing why. While I would rant and argue without having all the facts, she would calmly bring me back in line by providing reasoning followed with a hug and a kiss. Drew didn't have it in him for the latter, but what he did have was the patience to try and make me understand what he'd seen since the day the Rosens showed up at the coffin factory.

"Remember when you passed out from all the smoke during Maudie's fire?"

"Barely."

"You remember being carried off the porch to safety, don't you?"

"Yeah."

"Do you know who carried you?"

"It was you."

"No. It was Slate."

"Slate?"

"That's right, and it was a lucky thing too because that part of the porch collapsed right after he got you."

"I'm sure someone else would've shown up if he hadn't."

"Maybe, but he's the one who did."

I shrugged, unconvinced his actions were redeeming.

"Have you also noticed Ozzy hasn't been around in a while?"

"Yeah, I was kinda wondering about that."

"It's because he and Slate had a falling out. I heard them arguing one day outside."

"About what?"

"Slate was threatening him, saying that if he ever came back to the factory with his machete, he'd take it and shove it up—anyway, he let him have it."

"I thought he wasn't coming around because Mr. Rosen was taking him fishing and wanted to hang out with him."

Drew bobbed his head. "And there you have it."

"Have what?"

He rolled his eyes at me. "Cody, are you really that blind? Slate has had to put up with a father who's abused him probably most of his life, with his fists and his words. I'd bet he's never got a single attaboy from his father and I've never seen him come close to a hug. As far as I can tell, the only time he wants to spend with him is watching him play baseball, and even then he just yells at him."

It was then that I realized Drew's memories of our father were clouding his judgment. No one could compare to what he remembered of him, and because of it he poured out forgiveness on someone he thought deserved the same thing our father gave him. Because I never knew our dad and had no way to make the comparison, I continued to look at Slate as simply someone involved in the murder of a young boy. I listened to Drew and I got what he was saying, but my heart wouldn't budge. "Can we go now?"

He sighed, "Didn't make a dent, did I?"

"It's just a lot to think about," was all I could come up with.

"Well, after what we're able to do tonight, things will be changing for all of us."

"Are you going to tell me what's going on?"

He started the van back up and slowly pulled away from the curb. "You'll know soon enough."

Several minutes later we were on the edge of town, winding our way into the countryside. A quarter moon provided just enough light to reveal gently rolling hills past huge oak trees that lined the road. Another minute later we pulled through a stone archway. On the right, a sign etched in granite read, "Oakwood Cemetery."

Chapter 29

"What're we doing here?"

Drew peered out the window, squinting at the rows of gravestones as the headlights illuminated them. "Right now, we're searching for him."

"Who—Slate?"

"No," he said, bringing the van to a stop. "Irvin-Dell."

"This isn't funny, Drew. We need to go." I stared at him as if he were a stranger. "What's wrong with you anyway?"

"Nothing's wrong with me. I told you I finally realized what we needed to do." He paused, filling his lungs with a frustrated breath. "What've we been doing all this time with the coffins?"

"Seeing visions."

"What else?"

"I-I don't know."

"We've been learning how to use them, right?"

I nodded.

"Do you think we can bring President Kennedy back?"

"Well, yeah…"

"So, if we're going to bring him back, then why not

Irvin-Dell too? We know how to do it. And Mr. Merriweather's story about what he did with Maudie's coffin proved it."

His logic had my head spinning as I put together the reason we were sitting in the middle of the road in a dark cemetery—the cemetery where Irvin-Dell was buried. "We're here to dig him up?"

He leaped out of the van and slid the side door open. "Come on," he said, pulling out two shovels and a flashlight. "This could take a while."

I ran around the front of the van, holding out my hands. "Wait, just—just hold on a minute." I swallowed and I thought of the gruesome task ahead. "So after we dig him up, we'll have to take him out of the coffin…"

"That's right."

"And then somebody's got to get into it, right?"

"Yes, Cody, somebody's got to get into it. But don't worry, it's not going to be you. Here," he said, pushing the shovel into my hands, "now follow me."

Sweaty palms and a sudden case of the shakes caused me to drop the tool. "We forgot the most important thing. We need Happy."

"That's also what the van's for," he said, continuing to walk. "Once we've brought Irvin-Dell up, we'll take him out of the coffin and put him back in the hole. Then we'll take the coffin back to the factory. I didn't want to bring Happy and chance him running off or getting spooked." He swept the flashlight's beam down the row of headstones. "Can't see it so good from here, but I think he's the last one over there."

I had dug my heels into the idea of bringing Kennedy back, and its chance of success, as Drew said, had been proven by Mr. Merriweather's story. All the steps made sense, but there was one giant flaw. "Stop a minute."

"No more stopping. We have to get on with this."

I threw the spade down, freezing on the spot. "If you don't stop, I'm not gonna help."

"What?"

"Mr. Merriweather said there'd be consequences."

"I know."

"They could be bad—really, really bad."

"Maybe."

"And you still want to go through with this?"

"Yes."

"But—"

"No buts, little brother," he said calmly. "If I have to do this alone, I will. It has to be done though."

"Does it really?"

He jabbed the tip of the shovel into the ground. "Listen, if we can save Irvin-Dell, it'll be worth it. His parents would have him back, and if it was Mr. Rosen who was driving that car, then his guilt will be gone. His life will be better and hopefully so will Slate's. Who knows? Maybe that's part of why he's continued to drink and be the way he's been. Each day from the day Irvin-Dell was killed will be different, which means it should be for Maudie as well. She might not even be in her house the day of the fire or maybe the fire won't even happen. And before you say anything, I know none of that's guaranteed, but I'm going to try."

"Well, I'm not gonna let you."

"Come again?"

"I said I'm not going to let you. You're not getting in that coffin."

"Just watch me," he said, turning around.

I grabbed his arm. "I said no! I-I mean you can't because…"

"Because why?"

I lifted my chin. "Because I am."

He rocked back on his heels. "No, you're not. This was my idea so I'm doing it."

Before he could turn back, I grabbed him again, this time rearing back a step in anticipation of flying fists. "I said I'm gonna do it."

He brushed my hand off. "And I said no."

"Well, you won't be able to anyway."

"What?"

"You won't be able to because you won't fit."

He took two steps then stopped cold, his head falling. As I waited for my reasoning to sink in, he suddenly dropped the flashlight, then with both hands hurled the shovel out into the darkness. He groaned then kicked the light, launching it into a grave's floral arrangement, scattering flowers in all directions.

Never having seen his temper reach this boiling point, I stepped behind a gravestone. "Drew," I said, my tone as soothing as I could make it, "it's going to be okay."

"How?" he replied pitifully.

"I've already told you. I'll do it. It'll be a tight squeeze, but if I squinch up enough, I can fit. Besides, I've already done it once, remember?"

He swung his head. "I know, but I still can't let you."

"But I really want to. All that stuff you said is right. We can make things better for everybody." I picked up the flashlight then ran out into the dark, returning with his shovel. "Here, let's get this show on the road."

"But Cody…"

"But what?"

"You're—You're my brother."

My heart warmed as I realized what I failed to see so many times. Others would come in and out of our lives. He'd have his friends, even ones like Slate, and I'd have mine, but no one would ever break our bond.

Just as he was about to speak, he stopped. He angled his head down the row of graves. "Did you hear that?"

"Yeah. It sounded like a baby's cry. And it came from that direction."

We slowly began walking to where Irvin-Dell's burial site was supposed to be. A cloud rolled across the moon, leaving us in a black void. We continued, Drew leading with his flashlight. Its batteries running low, it cast an eerie glow on the gravestones creating ghostly guideposts for us to follow. The only sounds other than my heartbeat pounding in my ears were the sounds of crickets chirping from some faraway field.

As we grew closer, a loud wail pierced the night air, silencing the crickets. "There," Drew said, swinging the flashlight past a large oak tree, catching the tail end of an object scurrying off into a dark patch of bushes. "It was a fox."

"Was he making that noise?"

"Musta been. I heard when they're calling each other they sound like babies."

A moment later the crickets started again. Along with them the moon came back, shining its light down on the only two gravesites left in the row. The one nearest us had a headstone that read Hellen R. Kensington, 1886 to 1960. The other, barely visible, appeared to be awaiting its tenant. A large dark rectangle with a fresh mound of dirt lay next to it.

Drew huffed. "I could've sworn this was the row."

"What's going on with that one?"

"They must be preparing for a funeral in the next couple days." We walked closer. "That's exactly it," he said, shining the light down into the hole from which the dirt had been removed.

"Drew!" I shouted as I staggered backward.

"Would you hush? You're gonna get us caught."

"Sh-shine it there."

He spun around. Following my outstretched arm, he turned the flashlight in the direction of my shaking finger and onto the empty grave's headstone. His eyes widened as he read out the name in a slow, hushed voice. "Mathew I. Dellsworth."

"Irvin-Dell," I muttered.

Drew's face paled. "But where is he?"

Chapter 30

We filled the drive back to the coffin factory with a series of endless theories on why Irvin-Dell was not where he was supposed to be. Each one ended with, "Nah, it can't be that." The only one we could halfway settle on was that his parents had taken him.

"When they exhume a body," Drew explained, "it's usually to find out how they died."

"But we know how. Rosen hit him with his car. The little boy said so."

"We know that, but they don't. And don't forget, all we really know is that it was a Cadillac that hit him."

"I still don't understand why we can't go to the police about it. Rosen's the only person in town with a..." My mouth fell open as the image of another Cadillac rolled into my memory.

"What is it?" he asked.

I closed my eyes, working my way back to the moment. "Oh my gosh, Rosen's not the only one in town with a car like that."

"How do you know?"

"Because I met the owner of another one. It belongs

to the guy with the big mustache. His name was one of the planets."

"That's gotta be Cederic Mars?" Drew said. "He's that guy who's been talking to Mr. Merriweather."

"That's him alright. He was parked outside Maudie's house one day. I talked to him."

"So he's got the same exact Cadillac?"

"The exact same. But his is gray, not silver."

"Cody, those are two different colors."

"I know, but the gray was so close to looking like silver it could be…" I threw my hands over my face as doubt suddenly reared an ugly possibility. I shook my head, trying to convince myself it was a silver car Timothy had identified, not gray. "I-I don't know now. Maybe I was wrong. Maybe…" I dropped my head. "I'm sorry, Drew."

"There's no need to be sorry. This just means somebody's probably thinking there's more to his death than first thought. Whether the car was gray or silver is beside the point, as long as they're investigating it now."

By the time we pulled into the factory's back parking lot, I'd beaten myself to a mental pulp over how quick I had been to condemn Rosen for killing Irvin-Dell. Could I have become that unhinged? Why couldn't I have Drew's patience? What was wrong with me? I stared out the windshield straight ahead to a flickering light coming from the showroom window, all while my thoughts banged around in my head questioning my own character.

"You okay?" Drew said, snapping me out of my trance.

"Yeah, I-I'm alright. Is someone here?"

"There shouldn't be, why?"

"There's a light coming from the showroom."

Drew killed the engine and sat for a minute, studying the window from where the light was coming. He suddenly leaped from the van. "Come on," he said, grabbing the flashlight. "It could be the start of a fire."

Within seconds we had circled the building to the side door. Drew fumbled with the keys for an eternity. When he finally opened the door, he left me behind and raced across the factory floor, the beam from his flashlight jostling wildly about.

By the time I reached him, he was already inside. As I was about to enter, Happy came flying out, colliding into my chest. He flung his arms around my neck, smothering me in his grip. I gently shifted him onto my shoulder. "Easy boy," I said as I walked through the door.

In front of me, Drew stood frozen next to a lone candle, looking to the floor where Slate was struggling to free himself from a small white coffin that had been carved up to allow him to fit inside. Where the bottom end of the coffin had been, his legs from the knees down stuck out. A section on the side had also been cut away, enabling his torso to fit. The lid dangled open, a single hinge keeping it from falling off.

Twice he lunged halfway up, grappling with the sides for leverage only to flop back inside. On the third attempt Drew jerked him up by the collar. Just as he began to fall back, Drew reached under his arm and pulled him out onto the floor.

"Slate, what the heck are you doin'?" he said.

The edges of Slate's mouth slowly curled upward. "It's done."

"What's done?"

He lumbered toward the door as if sleepwalking, still smiling, seemingly unaware we were there.

Drew took him by the elbow. "What're you talking about?"

Slate looked past him to me. "I did it, Cody."

The shock of him calling me by my correct name for the first time was nice but alarming. "Are you okay?" I asked.

His smile widened, his eyes crinkling at the corners. In an instant his hand was over his mouth, and he was giggling like a little girl.

"I think he needs to go to the hospital," I said.

Slate's laughing petered out with a long, final sigh. "No, fellas. I'm fine. I couldn't be better."

"What's going on?" Drew asked. "Why were you in that coffin? How come it's all chopped up like that?"

"It was the only way I could fit."

"Look!" I yelled, pointing to the sides. "That's Irvin-Dell's coffin. Those are the maple-leaf handles." I looked at Slate. "You're the one who dug him up."

"Me and Frankie," he said.

"Somebody helped you?"

"Of course. I couldn't do all that digging by myself. I had to get one of my father's goons to help."

"And he knows too?"

"Don't worry. I paid the guy enough to keep him quiet. Besides, it won't matter if he tells him now anyway."

"So what's all this about? Where's Irvin-Dell's body?"

"Hello!" came a distant voice. "Is somebody here?"

"Shoot—it's that new night watchman," Drew whispered.

"I'll talk to you guys tomorrow," Slate said already halfway out the window.

"Wait for us," I said.

"Sorry, I gotta go."

"But we wanna—"

"Just come see me after the game tomorrow. I'll tell you everything." Then he was gone.

Our sprint back to the house came to a hard stop when we saw one beam of light flashing through the pecan orchard, one coming from around the house, and another all the way down in Mrs. Clegg's garden.

"Drew! Cody!" voices cried out. "Drew, Cody, where are you?"

We slipped behind a tree. "What do we do?" I said, tugging at Drew's sleeve.

"There they are," one of our uncles shouted.

"Just follow my lead," Drew said, stepping out into the moonlight and holding up his hands like he'd just been arrested.

"Where've you boys been?" Mom said, stomping up to us. "We've been worried sick."

"We couldn't sleep," Drew began. "With everything going on, we were wide awake, so we decided to walk around the block."

"And stuff your bed with pillows before you left?"

"We didn't want you to worry if you came home and found us gone. I'm sorry. It was my idea to make decoys."

My uncle's snicker broke the tension.

"You think this is funny, Dean?" she said.

"Come on, sis, the boys have been through a lot. Give 'em a break."

She stood stewing. "You two are going to give me a heart attack one of these days. Now get to bed right now. And don't leave your rooms until tomorrow morning. You hear me?"

"Yes ma'am," we answered as one.

The next morning, I woke to find a note from Drew on my bedside table.

Had to leave early to get rid of Irvin-Dell's coffin before Mr. M gets there. I won't be off until 3:45. Remember Slate's game at 4:00. See you there.

As I was reading the note, Mom popped her head through the door. "Has Drew already left?"

"Yeah."

"I told him he didn't have to go today if he didn't want to, considering, well—you know."

"It's okay, Mom. You can say it."

"Thanks, honey. It's just hard to believe she's gone."

"I know."

She paused, struggling for a comforting word. "Anyway, if you don't want to go to school the rest of the week, it's okay."

Normally, I would've been all about this kind of offer but too much was racing through my mind. With Drew gone and all my friends in school, I had to have something to occupy my thoughts. "I actually think I'll go if that's okay."

"Of course. On Friday, though, you'll need to leave before noon. That's when her funeral is."

Sitting in class that day was of little help. If the teacher was speaking, I'd try and listen but as soon as we were left on our own to solve a problem or do our work, my mind was back to finding Slate jammed into Irvin-Dell's coffin. Had he pulled off what I was thinking? Could Happy have helped send him back to save Irvin-Dell? Throughout the day I looked for signs of things being different or anything that could indicate a miracle had happened, but there were no surprises or revelations. The only things that were different were the strained conversations and uneasy glances from other students who didn't know how to engage with someone who had just lost a family member. By the time the final bell of the day rang, I was more than ready to meet Drew at the ballfield.

"You going to the game?" Mary Lib said, bouncing up beside me.

"Yeah. I'm supposed to meet Drew there."

"Mind if I tag along?"

My skills at politely telling her no without letting on that we had important business with Slate were lacking. "Well, he and I really needed to…you see, it's just that Drew, Slate, and I need to…"

Her eyes fell away. "Oh, I'm sorry. I, uh…I'll just catch you later."

I watched her slowly walk away, dejected that her attempt to make me feel better had failed.

"Get on over here, girl." What the heck, I thought. We couldn't talk to Slate during the game anyway.

"You sure?" she said, trotting back.

"Sure, I'm sure."

Five minutes later we were sitting ten rows up directly behind the Bulldogs' dugout. Mr. Rosen was a safe distance below us in his usual seat behind the players. Why he had not been banned from the games was mystifying, but it was a safe bet it had something to do with financial contributions to the athletic department.

"He's already going at it," Mary Lib said.

"Yeah, all his practice pitches are smokin'."

"I wasn't talking about Slate." She motioned to Mr. Rosen. "He's already got his brown bag out." Her attention suddenly moved to the entrance ramp. She jumped up and waved her hands. "Up here!" A moment later Drew was squeezing down the aisle to the empty seat I'd saved for him.

As he sat, I leaned into him. "Did you get rid of the coffin in time?

"Barely."

"Play ball!" The announcer's voice boomed out into the stadium.

"Who's batting first?" I asked.

"Yuck," Mary Lib said as Ozzy stepped up to the plate. "It's the meathead."

"Well, I'm gonna get a hot dog then. You guys want anything?"

"I'll take a Coke," Drew said.

"Thanks, but I'm good," Mary Lib replied.

As I made my way to the exit, the crack of the bat turned me around just in time to dodge the foul ball Ozzy had hit into the stands. As if it was a loaded grenade, the crowd around me scattered as it bounced off the cement then ricocheted off the wall straight at an unsuspecting little boy's head. Just before it smacked him, I threw up my hand, snagging it midair to the crowd's delight. Hoots and hollers filled half the stadium.

"Sign him up!" shouted a man behind me.

I looked back and waved my prize toward Mary Lib and

Drew. Both were smiling and clapping as if I'd just made the game's winning catch.

"Thank you, young fella," said a man extending his hand to me. "That could've meant some stitches for my nephew." He rubbed the boy's baseball cap. "Don't you want to thank him," he coaxed.

Too shy or embarrassed by the sudden attention, the boy hid himself under his cap without looking up. "Thank you."

The man smiled, "Enjoy the game, and thanks again." Taking the boy by the hand, he led him through the crowd. The little boy's head continued to hang low.

Foul balls were the equivalent to gold bars in our neighborhood, especially when they came with a story of such athletic heroics. I stood, rotating it in my hand, admiring the red stitching, thinking how proud PaPa would be upon hearing about it.

"Whatcha going to do with it?" a cute girl from my homeroom said, bopping up beside me.

I rubbed it with my palm, giving it another once-over. "I, uh—I don't know," I muttered as I watched the man and little boy disappear into the crowd. "Wait a minute. I know exactly what I'm gonna do with it."

"What?"

"I'll tell ya later," I said, bolting off in the direction of the concession area. A minute later I was standing at the corner of the hot-dog table, waiting for the man and the boy to finish their order. Upon seeing me, the man yelled over, "Can I get you something?"

"No, thank you."

With an arm full of snacks and drinks, the man nudged his way through the line to me. The little boy trailed after him, his head down as he chomped on a chili dog.

"You sure you don't want anything? I think you've earned at least a bag of chips."

"Thank you, but I'm fine. The reason I'm here is I wanted to give something to your nephew." I reached into my pocket and pulled out the foul ball. I bent down and held it in front of him. "I think this really belongs to you." I looked up to the man. "I just happened to be in the way."

"That's real nice of you," the man said. "Are you sure?"

"Of course."

"What do you say to the nice young man?"

The little boy handed his half-eaten chili dog to his uncle. With both hands he reached up and wrapped his fingers around the ball. The bill of his hat slowly rose, revealing the blue eyes of the boy that had lain in the white coffin, the coffin Slate had dug up and climbed into.

My legs wobbled. I stumbled back against the hot-dog table, spilling condiments onto the ground.

"Are you okay?" the man said, taking me by the shoulders.

My lungs collapsed as the air sucked from me. "Is—Is that really you?"

"What's your name?" the man said in a concerned voice.

"That's Cody," the boy said. "He lives down the street."

I took a shaky breath, then murmured, "Hello, Irvin-Dell."

Chapter 31

I'm not sure how long it took me to return to my seat or even how I got there, but when I did, Drew and Mary Lib were staring at me in a way that did little to bring me out of my trance. I sat down without hearing the roar of the crowd or noticing the fans jumping up and down in the aisles. The announcer could have been miles away. The only feeling I had was Drew and Mary Lib's eyes on me. Could this be how a ghost felt? Could it be how Irvin-Dell had just felt upon seeing me?

"Hey, buddy, what's wrong?" Drew said, tweaking my arm.

I looked out onto the field and watched as Slate took the mound. "He did it," I mumbled.

Drew leaned toward me. "What'd you say?"

"Strike one!" yelled the umpire as Slate recoiled from his first pitch.

"I said, 'He did it.'"

"Who did what?"

"Strike two," the umpire came again. The crowd roared.

"Slate," I muttered. "He—brought—Irvin-Dell—back."

"Guys, pay attention," Mary Lib chided. "These pitches are on fire."

"How do you know?"

"I just saw him. I talked to him and his uncle. He's down in the concession stands right now."

Drew's jaw couldn't have fallen any lower. He turned back to the field, fixated on the pitcher's mound.

The intercom squealed as the announcer called the next pitch. Slate rocked back, pulling the ball into his side.

"Here comes the windup," began the play-by-play.

Slate raised his glove above his right shoulder and coiled his torso into a pressure-packed cannon. He pumped the glove-covered ball once into the air, then with the speed of a bullwhip, his arm unleashed around his side in a fury of energy that somehow went wrong. Just as the ball was leaving his fingertips, a pop, like the sound of a firecracker, pierced the air. The ball didn't even make it to home plate. Slate fell to the ground, curled up and holding his elbow, moaning.

Behind the dugout, Mr. Rosen flung his paper-wrapped liquor bottle against the fence, barely missing the team doctor rushing onto the field. As Slate was being attended to, a hush fell over the stadium, the only sound coming from his father's cursing.

"What's happening?" I said.

"Can't you see? Slate's hurt," Mary Lib replied. "I think he threw out his arm."

I turned to Drew, my eyes pleading for the real answer. He stood expressionless, staring along with everyone else.

A minute later Slate was walked off the field, cradling his arm. The doctor strode alongside him, adding a supporting hand under his. The crowd erupted in sympathetic applause. A few minutes later an ambulance arrived and whisked him away.

As another pitcher took the mound, Drew asked, "Are you thinking what I am?"

"All I know is that Irvin-Dell's here, right this very minute, eating a hot dog, and Slate's been taken to the hospital."

Mary Lib leaned in. "What're you guys talking about?"

"Nothing," Drew replied.

I stared out onto the field, watching the replacement pitcher warm up, but I never saw a single throw. All I saw was Slate in that white coffin, fast-forwarding to the pitch that drove him to the ground. My lip began to quiver. My eyes welled with tears. "I wanna go. I wanna go now."

Mary Lib stood up. "I don't want to stay either."

"Yeah," Drew said. "I'm ready to go home too."

I shook my head. "No, I'm talking about the hospital."

"You want to go see how he is?"

I swiped my sleeve across my eyes and nodded quickly.

"You want to come too?" he asked Mary Lib.

"Of course."

"Then let's go," he said, scooting down the aisle. "We'll see if somebody can take us."

Three hours later Mom was pulling us up to the Alamance County Hospital emergency room in her beat-up Chevy. "Are you sure he's here?" she asked.

"Yes," Drew said, "I asked the team's coach before we left the game."

"Okay, then I'll be back in an hour to pick you up."

A frumpy lady chewing gum at the speed of a cow

grinding cud greeted us from behind the reception desk. "Can I help you?"

Drew stepped forward. "Yes ma'am, we're here to see Slate Rosen."

"You kids with his dad?"

"No. Is his father not here?"

The lady gave the gum a few chomps, a tiny bubble bursting between her pinched lips. "Nope. Other than the team doctor who came in with him, you three are his first visitors."

"Can we see him?"

"Sure, just take a visitor's tag and sign this sheet. He's through the double doors behind me, room 103."

Ever since I stepped on a rusty nail four years earlier, I'd come to despise the sterile walls of our city's hospital. I hated the smell and how clean it all was. Any place that was so germ-free was no fun. Today, though, I hated it far more than the hole in my foot and the accompanying tetanus shot.

We were standing outside Slate's door, hesitating to enter, when a nurse whizzed past carrying a plastic cup in each hand. "You all can come in. I'm just giving him his medicine." She pushed the door open and one by one we filed in. The drapes were closed, the only light coming from a small TV crammed into the corner, the sound barely audible.

"Slate, you've got visitors."

He rolled his head toward us, a weak smile appearing as he adjusted the sling wrapped around his arm. "Hi."

"We've got him on some mild pain meds so he may be a tad loopy," the nurse said, holding up the cups to him. "Time for another round, dear. Then you can visit with your friends."

After he swallowed the last pill, the nurse departed, leaving us in awkward silence.

"We would've been here sooner," Drew finally said, "but our mom was out visiting some of Maudie's relatives."

"How're you feeling?" Mary Lib blurted.

"Okay I guess," he said, stretching his eyelids, forcing himself to stay awake.

"What happened? Did you throw out your arm?"

"You might say that."

"Is it going to be okay?" Drew asked.

He turned to the window, then looked back, a tear appearing on his cheek.

"What happened?"

"The elbow's fractured and I've got something called a torn labrum. Doctor said he's seen both, but never at the same time."

"They'll heal, won't they?"

"In time. I'll have to have surgery though. But…"

Drew leaned forward. "But what?"

"I won't be able to pitch again—not ever."

My heart sank as I stood watching a boy I'd grown to hate tell us something I'd have easily wished upon him two days earlier. But now things were different. "Why'd you do it?" I shouted.

Mary Lib scowled at me. "What's wrong with you, Cody? Why would anyone want to throw out their arm?"

"That's not what he means," Drew said.

"Then what *do* you mean?"

The angst rose in my body as my chest tightened, taking away my breath. "He saved Irvin-Dell. He did something to keep him from being killed."

"What on God's green earth are you talking about?" Mary Lib said.

"Don't you get it? Slate used Happy and Irvin-Dell's coffin to go back and save him and now he's paid the price."

She reared back, eyes bulging.

Drew held out a calming hand. "She doesn't know, Cody."

"How can she not—"

"Remember, when Mr. Merriweather saved Maudie? Everything changed from that point on. Only he knew because he was the one in the coffin and Thiago knew because he was there, but for everyone else all things went on as if she'd never gotten sick—"

"Because he stole the letter." I paused, taking a needed breath. "And you and I only know about Irvin-Dell because we were there at Slate's coffin-jump."

By this time, Mary Lib had collapsed into a chair and was gazing up at us as if we'd been talking in tongues.

"Don't worry," Drew said. "We'll tell you everything later."

"But..."

"It's too long of a story," he said. "Trust me. You'll know everything soon enough."

I turned back to Slate. "Why'd you do it?" I asked again.

"You mean why did I go back and hide my father's car keys that day so he couldn't drive drunk? Because he did it! My father killed that little boy!" Suddenly his voice was clear, showing no trace of the sedating effects of his medication. Tears began to flow. "Nobody knew, did they?"

"We actually had a feeling," Drew said.

"So you were probably still there when Mr. Merriweather told us about the consequences, weren't you?" I said.

He nodded.

"And you went ahead and sacrificed your arm and probably your future to save him."

"I didn't know what would happen to me. All I knew was that I had to right his wrong." He wiped his eyes. "I'm so sorry."

"Why?" I said. "You don't have anything to be sorry for."

"I'm sorry for him."

"For who?"

"My father. I'm sorry for him being such a hateful, despicable, evil person." He buried his face in his hands. "There's something else you need to know." He slowly raised his head. "I-I don't know for sure, but I think he's responsible for burning down your great-grandmother's house."

"To get it for his parking lot?" Drew said.

"Yes."

I began pacing. I had to do something to keep from screaming or throwing something.

"Are you sure?" Drew asked.

"I don't have any proof, but I know he or one of his hired thugs is capable of it. Before we moved, he was accused of something similar but was never charged. Cody's right, he's evil."

"Look who's here to take you home," the nurse said from the doorway. Next to her stood Mr. Rosen.

"Who's evil?" he said flatly.

Drew grabbed me and Mary Lib by our sleeves. "We'd better get going now."

Rosen's arm stretched across the door. "Why the rush? Don't you want to stay and continue your chat with my boy? Don't you want to find out why I've told him over and over why he needed to change that stupid sidearm pitching of his?"

"I'm sorry, sir," Mary Lib said, shoving past him into the hall, "I've got to get home. Come on, guys. Let's go!"

"Excuse us," Drew said, pulling me along behind her. He turned back. "See ya soon, Sl—"

The door slammed shut, leaving him hanging mid-sentence. For the first time in my life, I heard my brother curse.

Chapter 32

Over the next few weeks Drew spent most of his spare time at the factory, his bond with Mr. Merriweather growing even stronger now that they shared the mystery of the coffins. Slate supposedly had surgery and because of his prolonged absence, we believed him to be recuperating at home.

As the days fell away, summer slowly faded into autumn, and with it came the excitement of our school's biggest event—the annual Fall Festival, a weeklong extravaganza of after-school fun and games culminating in Saturday's main event, The Show of Shows.

Always with a Halloween theme, The Show of Shows was held on the baseball field and remained a mystery right up to showtime. One year it was a mini circus, complete with baby kangaroos, clowns, jugglers, and a bear-wrestling contest. Another year it was a Halloween rodeo featuring ghosts and goblins doing trick riding, barrel racing and lassoing baby goats. This year's event was rumored to be a haunted Wild West show. According to Cackles, she'd seen a dozen leather-clad cowboys camped down by Old Man Kelsey's creek, practicing trick shots. And with the festival starting the following day, there was no reason to doubt her.

"Maybe they'll have a shootout like in that movie *High Noon*," she said one afternoon while helping me rake leaves onto blankets that we pulled off into a ditch to burn.

"Yeah, could be," I replied.

"Maybe they'll ride sideways on a horse, shooting tin cans."

"That's possible."

"Maybe they'll do some knife throwin'. Maybe even split an apple off some kid's head."

"Yeah, sure."

"Maybe Martians will come down from outer space and tap dance while chugging Cokes and balancing teacups on their green heads."

"I reckon."

"Dagnabbit, Cody. What's the matter with ya? You haven't heard a word I've said."

I ran my hand through my hair. "Sorry about that. My mind musta been someplace else."

"Ya thunk! It's been someplace else ever since Slate tore up his wing."

Cackles was right. I *had* been preoccupied ever since Slate's accident, but today's lack of focus had more to do with the hour-long session I'd spent with the mysterious Mr. Mars earlier that morning. Seeing me across the street rummaging through the remains of Maudie's house, he called me over to the coffin factory, ushered me inside, and proceeded to enlighten me on the marvels of his occupation, ending with a request that left me dumbfounded.

"Seriously, what's up with you?" Cackles prodded.

I searched for prying eyes. Convinced no one was in earshot, I drew a quick breath, ready to share my encounter, when the image of Mars's arched brow suddenly appeared staring down on me. The tips of his moustache whipped his cheeks as he explained the importance of secrecy.

"I'm sorry but I told—" I cut my thought short, realizing saying anything else would require more explanation than I felt like getting into. Besides, I'd sworn not to tell anyone about our talk, not even Drew.

"You're sorry for what?" she asked.

"I'm just sorry for being so—you know—out of it."

"Anything you want to talk about?"

"No, it's all good." Taking advantage of her typical short attention span, I switched gears back to The Show of Shows and its big finale. "What do you think they'll end with?"

"Maybe that shootout I mentioned. I'm pretty sure about those cowboys I saw at the creek. I'd bet my new first-baseman's mitt that it'll be something like that."

"Nah, it's gonna be bigger."

"So what do you think it'll be?" she said, suddenly tilting her head around my shoulder. "Well, looky there…"

I turned and followed her gaze across the backyard toward the coffin factory. Coming up over the ridge was Drew. Nudged up alongside him was Slate, Drew's arm wrapped around him. They walked in a staggered lock-step that from a distance looked more like a slow-motion sack race.

"Stay here," I told Cackles as I sprinted off toward them.

Meeting them on the other side of the driveway, I stopped when I realized there was a reason for their odd gait.

Slate's face was hidden in a downward gaze. From all angles it appeared Drew was dragging him along.

"What's wrong with him?" Cackles wheezed as she came running up behind me.

"Nothing's wrong," Drew said. "He's just tired's all."

"Tired from what?"

"He came to see us at the factory, and it was just a little too much."

"Too much for what?"

"It was the first time he's been out of his house since the accident."

Slate's head slowly moved up and down in a way I took for a nod.

"Where ya going then?" Cackles continued.

"I'm taking him inside for something to drink and to rest a spell."

"Did the surgery hurt much?" she asked. "Are you better now?"

"Would you hush it?" I said. "Geez, you're as bad as one of those squawky parrots down at the pet store."

"Don't get snappy at me, Cody boy. I'm just askin'."

Slate mustered just enough of a raised hand to say it was okay.

Drew continued to assist him to the house. "You guys go on about your leaf raking."

I started to follow them until Drew stopped me with a stern face. "Go on now. You still got some raking left."

Twenty minutes later, after heaving another three bundles of leaves to the ditch, I was ready for a break, not only from my labors, but also from Cackles' continuous need for details about Slate's unexpected visit.

"I think this is good enough for now," I said, tossing my rake to the ground.

"You wanna get a game of roller-bat going? I'll round up the gang."

"You go ahead," I said, dashing back to the house. "I think I'm gonna get something to drink."

Instead of finding Drew and Slate sitting inside chugging lemonades, all I found was an empty kitchen. The only sign of anyone being home was the murmur of Gonny's voice coming from one of our rooms down the hall. I couldn't make out what she was saying, but the tone was familiar—the soothing cadence of a caring grandmother addressing someone in distress. It was the same tone she always used with Drew and me after we scraped a knee, cut a finger, or got any number of childhood injuries. I silently made my way through the house.

As I approached Drew's room, her words became clearer. "It's going to be alright. You'll see." A moment later I heard sobbing and more consoling. I stood outside the door, wondering if I should go in. I reached for the knob, then pulled back. Just as I did, it opened a third of the way. Drew squeezed through, shielding me from seeing behind him.

"What's going on?" I said, stretching my chin over his shoulder and trying to look inside.

Without a word, he pulled me to the kitchen toward the back door. By the pressure of his grip on my wrist and the speed at which I was being dragged, I prepared to be flung outside. Instead, we stopped just short of the screen door where he spun me around by the shoulders. I stood motionless, hoping my silence would remedy whatever violation I'd committed. He wiped his hand over his forehead, took a half step back, then paused before whispering, "Slate's father almost killed him this afternoon."

"What!"

His hand was suddenly covering my mouth. "Shhh,"

he said, glancing back down the hall. He slowly pulled it away. "You gotta be calm."

"Was it an accident?"

"No. He actually tried to *kill* him, Cody."

Before I could blurt out a horrified response, he grabbed me by the wrist and pulled me outside.

"What do you mean he tried to kill him?" I said, stumbling loose of his grip.

"He tried to kill him with a broken whiskey bottle. They were arguing and it got to where Mr. Rosen broke the bottle on a table then swung at him. Maybe he was too drunk to know he still had the bottle in his hand, but it slashed Slate from below his ear to his chin. Luckily it wasn't deep, but any farther down and it probably would've got his jugular."

I stared through the screen door, unable to speak.

"And what I said about him coming to see us at the factory today was a lie. He was already there. He snuck in yesterday after work and spent the night in one of the storage rooms. I just happened to find him while cleaning up."

"Does Gonny know all this?

"I had to tell her."

"What'd she say?"

"She wanted to go to the police, but Slate said no. He said that if she did, his father would have one of his henchmen kill her or somebody in our family."

I continued looking back at the house, envisioning my former enemy sitting on the bed with our grandmother kneeling next to him, soothing him with the same love and care she'd given us all those years. All I could do was shake my head.

"That's not all," Drew said. "He's not going to have his surgery."

"I thought he already had."

"I did too, but come to find out his dad doesn't want to pay for it. He says it won't heal well enough for him to pitch again so what's the use?"

"Then he'll have an arm that won't work."

"It'll heal to a point, but he'll probably always have pain and won't be able to move it like he used to."

"And all because he did the right thing."

Drew nodded.

"So what's he going to do now? He can't go home."

"He's going to stay with us. Gonny said he could have my room and I'll sleep in yours."

"What if his dad comes looking for him?"

"We'll just have to keep him outta sight."

"But he can't stay with us forever. Sooner or later, he'll have to go home."

"I don't know. I'm just glad PaPa will be back this Thursday."

"For how long?"

"Just 'til Saturday. He's staying until after The Show of Shows, then he's off on another long haul out west." Drew gave me a look I'd seen a thousand times before. More than just a look, it was a way of examining my soul.

I waited as I always had, then broke the silence with a baffled shrug. "What?"

"Are you okay with him being here?"

"Of course! Why wouldn't I?"

"Just checking, that's all."

"Well, you can quit your checkin'—geez." Another moment passed. "You said they were arguing. Do you know about what?"

"Slate accused him of burning down Maudie's house.

He said he should've waited until he wasn't drinking but for the past six months, he'd pretty much been drunk all the time."

"I don't get it. Why do some people drink so much?"

"I think I might know why *he* does."

"Really?"

"Seems he blames Slate for ending his own baseball career. That and his marriage."

"How could a kid do either of those?"

"Apparently Mr. Rosen was a good pitcher himself. In fact, he was on his way to the majors until he found out he got a girl pregnant."

"With Slate?"

"Yep. Supposedly the girl forced him to get married and said she wasn't about to go on the road with what she called a 'baseball-playing gypsy.'"

"So what happened?"

"I guess he loved her because he gave up the game and tried to settle down. Slate said he thinks that's when his drinking started. Five years later his mother took up with some French businessman and just up and left the country, leaving them high and dry. Just up and bolted."

"So why didn't Rosen go back to baseball?"

"Cody, you know how competitive it is—five years away from playing ball is like twenty. He'd lost all his skills. No team would ever think about bringing him on. But the main thing is he had to raise Slate on his own."

"And he resents him for it?"

"In the biggest way," Drew said. "And the alcohol only makes it worse."

My brother's story left me with an empty space in my heart that suddenly filled with anger—anger for a father who was anything but. Slate's place in this world was doomed with John Rosen in that role. If he invited him back in, he would surely die, either by his hand—or worse, by his words and the slow agonizing torture of constant humiliation.

"If there was only something we could do," Drew said.

"His father just needs to leave. If he did, Slate could live with us."

"Wouldn't that be something? To see old man Rosen's name on a missing person's poster?"

I turned back to the coffin factory. "Yeah, that would be something, wouldn't it?"

Chapter 33

The next day was the start of a long week of deception. What should've been a raucous good time, hanging with our friends at the festival's after-school events, was more of a chore in dodging them. As much as it pained me, Drew and I agreed that someone had to stand guard and keep an eye out for Slate's father. And since Drew had to work in the afternoons, the job fell upon me.

Several times Mary Lib caught me sitting cross-legged on the front porch, scanning the street, waiting for Rosen's dreaded silver Cadillac to come screeching into the driveway. On Monday and Tuesday, she dropped by asking if I wanted to go with her to the festival, to which I replied with a theatrical moan that I wasn't feeling well. On Wednesday I told her I had too much homework. By Thursday, I assumed she'd given up but had sent Reubin and Peeps in her place. My excuse for them was that I'd been grounded but I was definitely in for The Show of Shows on Saturday.

Every night that week Drew and I took turns sitting with Slate and making sure he was okay while the other manned a lookout post. With Gonny's approval we brought his meals to Drew's room and even did his wash. Without us knowing it, she also went to Weaver's Menswear and bought him several sets of clothes. I had never heard him say thank you before, but during those five days he wore the words out. It was also during this week we learned more about his father's verbal abuse, the countless beatings Slate had taken, and other horrors too traumatic for him to express.

When PaPa finally got home late Thursday evening, he dispensed with his customary settling-in period of a shower and dinner followed by an hour of TV in his favorite rocking chair. To my surprise, what he wanted was to know which room Slate was in. Drew later reminded me that he and Gonny always talked every night on the phone whenever he was on the road, and that our new housemate would have surely been their number-one topic.

"He's in my room," Drew said.

PaPa patted him on the head and began down the hallway.

"What all did Gonny tell you?" Drew asked as we tagged along after him.

He stopped outside the door and looked warmly back at us. "Enough to know he's got some good friends. Now you boys wait in Cody's room. I'd like to talk to the young man alone."

Forty-five minutes later he peeked his head inside my door. His eyes were a tinge redder and a bit puffier than when he'd gone in to see Slate.

"Well," he said, drawing the word out with a slow breath, "that's a heavy heart we have next door."

Drew left his chair and joined me on the bed. PaPa sat down in his place, pulling closer to us. For the longest time he sat silent before finally speaking in a low baritone, every syllable rolling over us like a warm blanket. "Do you know what a wonderful father you had?"

"I know I was little, but I remember," Drew said. "I do. I really do."

I hung my head. "I don't."

My grandfather's face glowed. "Cody, you don't remember because you weren't born yet, but Drew can tell you his love ran deep for him and your mom. Had he been there for you, I'm sure he'd have loved you just as much."

My brother's nod came with a tear rolling down his cheek.

PaPa looked at the wall that divided our rooms, inspecting it as if trying to see through it. "I'm afraid Slate's never experienced the type of love your father gave."

"But he knows we care about him now," Drew said, wiping his eyes.

My head fell under the weight of the guilt I carried for hating him so long.

"What's wrong?" PaPa asked.

My mouth clamped shut as my eyes welled with my own tears. I looked away, hiding my reaction from myself as much as from my grandfather.

As he'd done so often, Drew came to my aid. "He's been beating himself up for a long time about Slate."

"Why?"

"He never really got to know him and feels he judged him wrongly. But in all fairness, I should've told him sooner about what was going on with him and his father. I just wanted him to see it for himself." Drew put his hand on my shoulder. "I'm sorry, brother. I thought it'd be better if you learned what grace was on your own without someone forcing it on you."

I wiped my face, then looked him in the eyes and smiled, knowing how right he was. I turned to PaPa. "We're gonna replace that pain he has with something better, aren't we?"

"That's right," he said. "We're going to get rid of it and make sure that father of his can never hurt him ever again."

The image of Rosen's face on a missing person's poster suddenly flashed in my mind. But before I could smile, the conviction of my grandfather's words hit me. They were like something a gangster would say when planning to rub somebody out. "What do you mean? How can we make sure he'll never hurt him?"

"There're people that protect kids like Slate. They work for a department called Social Services. They take them away from abusive parents and put them someplace safe. He's a perfect case for something like that."

Drew was shaking his head.

"You haven't heard of them?" PaPa asked.

"I have, sir, but I'm afraid Slate has too. In fact, he said they'd been to his house before and his dad put on this whole lovey-dovey father thing and convinced them everything was alright. He was so good at it he had them believing there was something wrong with Slate. All it did was humiliate him. The worst part is that after things cooled down, Mr. Rosen beat him to a pulp. And to top it off, he said if they ever came back, he'd just as soon kill him before he let them take him away."

I threw up my hands. "I don't get it. If his father hates him so much, then why doesn't he just let him go? I don't think he ever wanted him in the first place."

Drew stood. "What gets me is how somebody like him can go from being such a monster to putting on airs like he's the world's best dad."

"I don't know either," PaPa said. "A man's inner demons can sometimes sprout angel wings when needed." He patted his fingertips together. "I think we're still going to have to call Social Services."

"But, sir, Slate told me point-blank he didn't want to go down that road again. He's sure his dad'll kill him."

"Does he have any relatives we can call?"

"None that I know of."

PaPa rose from his chair, then walked to the window where he stood staring out into the darkness. "We don't have a choice."

"But he said—"

"It's our only option, Drew. I'll contact them tomorrow. In the meantime, we'll just have to keep him out of sight."

"There's got to be another way. We'll get him killed if we don't find it. And if Rosen knew it was us who called, I'm sure he'd do something to us too. According to Slate, he's got people on his payroll that do that sort of thing."

"I'm sorry. This is all we can do. Anything else is just an illusion."

It was then that a speck of a thought, like a tiny cinder from a fire, floated into my brain. I closed my eyes hoping for it to ignite.

"Are you alright?" PaPa said.

I dared not answer for fear of it vanishing. I squeezed my eyes tighter, forcing myself to block him out as he asked again.

"Cody—are you alright?"

All at once it came to me—a daring idea burning brightly with all the details in place. "That's it!" I shouted. I opened my eyes to find them gawking at me the same way we did ole Bullet just before he broke free of his chain.

"What do you mean, *that's it*?" Drew asked.

My heart raced. "We don't have to get those social people

involved. I know a better way!" I turned to PaPa. "We can do it. It'll work. I know it will."

Without saying a word, he stood studying me in a way that told me he was searching for a nice way to say, "Shut your trap." I nervously waited as he eased back into his chair. Without emotion, he clasped his hands over his lap and said, "What's your plan?"

Chapter 34

The following day no one called Social Services and neither Drew nor I had to take turns guarding the house. When school let out, I was able to accompany Mary Lib to the last day of the after-school festivities. Drew got off work early and was even able to join us for the last hour. PaPa banged around in the dungeon showing Peeps and Reubin how to change a lawn mower's spark plug. And across town Gonny spent the afternoon with Uncle Dean and Aunt Sally. As the sun began to set, she slid into the seat of her old Plymouth, adjusted the rearview mirror and waved goodbye. With the sun behind them, Uncle Dean and Aunt Sally stood silhouetted, waving. Between them, Slate waved along.

Saturday morning came early with a banging at our front door that woke everyone in the house. From out in the hall, I could hear PaPa's feet stomping past my room at the same volume as the banging.

"Hold your horses!" he shouted.

We heard the sound of the door being opened and then an abrupt, "Where's he at?"

"Where's who?" PaPa replied.

"My boy. That's who."

The door suddenly slammed shut and all we could hear from the other side was the muffled exchange of one angry man and the even tones of another. I peeked my head out my door just as Drew opened his. I stayed put, peering out while he marched down the hall toward the action. "Where you goin'?" I said as he passed by, but I knew by his determined look he was going to the aid of our grandfather. I took a deep breath and fell in behind him. "I knew he'd show up sooner or later. I just knew it."

"Shhhh," Drew said, stopping just short of the door. He slowly leaned forward and pressed his ear against it.

"That's Rosen out there! He's gonna—"

"Hush, dang it," he said, flashing me a fiery gaze.

Several minutes passed as I stood watching him try to decipher the garbled conversation coming from outside. His eyes widened as the sounds grew louder, his brow beginning to fold into deep concentration just as the door opened. He jumped back, barely missing being whacked in the head as it swung inward. PaPa quickly closed it behind him.

"Is everything alright?" Gonny shouted from the back of the house.

"Yes, dear. Just a pushy salesperson. You can go back to bed."

"What did he say?" I asked. "Does he know Slate was here?"

"You were right. He does have people working for him, the kind that I'm sure will do what you said."

I cupped my hands to the back of my head. "This is bad. He's a Mafia guy, isn't he? I knew it. He's gonna kill us."

PaPa's voice grew solemn. "I don't know about the Mafia, but he does know Slate was here."

"I heard what you told him," Drew said. "Do you think he believed it?"

"Believe what?" I asked.

"I told him that Slate had been here, that in fact he'd been here several days."

"Why?" I shouted.

"Just listen," Drew said.

"I told him he'd come by to see if he could spend a few nights with us while his father was out of town."

"But he wasn't out of town."

"You're not getting it," Drew said. "PaPa had to make up a story that sounded like it was coming from Slate. He had to make it sound like Slate was even covering for him. Go on, sir, tell him what else you said."

"I said Slate told us he'd slipped off a street curb and fell on his face into a metal sewer grate—"

"But if he had an accident," I said, "why wouldn't he have gone to Mr. Merriweather to find out where his father was? Wouldn't he have gone there before coming here?"

PaPa smiled. "Smart boy. I just figured Rosen's intelligent enough to know he would avoid Merriweather because Avel would've called him, which means he'd probably be upset."

I threw open my hands. "So?"

"So he has to know how scared his son is of him. It's only logical that Slate would've gone anywhere else instead of chancing another beating. Besides, he knows that he considers your brother his best friend, which is another reason he'd come here instead."

I jerked my head toward Drew. "Is that true? Is he your best friend?"

He stood wide-eyed. "This is the first time I've heard that." He turned to PaPa. "Is that just part of the made-up story?"

"Nope. Seems it's what he's told his father."

"Well, I'll be," Drew said.

"Is he your best friend?" I repeated.

"I don't know about best friends. I've just been trying to be nice to him." He paused. "What if he was? Would you be okay with that?"

I could suddenly hear his speech on the importance of grace. My lips curved upward. "Of course, I would."

Drew smiled, then turned back to PaPa. "Do you think he's going to be okay at Uncle Dean's house?"

"I think so. At least until…" Instead of completing his thought, he opened the front door and stuck his head out for a moment before pulling back in. "Looks like it's going to be a good night for The Show of Shows. Are you boys ready for it?"

Drew put his hand on my shoulder. "It's going to be the best one ever."

At six that evening our neighborhood crew began to show up at the house for our traditional pre-show cookies and coffee, a special activity Gonny concocted years ago to add excitement to the evening. As simple as it was, we all looked forward to it mainly because it was the only time of year our parents allowed us to drink the beverage, rationalizing the caffeine would be out of our system by show's end.

The first to arrive was Mary Lib, followed by Cackles who brought her father's twenty-ounce beer stein.

"Fill 'er up, Miss Gonny," she said, thrusting the ceramic mug in front of her.

"Deary, if I fill that thing up, there won't be enough for anyone else."

Cackles frowned as Gonny stopped pouring halfway up.

A Styrofoam cup appeared from around Gonny's back.

"Excuse me, waitress, how about some for a workin' man." PaPa smiled broadly. "It's going to be a long one so don't go shorting your old man like little missy there."

Gonny laughed as she filled his cup.

"You're not going to the show, Mr. Edwards?" Mary Lib said.

"I'm afraid not, young lady."

"PaPa's got a long haul," I said, running up behind them.

"Where ya going this time?" Cackles said.

His eyes grew big as he bent down in front of her. In his best theatrical voice he said, "To a land far, far away."

Unimpressed, Cackles replied with a simple, "Okay, have a nice trip," and walked off.

PaPa chuckled. "Where's your brother?" he asked.

I pointed to the pecan orchard where he was standing over Reubin and Peeps who were locked in a heated battle of marbles.

"Would you fetch him for me? Tell him I'm leaving to get the truck in five minutes."

A minute later I was in Drew's spot, watching Reubin school Peeps with his special tiger eyes.

"Those marbles ain't fair," Peeps whined.

"Are too," Reubin retorted.

"Are not," Peeps snapped.

"Are too," Reubin came again.

Bored with several more rounds of *are too, are not,* I turned from their bickering to find Drew embraced in a long hug with our grandfather in front of his car. Just as

Gonny had her special coffee-infused tradition, he and PaPa had their own personal one. Before he left on any trip, he saw to it that Drew was the last person to give him a hug, each lasting as long as the first one that began it all. Over the years the tears had ceased to flow, but the need for the hug remained.

"Thirty minutes, everybody," Mom said, coming out the back door carrying a large silver tray. "Get your cookies while they're hot."

Reubin's and Peeps' heads popped up like a couple groundhogs. "Cookies!" they screamed then dashed out of the orchard, abandoning their marbles. Fifteen minutes later, after gorging ourselves on lemon drops, gingersnaps, and chocolate chip cookies, and with a tank of coffee running through our veins, we were fully amped and ready to get to the big event.

"What time is it, Mrs. Edwards?" Reubin asked.

Mom checked her watch. "Oh my! We better be going." She cupped her hands around her mouth and shouted, "We've got fifteen minutes before the show begins. Time to go!"

Cackles ran to the switch bush, pulled off a big one and began running around swatting people's rears and yelling, "Get along, little doggy!" Oddly enough it seemed to work as our group came in a line any military unit would be proud of. A minute later everyone was marching down the side-walk—that is, if skipping and dancing could be considered a form of marching.

Drew lagged behind. "But he's not here," he called out, staring back at the coffin factory.

"He'll be there. Now come on, we gotta go."

"No, I'm gonna wait."

"But—"

"Just go on. I gotta make sure he's coming."

The cool autumn air didn't prevent me from beginning to sweat. I'd expected to have my brother beside me tonight.

Chapter 35

Five minutes later we were cramming our way into line with several hundred other clamoring showgoers.

"Ten minutes to showtime!" The announcer's voice boomed from inside the stadium.

I ran up and down the line, handing out tickets to everyone in our group. "Don't lose 'em. There's a raffle at the end of the show."

"How'd you get such good seats, Cody boy?" Cackles said, tapping my shoulder with the switch she still carried. "These are front row right behind home plate."

"Connections," I said, grinning nervously.

Whether it was the coffee, cookies, or what lay inside, my heart was now thumping faster than the drumbeats coming from the Bulldogs marching band. Combined with the hoots and hollers and the pushing and shoving to squeeze through a one-person gate, the simple act of entering the stadium was maddening.

"Five minutes to showtime!" The announcer's voice came again.

I scanned the crowd for a glimpse of my brother.

"Do you see him?" Mary Lib shouted over the rising noise.

I shook my head just as Mom pulled me through the gate. "Don't worry, he'll be here," she said, taking my ticket and handing it to the girl at the counter. "Right now, we need to get to our seats before somebody takes them."

"They're pre-assigned, Mom. Nobody's going to take them."

Cackles came pushing back through the crowd. "Tell that to the family who just popped a squat in the middle of our row."

A minute later I was staring up at a barrel-chested man, explaining the rules of assigned seating. "See here, sir, the number on my ticket is for the seat you're in now." I looked at his, then searched the stadium. "I think you and your family are up there." I directed him to the farthest row back.

"We won't see a darn thing from way back yonder."

I shrugged while smiling as pleasantly as I could without getting clobbered.

"Three minutes to showtime!" came the announcer.

"Well, I count you got six with ya," he said. "Since there's ten seats in this here row, we'll just be taking the four on the end."

"I'm sorry, sir, but those are ours too."

His glare did nothing to help calm my fraying nerves.

"You got six. You use six," he snarled.

"No! Those seats are—"

"Pardon me," a man in a blue blazer said, sidestepping down the aisle to us. "Is there a problem with the seating?"

"No sir," Mom said, coming up alongside me. "We're just getting situated is all, but if you could help this nice gentleman with his tickets, we sure would appreciate it."

A minute later the man was grumbling obscenities and dragging his wife up the stairs while his two kids stumbled after him, occasionally turning back to ogle the four vacant seats.

"Mom, I'm gonna sit over there to hold these other four," I said, scooting to the empty seats at the end of our row.

"Probably a good idea. But isn't that too many seats?"

"No ma'am, they're all ours."

The stadium speakers crackled as a tall, lanky man in an Abraham Lincoln top hat walked to home plate. Dressed in a long black duster, his face was painted a grayish white, his eyes set in large black ovals. A streak of crimson ran from under his hat down the side of his face. Holding a mic in his hand, he arched his back, surveyed the crowd, then jerked it to his mouth. "Welcome and good evening, ladies and gentlemen, to this year's Show of Shows!" The crowd erupted in applause. "Prepare to be amazed at the brilliance, the skill and daring of this year's troupe of haunted cowboys brought to you by the Atlantic Coast Cowboy Entertainment Company! My name is Edgar Pulman and I'll be your host this evening." Before he could finish, the field was suddenly swarming with dozens of cowboys and cowgirls decked out in tattered Western outfits, complete with ghoulish makeup befitting the event's haunted theme.

Down the aisle, Cackles sat sticking her tongue out at me. "Told you it was gonna be them," she squawked.

I dismissed her gesture with a roll of my eyes, then began searching the stadium. "Please, please be here," I mumbled to myself.

Just then Drew appeared from out of the crowd on the other side of the stadium. Behind him was Mr. Merriweather. I jumped up and began waving wildly, which was pretty much the same thing everybody else was doing. The only difference was their attention was focused on the dozen brown and white horses circling the infield carrying zombie-faced cowboy acrobats standing in their saddles, sitting sideways, or doing flips.

When they finally reached me, Mr. Merriweather gave me a hug then plopped down into a seat, his chest heaving.

"Are you okay, sir?"

"I'm fine," he said, patting my forearm. "Please don't tell me we missed the cowboy clowns!"

"No sir. No cowboy clowns have been out yet."

Drew waved to the others down the aisle then sat beside me. "Anybody else here?" He craned his neck around behind him.

"No sign so far."

I watched him close his eyes and bow his head, waiting patiently as he mouthed a silent prayer. A minute passed, then two. When he reopened them, I was staring past him, my finger stretched out toward the Bulldogs' dugout. In his usual seat, as if all was right with the world, sat Mr. Rosen and his friend in the brown paper bag.

Drew let out a long sigh. "Thank goodness. He showed up. Let's just pray he doesn't get thrown out."

"Put your hands together for those magnificent stunt-riding zombies," the host blared. "Next up, be prepared to witness the dead cowgirl as she floats through the air while spinning death-defying circles on her way to the afterlife." A hush came over the stadium. A drumroll followed, drawing the crowd into cheers as a girl—dressed more like a witch in a black robe—zipped down a line across the diamond and out to a light pole in center field. With only two death-defying spins, the crowd's reaction was less than enthusiastic. The roar produced by the host's setup faded into a dull murmur. Just then a metallic thud followed by a series of synchronized clanks broke the lull. Instantly the baseball field was washed in an orange hue as the stadium lights sent the crowd cheering again.

Drew eyed Rosen, then checked his watch. "It's already seven twenty. Do you think the finale's still going off at eight?"

"There's supposed to be four more ten-minute-long performances so…" I paused doing the math.

"That'd be eight o'clock on the button," Drew said, fidgeting in his seat.

"Yeah, I think we're gonna be okay." I rubbed my sweaty palms up and down my pants.

Down on the field several cowboys were towing a large vertical wooden wheel toward the pitcher's mound, a cowgirl following behind them. The crowd's roar slowly evolved into a whispery wave of anticipation as the cowboys strapped her to it, her arms and legs stretched out like a starfish.

"Spin'er good, boys!" the host howled.

Faster and faster the wheel turned as one of the cowboys threw perfectly placed bowie knives between her outstretched limbs, all to the crowd's delight.

Drew checked his watch, then turned to the entrance from where he'd come. At the same time, I turned toward the one I'd used.

"What's wrong with you boys?" Mr. Merriweather said. "You're going to strain your necks, stretching them all over the place like that. Aren't you interested in the show?"

"No sir, I-I mean, yes sir," I stammered. "We're just checkin' out who's here."

Two more performances followed—another knife-throwing act that almost left one cowboy without an ear, and a sharpshooting contest between the host and a cowgirl. Drew and I failed to notice either.

Just as Mr. Merriweather was about to get on us again for our lack of interest, Drew shouted, "There they are!"

A skinny clown with a huge red nose and oversized cowboy hat went bolting across the infield, fake money fluttering out of his pockets. Behind him, a fat cowboy with an even bigger red nose and hat with a star on it chased him around, firing a revolver in the air howling, "Stop 'im! He robbed the bank!" From base to base they stumbled and bumbled as other clowns rushed to aid the hefty sheriff, only to be thwarted by some comic mishap.

I tugged at Drew's arm. "What do we do? The finale's in five minutes."

The look of defeat was written on his face.

Chapter 36

A hand suddenly appeared on Drew's shoulder.

"Sorry we're late," Uncle Dean said. "We had car trouble."

Through the crowd's roar I could hear Drew's sigh of relief. Behind my uncle, Slate stood smiling under the brim of his own cowboy hat.

"Nice touch," Drew said.

Mr. Merriweather introduced himself to our uncle then with both hands grabbed Slate's and squeezed it tight. "My dear boy. It's so nice to see you. We've missed you at the factory."

"You guys got here just in time," Drew said. "The finale's starting any minute.

"Uncle, would you mind if I sit next to Slate?" I said.

"Not at all."

"Like my camouflage?" Slate said with a welcoming touch to his hat's brim.

"Love it." I smiled. "How ya doin'?"

"I'm good." His eyes glistened. "Thank you for this, Cody. I don't know what I'd do without—"

"Are—you—ready?" The host's voice echoed through the stadium.

All eyes turned to the field where he was standing at home plate, his mic in one hand, his stovepipe hat in the other. A horse-drawn covered wagon barreled up behind him.

"Prepare to be dazzled, amazed, and bewildered." The Bulldogs marching band rolled out a drumbeat that rose with every word. "Introducing, the one—the only—" The beat grew louder then stopped cold. "The magnificent, marvelous Mr. Mars—magician extraordinaire!"

Mr. Merriweather patted my knee, then pointed to the wagon where the man I knew as Cederic, the man with the huge, overhanging moustache, appeared from the back of the wagon. Just as when we first met, he was dressed all in black, including the same floppy black hat. *Of course,* I thought, *what could be more appropriate than a cowboy undertaker magician at a haunted-cowboy-themed festival?*

The host handed the mic to him. "They're all yours, Mr. Mars."

"Thank you, kind sir!" he bellowed. Suddenly he was spinning in place. On his third turn he cast his hand down as if striking the earth with an imaginary hammer. A firecracker exploded with a huge puff of smoke that engulfed him. The crowd cheered then gasped as one, finding him not there when the smoke cleared. Seconds later he sauntered out from behind the wagon, sporting a wicked grin. "Miss me?" he snickered into the mic. A wave of applause went out over the stadium. "Ready for some magic?" he teased.

The crowd went wild.

"Then let's get started! For my first endeavor we'll—" He stopped mid-sentence, looked up under his slouching brim then began patting the top of his hat. "Is that you up there, Milo?" He placed his mic into its stand then pulled off his hat and looked inside it. "Why, there you are." He reached in and pulled out a fluffy, white rabbit.

Another round of screaming approval went up.

After handing Milo to a pretty young cowgirl, he continued to wow the audience with a rapid-fire series of exhibitions including levitations, bending metal bars, and moving objects with only the power of his mind. He even grew a full-sized shrub from a seed and single drop of water. For his final trick he sawed his cowgirl assistant in half, only to have her pop out of a box in one piece. For a full two minutes the mysterious Mr. Mars relished his standing ovation. After more than a dozen head-bobbing bows, he grabbed his hat and in an exaggerated swooping motion, swung it behind him while bending over for his final farewell. As the crowd cheered on, he slowly backed up to the wagon and disappeared to the other side.

Drew and I clapped and cheered along, all while keeping an eye on Mr. Rosen who was now clinging to the dugout's chain-link fence. At his feet lay the empty bottle, hanging halfway out of its brown bag.

With no letup, the crowd's cheer-filled appreciation slowly changed to chants of, "We want more!"

Drew grinned at me as I'd never seen him do before, like it was Christmas and he'd just caught a glimpse of Santa's boots scooching down the chimney. Instead of Mr. Claus, he was watching Mr. Mars striding back to home plate.

"You want more?" the magician said, stretching his arms wide. The response was a deafening uproar. Every man, woman, and child bounced in their seats and shouted back that they did.

"Then I'll give you more!" He looked to the back of the wagon where two beefy cowboys stood with their hands crossed. He nodded to them, a signal that sent one of them leaping into the wagon. A moment later they were sliding a long black box out onto the ground. On each side were two gold handles. Between them, etched in matching gold leafing, were the words, *Peace Awaits*.

Mr. Merriweather beamed as he poked my arm. "Now that's a mighty fine coffin if I do say so myself."

With a wave of Mars's hand, the men lifted the coffin and placed it on a shelf on the side of the of the wagon, giving the appearance it was floating in air. "Observe," he said, running a hula hoop over and around the coffin at every possible angle. He then opened the coffin's lid. "I submit to you the only way in—the only way out."

A hush fell over the stadium as the young cowgirl walked up and placed a small step stool next to it.

"If you would, my dear," he said.

She placed one foot on the bottom step. "Wait!" he said, holding up his hand. "I have a better idea."

A murmur rippled through the crowd.

"Ladies and gentlemen, I understand your tickets to this evening's event will be used for a raffle and carry a series of numbers on them. If you'll permit me, I'd like to use those tickets for any skeptics in the house who may believe my lovely assistant is privy to a secret exit in my coffin." He turned to a table that had been rolled out next to him during his speech. On it was a fishbowl full of the matching stub ends to all the tickets. "With that in mind, I will now draw from this jar to randomly pick one brave soul to enter my coffin for the purpose of sending them to the afterlife—and then bringing them back safe and sound."

The crowd cheered with a smattering of hopeful volunteers yelling to be picked.

"Then let us proceed." He stretched out his hand, letting it hover above the bowl long enough for everyone in the stadium to retrieve their tickets. As Mars plunged his hand inside, I inched mine next to Slate's, releasing my tiny red-and-black piece of paper into his palm.

A drumroll rose and fell with each swirl of the magician's hand in the jar, accented by a trumpet's blast when he jerked it out.

"And the lucky victim, I-I mean volunteer is…" He paused, chuckling along with the crowd, then started again. "Our lucky volunteer's ticket is number—8673."

The audience went silent, the only sounds coming from disappointed spectators grumbling about not being picked.

I turned to Slate. "Well?"

He sat holding the red-and-black ticket with both hands, took a deep breath then flashed me a smile. "Okay, here we go." He pulled his hat down, then with the ticket clutched tight, he stood raising it above his head.

"There you are!" Mars shouted. "And how about that, folks? We've got another cowboy to help us out. Come on out here, buckaroo!"

The pretty cowgirl assistant walked to a small gate behind home plate and opened it, ushering him to it.

Slate shuffled out into the aisle, then made his way to her while keeping his eyes fixed to the ground.

"Don't be shy, young man. Come on in."

As he walked out onto the field, Slate glanced back at me with a look I couldn't pin to either fear or excitement. All I knew was that his fate was now in the hands of Mars—magician extraordinaire.

Chapter 37

When he was close enough, Mars wrapped his arm around Slate's shoulder. "Let's give it up for this brave lad, shall we?"

The crowd applauded wildly.

Mars bent down to look under the brim of Slate's hat. "Who exactly do we have under there?" He spun back to the crowd, seizing the comedic opportunity. "I'm afraid our hero's hat won't be able to make the journey. The dearly departed usually don't leave this world wearing their Stetsons."

Laughter filled the stadium.

He turned to the cowgirl. "Gloria, would you mind holding on to Mr.—" He smacked his forehead. "I'm sorry, we never got this young man's name. Would you mind telling us—"

"Slate," he said, pulling off the hat. He leaned into the mic. "My name's Slate Rosen."

The crowd exploded. The entire stadium was suddenly on its feet shouting and cheering. Girls squealed and guys chanted his name.

Mars rocked back on his heels, glanced up at me, then

back to Slate. His mouth hung open as the thundering jubilation continued.

Behind the dugout Mr. Rosen sat staring blankly at his son and a magician who was as baffled as he was.

"Drew, look at his expression," I snickered.

"Whose? Cedric's or Rosen's?"

Mars glared at me out of the corner of his eye. Time seemed to crawl as I watched him steaming over the curveball I'd thrown him.

Rosen, on the other hand, was not as calm. He paced back and forth along the fence line like a caged animal. "That's my son! He's got my boy out there!"

"Shut up, Rosen!" someone yelled. "Let the man do his trick."

Mars raised his hand toward the audience, then gradually lowered it, bringing their excitement to a simmer. Holding the mic behind him, he pressed into Slate and appeared to whisper something. Then he whipped the mic back to his lips, and with the drama of a circus ringmaster thundered, "Afterlife—prepare to welcome the brave and daring Slate Rooo—ssssen!" He held his last name, extending the two syllables, prodding the crowd into a frenzy. "And now, if you would, good sir, allow me to introduce you to your final—I mean temporary—resting place."

Slate followed him toward the wagon as the stadium grew quiet. The cowgirl walked ahead of them, holding out her arms, introducing him to the coffin that lay suspended on the side of the wagon. Just before taking his final steps up into it, Slate turned toward his father and smiled.

Mr. Rosen made a crazed attempt to tear through the fence while ranting, "Don't you dare get in that thing! You hear me? Don't you do it!"

The roar of the crowd drowned out his tirade as Mars slowly closed the lid.

"And now, if you would please assist me in counting our dear friend into the hereafter."

As he spoke, the two cowboys who had transferred the black box out of the wagon pulled off its canvas cover and stretched it over the coffin, hiding it from view.

"Everyone ready?" Mars banged his fist on the side of the coffin then bent over it, shooting a playful grin back at his audience. "Put a good word in for me with the Almighty." He then stood back and raised his hand. "Here we go. One—two…" On three he swung his hand down like before, this time producing an even louder blast with an even larger smoke cloud, this one engulfing the entire wagon.

The crowd howled. A minute passed before the smoke cleared. The wagon, with its cover draped over the side, remained. The only thing different was Mars now stood clutching a corner of the canvas in his hand. "Farewell, dear boy!" he shouted and yanked off the cover, revealing a vacant spot where the coffin had been. The crowd applauded as Mars took a bow.

A young boy in front of us jumped to his feet, pointing. "It's in the wagon! They put it back inside."

Mars cupped his hand to his ear. "What's that you say?" He patted the side of the wagon. "You think it's on the other side?" He peered over the edge. "Maybe you're right." He turned to one of his cowboy assistants. "Would you mind taking her for a spin?"

Immediately the assistant climbed onto the bench seat. With a flick of the reins, off he went, circling the infield and displaying the wagon. Everyone could see that it was nothing more than an empty wooden rectangle with three-foot-high sides set on top of wheels.

"As you can plainly see, our dearly departed has done just that—departed. But! Not to worry, for as promised, I will bring him back. Gentlemen, once again if you would."

The cowboys grabbed the covering and replaced it over the top of the wagon.

Mars raised his hand over his head again. "Ladies and gentlemen, on three once more. One—two…" On three he swung his hand down again, but this time there was no blast or cloud of smoke, only a dull murmur from the crowd. Mars scratched his head, pretending to inspect the empty shelf where the coffin should have been. "One moment please," he said, motioning to the back of the wagon where his assistants were pulling the coffin back out and onto the shelf.

Mars gave his forehead an exaggerated wipe of his sleeve. "Phewww, I thought for a minute we forgot something." The crowd returned a mixed round of applause and laughter. As it slowly died off, he swung his arm toward the coffin. "Gloria, would you welcome our brave young friend back to the living?"

She nodded, leaned against the coffin, and with all her might shoved the lid open. "Welcome back, Mr. Rosen," she said, spinning back toward the crowd. Her hands shot above her head as if signaling a touchdown, but there was no burst of applause, only thousands of eyes on her. She turned back to the coffin and gasped in an unconvincing state of shock.

"What's wrong, my dear?" Mars said.

"He-he's not there."

On cue, the two beefy cowboys ran up and tilted the empty vessel toward the audience, showcasing the obviously planned hiccup. Mars gave the crowd a puzzled look. "Outta the way, boys," he said, striding up to the coffin. With the palm of his hand, he slapped between the words *Peace Awaits*, causing the lid to slam shut. He took a step back, stretched his arms wide and howled, "From the great beyond—he returns!"

The crowd went silent. All eyes fixed on the coffin again, waiting for Slate to bolt out of it in triumph.

Mars slapped the coffin again. "Welcome back!"

"Did ya lose something, Mr. Magic Man?" a voice pierced the silence.

Laughter rippled through the stadium.

Mars chuckled with them. "Looks like the other side isn't ready to give up our boy just yet." He cleared his throat, held the mic tight and shouted. "Time to come home—I command you." Instead of another slap he pounded the lid with his fist. "Arise *now*, Slate Rosen!"

The coffin sat with the lid shut, mocking the magician as a nervous wave of laughter rolled across the field.

"I don't understand," Mr. Merriweather said. "It should be working."

I held my breath and prayed, unable to take my eyes off the coffin's lid.

"Get him out," yelled Slate's father. "Get him out now!"

Mars looked to his assistants, but they only shrugged. His cowgirl bit her lip as she backpedaled off the field.

From the far end of the stadium, a faint call of, "We want Slate," filtered through the air. Before long the entire crowd was stomping their feet and chanting, "We want Slate, we want Slate…"

Mars's head twitched, then suddenly his hands went up. "Are you ready to bring Slate home?"

"We've been ready, you idiot," the man behind me replied.

"Then on the count of three, if you please."

"Oh, for heaven sakes, not again," grumbled another.

"Ready! One—two…" On three he threw his hand down, again producing another cloud of smoke and the wagon faded away. As the smoke cleared, the silhouette of someone crouching underneath it slowly emerged.

"Look, everybody, it's Slate!" someone shouted.

A man several rows away pointed to the figure. "No, it's not!"

Before he could conceal his motive for being under the wagon, a sudden gust of wind blew the remaining smoke away, revealing Mars examining a trap door that had sabotaged his illusion.

"Fake!"

"Fraud!"

"Two-bit magician!"

The heckling came fast and furious and without sympathy. The air echoed with boos, peppered with more heckling.

Unable to recover from a magician's worst nightmare, and without any explanation to give an increasingly hostile crowd, Mars chose to vanish along with Slate. He crawled out from under the wagon, took a humiliating bow and thanked everyone for coming. Then he swung both hands down at the same time. The blast that followed threw everyone back in their seats. When the cloud that came with it finally drifted away, only the wagon and coffin were left. Mars was gone.

Chapter 38

The paper's headline the following day read, "Magician's Trick Falls Short, Local Baseball Hero Missing." Drew and I took turns snatching the *Burlington Gazette* from one another, reading the article's details to our neighborhood crew on our front porch.

I stared into the fine print. "Says here, the police questioned Mars about kidnapping but later dismissed him of any wrongdoing."

"Kidnapping?" Cackles said. "How about practicing witchcraft without a license?"

Peeps shook his head. "It's too bad. He was doing pretty good up until he lost his mojo."

"It just doesn't make sense," Mary Lib said.

"What part?" I asked.

"All of it. The guy's just a magician who does tricks. This one backfired is all. He didn't actually do any real magic. Slate's here somewhere. He's gotta be. And don't say he's dead, Cackles. I swear if you say that, I'll clobber you."

"I wasn't gonna say that! Honest. He'll show up."

Just then the front door opened. Gonny stuck her head

out. "Drew, Mr. Merriweather just called. He needs you and Cody over at the factory."

Within minutes we were standing in front of his desk. In the corner was Mars's black coffin.

"How'd that get here?" I asked.

"Mars brought it back."

"Why?" Drew asked. "He paid good money for you to customize its trap door."

"He thinks it's cursed. He didn't even want his money back. He just wanted to wash his hands of it and get out of town after being so embarrassed." He turned to me. "And you," he said, narrowing his eyes, "he had some rather choice words about you."

I looked away, unable to face what I knew was coming.

"Did you give Slate your ticket?"

I nodded.

"Why on earth did you do that when your plan with Mars was that your number would be called? He spent all that time rehearsing the trick with you. He said you had it down cold."

"Yes sir, I did."

"So why did you give your ticket to Slate when he had no idea how to work the trap door, where the escape route was, and how to get back inside?"

"Because he did know."

"How?"

"I told him all the details the day before the show. He picked it up super-fast. He's incredibly smart, you know. Everybody thought he was a dumb jock, but he's actually—"

"Stop!" Mr. Merriweather threw up his hand. "Just tell me why you made the switch."

Drew stepped forward. "Because his father was going to kill him. If it wasn't now, he would eventually. You know some of his story, sir, but not everything. Not even a fraction. Mr. Rosen's an evil man. Cody just allowed him to use the coffin as a way to go into hiding."

"So where is he now?"

Drew looked to the ceiling, thinking. "Right about now, I'd say probably somewhere in Tennessee."

"Tennessee! How'd he get to Tennessee?"

"An eighteen-wheeler carrying a load of textiles."

"He's a stowaway on a tractor trailer?"

"No sir, a passenger."

"I'd hardly call bouncing around in the back of one of those trailers being a passenger."

"He's not in the trailer. He's in the cab sitting next to PaPa on the way to Grand Junction, Colorado, where he's going to live on Uncle Jake's ranch."

"So your grandfather's in on this too?"

"Yes sir. It was his idea to use his long-haul trip to get Slate out of town. Since the trick's exit route included a secret walkway to the stadium's service exit, all PaPa had to do was park his rig next to it and wait for him to walk out to him."

"But why did you have to concoct such an elaborate scheme and make it so public? Couldn't he have just run away? If he's as smart as Cody said, couldn't he have just done that?"

"His father has guys that would've tracked him down. It had to be done in front of him and in a way that would spook him enough to keep him from going any further with it. He knows the power of the coffins and what they can do. We figured he could easily convince himself that it could make him vanish. You heard him yelling for Slate not to get in it."

"What did you mean when you said, 'he knows what they can do'?"

Drew swallowed. "He knows about coffin-jumping."

He squeezed his eyes shut, shaking his head. "Oh no, please tell me that's not true."

"I'm afraid so."

"But how?"

"It's my fault, sir," I said. "He found out when—"

His hand went up. "You don't have to explain. What matters is he knows and can exploit them for the wrong reasons."

"Which he's already done," Drew added.

Mr. Merriweather's head fell. For a long minute he sat with his elbows on his desk, his hands covering his face.

Just as I was about to speak, Drew held me back with a quick head shake, allowing Mr. Merriweather time to take everything in. By degrees, his hands parted, revealing a deep sadness on his face. "If Rosen knows what the coffins can do, he knows the most important thing isn't them—it's Happy."

"Of course, without him doing his taps or turns, nothing happens."

"And since Rosen knows this, it's just a matter of time before he comes for him. I'm surprised he hasn't already."

"What do we do?"

"We have to get him out of here too."

"That's no problem," I said, bouncing on my toes. "I can take him. I'll hide him in the root cellar. Nobody'll ever know he's there."

"I'm sorry, Cody. As much as I hate it, we're going to

have to get him someplace far away—someplace far enough that Rosen won't think to go looking for him."

"But sir! I promise I'll take care of him. I'll keep him outta sight. I promise."

"He's right," Drew said. "Happy'd never be safe here."

"So what do we do?" I asked.

Mr. Merriweather scratched his chin. "Do you think he would enjoy life on a ranch?"

A faint smile fell across my brother's lips. "If it was out west and where he already knew someone. Yeah, I believe he'd enjoy that very much."

Mr. Merriweather walked to the tiny open door with the words *Happy's Place* written on it. He stopped and angled his ear outside, listening to the birds chirping as lonely autumn leaves of red, gold, and orange rustled past. But it was the childlike chattering of his longtime companion that broke him down into tearful sobs.

Drew put his arm around him. "He's going to be okay, sir. They both will."

He wiped his eyes with his palms. "You boys must think me an old fool."

"Of course not," Drew said.

"I don't think you're a fool. You're one of the smartest, nicest people I've ever known."

He patted my head.

"Do you have a plan, sir?" Drew asked.

"I think so, but we need to act on it immediately."

"Just tell me what you need us to do."

"Do you think you could contact your grandfather and see if he'll hold up his trip and let me meet him wherever he is now?"

"Sure, he usually calls Gonny around dinnertime whenever he's on the road. I'll ask to talk to him then."

"Good. If he's okay with it, I'll pack up Happy in the van this evening and drive to meet him."

"What happens when Rosen comes looking for him and doesn't find him?" I asked.

"Give me a minute," he said, rubbing his temples.

"What if we make it look like someone broke in and stole him?" Drew said.

"I think I have something better. We can say I sold him to Mars for his magic show. He made me an insane offer I couldn't pass up. How about that?"

"I think he'll send his goons to track Mars down," Drew said, "and when they find him without Happy, he'll take his vengeance out on you."

"No, he won't."

"Why?"

"Because they'll never find Mars."

"How's that, sir?"

"Because he's already out of the country. He was leaving this morning. He said his name and reputation are trashed here in the U.S. after what happened at the festival, so he's starting over in some other country."

"What country?"

"He wouldn't say."

"The ultimate vanishing act," Drew muttered.

Just after dinner Drew and I were back at the coffin factory, this time on the loading dock helping Mr. Merriweather put Happy's cage into the van. Sitting off to the side was Mars's coffin.

Mr. Merriweather turned to Drew. "How long did your grandfather say it took him to get where he's at?"

"About eleven hours." Drew handed Mr. Merriweather a folded piece of paper. "The town's called Camden. All the directions are on this."

"Eleven hours!" I said. "You'll be gone two days. What do we do if Rosen comes looking for you? Where do we tell him you've gone?"

"First of all, you both need to stay away from here. But if he does come up on you, tell him my cousin is ill and I went to see her and I'll be gone for a few days. I left him a note at the front desk stating the same thing. Are you boys going to be alright while I'm away?"

Drew put his hand on my shoulder. "Yes sir, we'll be fine."

"One last thing. I was going to take Mars's coffin and dump it someplace, but it won't fit in the van with Happy's cage in there. Can you destroy it for me? Just have Old Rip cut it down, then put all the pieces in the shredder."

"You don't want to sell it?"

"No." He took a deep breath as his gaze fell back onto the black box. "Mars said it was cursed. And to be honest… whether it's cursed or not, I want it gone. I want to make sure no one claims ownership of it. Can you make sure it's trashed?"

Drew turned to the coffin, studying it as if waiting for some unholy spirit to arise out of it. "Of course. I'll do it tonight."

"Good," he said. "Now bid your farewells to Happy and I'll be on my way. The sooner I get on the road, the sooner I'll be back."

After hugs and tears a few minutes later, we watched as the van pulled out of the back lot and headed west. I reached into my pocket and pulled out a pecan. "Shoot, I still had one left."

Drew chortled. "You gave him a whole bushel and a mountain of Pez candy—I think he'll be okay."

I wiped a final tear away. "I'm going to miss him."

"Me too, little brother…me too."

Chapter 39

When the van's taillights finally vanished into the distance, Drew turned to the black coffin. "I'm with Mr. Merriweather—I want it shredded."

"What do you think he meant by not wanting anyone to claim ownership of it?"

"I don't know," he said, rolling a dolly beside it. "Just help me get this thing to the saw."

A minute later we were heaving the coffin up onto two large wooden sawhorses. Looming over it, like a modern-day guillotine, was Old Rip, the factory's largest, most powerful buzz saw. A mill worker could swing its menacing, three-foot circular blade down by a handle and tear through chunks of wood the size of full-grown oak trees. Mars's coffin would be nothing more than a slab of butter for the fearsome beast.

"Help me center it. I wanna be able to saw it in half as close as we can."

After scooching the coffin back and forth a couple times, Drew stepped back to make sure the blade was centered directly between the words *Peace* and *Awaits* etched on the side. "We'll make this cut, then cut those two pieces in half and then throw it in the chipper."

"This thing's always scared me," I said. "Anybody ever been killed by one?"

"I did hear tell of a guy down in Greenville who accidently cut his arm off."

"What happened?"

"While the blade was running, he reached out to move his piece of wood. At the same time the blade's safety latch popped and it swung down across his forearm. Sliced it clean through."

My chest tightened at the thought of the man's bloody arm tumbling to the floor.

Drew pointed behind me to a large red mushroom-shaped button on the wall. "When I'm ready, I want you to start the saw by hitting that with your palm."

Standing in front of the coffin, he reached up with his left hand and flipped up the blade's safety latch. With his right he grabbed a curved metal bar sticking out from just above the blade and slowly pulled it down until the teeth were waiting an inch away from the coffin's edge. "Ready?" he shouted.

I returned three quick nods.

"Stop! Don't touch that button!"

I jerked my head to the right, thinking the voice had come from that direction. Drew's wide-eyed gaze over my left shoulder provided the direction I should have looked. A slap of cold metal against my cheek confirmed the person making the demand was right behind me. I slowly turned to find the tip of a two-foot-long machete leveled at my nose. On the other end was Ozzy. "Back away from that box—both of ya!"

Drew took a step back. I took five.

Out of the darkness the figure of a man slowly emerged. My heart raced, the beats doubling as his face came into view.

"Mr. Merriweather! What're you doing back?"

Before he could answer, Happy leaped out from behind him, running up and jumping into my arms, almost knocking me off my feet. The scent of liquor followed him in his rush to me, and I saw Mr. Rosen emerge from the corner of the factory.

"Why, you boys look like you just saw ole Grandel's ghost," he said, zigzagging toward us, a half-empty whisky bottle sloshing by his side. "You got the same look the old man had when we caught him down the road trying to skip town with his magic chimp." His eyes fell to the coffin. "What's this? What're you doing with my boy's coffin?"

"It's not your son's," Mr. Merriweather said.

Rosen flung the back of his hand across the old man's cheek, knocking him to his knees. "It took him, so it's his!" His open hand curled into a fist.

"Please don't!" Drew yelled. "We, uh…I mean I was just going to get rid of it to free up space for other inventory."

"You—will—not!" He pulled Mr. Merriweather up by the collar. Nose to nose he snarled, "If you sold it to the magician, then why do you still have it?"

"Because I bought it back from him."

"Why?"

"He didn't want it anymore. His trick failed so it was no good to him. He just wanted rid of it."

"You mean he wanted to get rid of the evidence." Rosen's voice grew louder with every word. "That's what you mean. That's why you were going to shred it." He twisted Mr. Merriweather's collar in his fist. "Isn't it!"

"I-I don't know what you're talking about," he wheezed.

Drew shot me a look that told me we were right in thinking Rosen's mental state would lead him to believing the coffins had more power than just producing visions. In his broken mind, they were weapons, the kind that could make men vanish.

"You built this thing that took my son, now you're going to use it to bring him back."

"I-I'm sorry…I really don't know what you want."

With both hands he spun Mr. Merriweather around, then shoved him down at my brother's feet. As Drew started to help him up, Rosen grabbed his hair and yanked him away from the old man. Dragging him to the coffin, he whipped Drew's head down in the saw's path. With his other hand he grabbed the blade's handle, pulling it down until its teeth rested across the back of my brother's neck. "Are you ready to bring my boy back?"

Mr. Merriweather wheezed. "I just don't know what you want. Tell me what you want me to do!"

Rosen turned to Ozzy. "Start this thing!"

"No!" I yelled and lunged toward the red knob. The butt of Ozzy's machete found my gut, sending me to the floor. Stradling me, he centered the blade over my chest. "Just give me the word, sir, and I'll start carvin'."

"Don't—do—anything," I said, gasping for air. "Please stop!" I sucked more wind into my lungs. "I'll tell you what happened to your son."

The factory went silent. Rosen glared at me, still holding a white-knuckled grip on Drew's hair while Ozzy stood with his weapon in striking position.

Before I could spew the details of Slate's escape, Rosen's eyes went black, his lip inching upward like a snake.

"I know what we'll do," he hissed, "we'll offer a sacrifice." His glare bored into me. "Your brother for my son."

"No," I said, shaking my head. "Please—no sacrifices!"

Rosen directed Ozzy to the red button. "Do it!"

"Wait!" Mr. Merriweather shouted. "We can bring him back. I know how."

Sweat poured down Rosen's face as his madness pulled him farther and farther from reality. "A sacrifice is the only way," he growled.

"Not yet!" Mr. Merriweather said, pushing himself up. "We'll use the coffin just as you said. We'll use *it and Happy* to change things. We'll bring him back, Mr. Rosen. I promise, you'll have your son again."

Rosen stood, his chest rising and falling in gradually slower breaths.

"You know what the coffins can do with Happy's help, don't you?" Mr. Merriweather said.

"Of course."

"But you don't know everything. You don't know that he can send someone into the past and when that happens, they can change things."

Rosen didn't move. He didn't fly into a rage or even blink. A mouse scurried past one of the sawhorses, the pattering of its feet breaking the silence. "So someone could prevent my son from getting into this coffin," he said flatly without a trace of emotion. "Is that what you're saying?"

"Yes."

Rosen pulled his hand from the blade but continued to cling to Drew's hair with the other. "Tell me how."

"Can you let Drew go first?"

"No. Now out with it or else Ozzy fires up the saw." He grabbed the blade's handle again.

"Alright, alright. I-I'm sorry," Mr. Merriweather said. He rubbed his hands, took a deep breath, and began. "It's simple. Someone gets into the coffin. When the lid closes, Happy climbs on and at Cody's prompt, he does his magic. That's when the one inside is transported back in time, usually somewhere right before the event that caused the person's death. While in the past, the one inside has to alter things in a way that will prevent Slate from getting into Mars's coffin."

"He's lyin', Mr. Rosen," Ozzy blurted. "You said that someone could only watch things and shouldn't touch or do anything."

"Is that right? Are you lying to me, old man?"

"No. This is different. The other times were only about observing or getting information. You can do more because you're changing destiny."

Rosen stood dissecting him with a suspicious glare. "You've done this before?"

"Yes."

"And…"

"I saved someone's life."

Rosen reared up. "Alright, let's do it!" He jerked Drew's head away from the blade and pulled him around to the other side of the coffin as Ozzy kicked a crate up beside it. Rosen let loose of Drew then shoved him up to the make-shift step. "Get in!"

"No!" Mr. Merriweather blurted. "It can't be him."

"Of course it can." Rosen held a threatening finger in front of Drew's face. "Whatever you have to do, you keep him out of this box."

From some unknown place Mr. Merriweather summoned

enough energy to reach out and pull Drew away from Rosen. "It won't work with him!"

Rosen turned toward Ozzy who had slowly crept into the shadows.

"It can't be him either."

"Then who?"

"It has to be *you*."

"Me! Why me?"

"Because you're his father. Only someone who's related can alter the destiny of another family member."

Rosen stared into the coffin. After a long moment, he stepped onto the crate, then turned to Mr. Merriweather. "Get the monkey ready."

Mr. Merriweather dug into his pocket and pulled out a pecan. Happy leaned around me, his fingers stretching out for the treat.

"He'll do it, won't he?" Rosen's eyes begged me for a positive reply.

"Yes."

He slowly arched a leg over and into the coffin. Before lying down, he turned to Ozzy. "Make sure this goes off exactly as he said." Reaching up, he grabbed the lid, keeping his eye on Mr. Merriweather. "If this doesn't work—there's going to be hell to pay."

Chapter 40

As Rosen pulled the lid shut, Mr. Merriweather leaned into me and placed the pecan in my hand. "Make sure Happy taps," he whispered.

"Don't you mean spin?"

"No. He has to tap."

"But—"

"Tap," he said, wrapping both hands around mine and squeezing it tight. "He has to hit that lid with no spinning—understood?"

I glanced back at Ozzy.

"Get on with it," he said, directing me to the coffin with the point of his machete.

"Okay, okay." With the pecan in hand, I stretched it over the top of the coffin and slapped it down. On cue, Happy leaped onto it, grabbed his prize and gobbled it down in a frenzy. No tap or turns followed. He sat with his arms crossed, as if waiting for more. "Go on, boy," I said. "Give it a smack." His tiny black eyes jetted between me and Mr. Merriweather. "Please, boy, give the box a whack."

Mr. Merriweather grabbed my elbow. "Why's he not—"

Just then, Happy raised his hand high, let out one of

his childlike giggles and smacked the lid. Before I could reach out for him, he was already climbing back onto my shoulders.

From the other end of the factory floor, the giant clock ticked off the seconds as we stood waiting for the coffin to explode open.

"It's been at least two minutes," Drew finally said.

"Patience," Mr. Merriweather replied, keeping his eyes fixed on the lid.

Another minute passed. "How long's he going to be in there?" Ozzy huffed.

I tapped Mr. Merriweather's sleeve. "It's never taken this long."

He motioned Drew to the coffin. "Would you take a look?"

My brother wiped the building sweat from his forehead as he stepped onto the crate. He wrung his hands together, then wedged them under the lid and slowly lifted. Before he had it halfway up, I could tell by the curious tilt of his head something was different.

"Mr. Rosen?" He said, bending toward the coffin.

We waited for his reply.

Drew leaned down farther. "Sir, are you alright?"

The factory clock continued to tick.

"Mr. Rosen," my brother's voice grew louder, "can you hear me?"

Mr. Merriweather grabbed my arm, using me as a crutch to take him to the coffin.

"What's wrong?" Ozzy said from behind the large metal beam where he was hiding.

Ignoring his question, Mr. Merriweather and I moved forward. As if a mortician had prepared him while we weren't looking, Rosen lay with his arms folded over his heart. Had it not been for the movement of his chest and his wide-eyed gaze, he could have been declared dead. But there he was, staring past us into the dark rafters above. From the corner of one eye, a single tear rolled down the side of his face.

"Mr. Rosen, can you hear us?" Mr. Merriweather said.

The only reaction was another tear. Then slowly he rolled his head to us. His expression was without emotion, except for the tears. He blinked once, grabbed the edge of the coffin and pulled himself upright. Without saying a word, he climbed out, brushed past Drew on the crate and stepped to the floor. He stood there, his arms hanging straight by his sides.

He turned to us and in the gentlest voice said, "You were the only ones." The shadow of a smile came and went. He took two steps then stopped. "Thank you for being there. Please, thank your grandmother too." His head dipped slightly as he walked across the factory floor. It was neither hurried nor slow, each step measured in a robotic stride that led him out the side door into the night. Ozzy held back for a minute then sprinted after him while Drew and I stood frozen, unable to comprehend Rosen's exit.

"What just happened?" I asked.

Drew's eyes followed Mr. Merriweather as he walked to the door where he remained, staring into the darkness.

A moment later a truck's horn blared from outside, tires screeched, then we heard a dull thud. Ozzy screamed for help.

Drew and I ran for the door, but Mr. Merriweather stopped us by holding up his hand. His head made a broad swing back and forth. "Don't go out there."

"But that sounded like an accident!" I said.

In the distance, Ozzy's cries for help continued to ring out.

"Somebody's been hurt!" Drew took a step but stopped as Mr. Merriweather's arm crossed the doorway.

"It's too late. He's already gone."

"Who's gone?"

Mr. Merriweather started to reply but nothing came out. He pressed his palm over his forehead and grabbed Drew's arm, desperate to keep from falling.

Fifteen minutes later, Mr. Merriweather was back in his office sitting behind his desk and sipping on a glass of water I'd brought him while Drew spread a cold compress on his head.

"I'm sorry, boys," he said in a labored breath, "I guess everything that's happened just caught up with me."

"Are you gonna be okay, sir?" I asked.

He reached out a feeble hand and placed it on mine. "Yes, I'm going to be fine."

"You had us scared," Drew said.

He pulled the compress off and angled his head toward the door. He grimaced as the sirens out on the street echoed through the factory in an ear-piercing chaos of sound. "Will you close that, please?"

Drew pulled the door shut.

"Thank you." He leaned forward onto his desk, then turned back to the door as if waiting for it to open. The reason soon became clear. "We're going to have to come up with a story before the police get here."

"What's happening, sir?" Drew said. "First, Rosen's back at the factory with you and Happy, then he's trying to save Slate, then he up and walks out like a zombie."

"Then there's that sound like a car crash," I added. "And now all these sirens."

"And what do you mean by a story for the police?" Drew said. "Are we in trouble?"

"But we didn't do anything wrong!" I pleaded.

"You're right, Cody—you didn't. I'm the only one who did."

"What's that mean?" Drew asked.

"Nothing—well, something…" He took a deep breath. "The reason Rosen left the coffin the way he did was because I didn't let him see the past. That's why I told Cody to get Happy to tap instead of spin." He looked at me. "You knew what was happening, didn't you?"

"I just knew that by tapping he'd be sent forward to the funeral of whoever's coffin it was meant for. And I knew it couldn't be Slate's because he was with PaPa."

"That's right. He'd be sent to the funeral of whoever had claimed it."

"But, sir, nobody had bought it."

"Correct, no one had, but it did get claimed."

"By who?"

"By Mr. Rosen. It was claimed the instant he stepped into it."

"What? How can that be?" Drew asked.

"If a coffin is never going to be purchased by or for someone, then whoever enters it with the sole purpose of altering the future claims it. Or to be more accurate, the *coffin claims them.*"

Drew's eyes had found the ceiling, and I knew his thoughts were churning away. He finally burst out, "Oh my God! Rosen saw his own funeral." He spun to Mr. Merriweather. "That's why he was in such a state."

He nodded. "And unfortunately, destiny doesn't wait. Death comes almost immediately after a coffin claims its owner." His head dropped. "There was nothing that could be done. He simply walked outside into the street knowing his last day was near, but not knowing when. He probably didn't even see the truck that hit him."

"What if he survived?"

"I'm sure he didn't."

"How do you know?"

"Because I've witnessed it too many times when I was in Panama. Thiago would warn people about the risks involved with Happy and the coffins. Those who wanted to change the future suffered the consequences like Slate and I did. All told, there were eleven who didn't know the coffins they chose were never going to be sold. Each of them died within minutes of leaving them." He looked up at us. "Rosen was number twelve."

Heavy stomping through the factory whipped our heads to the office door. Louder and louder they came, then silence, followed by three loud knocks. "Anybody in there?" Without waiting for a reply, the door flung open. Two policemen stood on the other side. One held a flashlight, the other a notepad. "Burlington Police Department—which one of you is Merriweather?" said the one with the pad.

"I am," Mr. Merriweather said, pushing himself up from his desk.

Drew wrapped his arm around him, holding him steady.

"Sir, I'm assuming you know about the accident that occurred at the corner of Maple Avenue and Davis Street this evening, correct?"

"Yes sir," he said, rubbing his arm. His skin had turned ashen. "I—I know about it."

"Well, we're here to gather information on it. A boy named Ozzy said you could give us everything we needed."

I looked at Mr. Merriweather, praying he'd have an alibi for the officers. Instead, I watched in horror as he collapsed into Drew's arms, clutching his chest and groaning.

Chapter 41

The following week there were no flags flying half-mast for John Rosen, no TV shows documenting his life's accomplishments, and no horde of mourners lining the streets, weeping for him as there had been for John Kennedy. The only difference was the coffin factory's dreadful silence and the sign on the front door that read "For Sale." Drew couldn't bear looking in its direction for fear of bursting into tears. Every day was painful. Saturday was the worst. That day the same policemen came for us.

The knock on the door was a series of three light taps, nothing like the pounding they delivered the night they barged into the factory demanding answers surrounding Rosen's death. They were subdued, even respectful.

"Are you boys ready?" one of them asked.

I looked down on my shoes, thinking how Mom would've liked them shinier, but I didn't really care. "Yes sir," I replied. "Drew, are you ready?"

He nodded.

Outside, standing beside the police car was our misfit crew. They were all lined up with their heads lowered, fidgeting, not knowing how to behave in front of the men in blue. Sandwiched between Cackles and Peeps was Irvin-Dell. I smiled as I passed him, thinking about the sacrifice that had been made for him and how long it took me to learn the true meaning of grace.

Just as we slid into the backseat, Mary Lib rushed to Drew's window. From behind her back, she produced a white orchid. Her lips parted but nothing came. Drew simply took the flower and placed it in his lap. "Thank you," he said.

As we pulled away, I looked down at the flower and for a second thought about taking his hand and telling him everything was going to be alright. But he had always been the stronger one and the one to provide comfort. It was his role ever since our father's death and something I would not dare take from him. I pulled my hand back and turned my gaze out to the giant maple trees that lined our street all the way to the edge of town. My mind wandered. Like the leaves floating past us, my thoughts flittered from one thing to the next, unable to light gently on anything. Why had Slate's father wanted to save his son? Why were Drew and I the only ones to bear today's burden? Why did heart attacks have to happen to good people?

"I wish Gonny was here," I said.

Drew didn't answer. He was staring out the window, deep in his own thoughts.

Minutes later we pulled up behind a long black car and parked under the shade of a willow tree.

The policeman on the passenger side leaned over the seat. "We'll wait for you here if that's okay?"

"That's fine," Drew replied, then stepped out into the midday sun. I followed him.

Side by side we walked to the corner of the burial plot where Pastor Wilson waited for us next to a coffin. "Thank you for coming," he said, forcing a smile I knew he'd summoned hundreds of times. In front of the coffin were three rows of five folding chairs. All empty.

"Did you boys want to say any—"

"No," Drew replied before he could finish.

"Cody?"

I shook my head.

"Well then, I guess we can begin."

"Wait sir," Drew said. "I do have something."

The pastor motioned him forward. "By all means."

He walked up to the coffin, pulled out Mary Lib's white orchid and placed it on the lid right above the words *Peace Awaits* etched on the side. His hand slowly curled into a fist as he lifted it over the flower. There it hung, shaking, his knuckles white with tension. I held my breath, waiting for it to slam back down, waiting for him to scream out in anger. Instead, his fingers slowly relaxed, spreading out as he eased his palm onto the lid. His head dropped and I watched as he whispered, "We forgive you."

Pastor Wilson's eyes glistened as he opened his Bible. "I have a verse I'd like to read that I believe is befitting for…" His thought died off as his eyes cut past us out to the willow tree. "Well, praise the Lord…"

Drew and I turned. Pulling up behind the police car was Gonny's '58 Plymouth Fury. In the passenger seat sat Mr. Merriweather.

"Drew, look!" I spun to him, but he was already halfway to the car. I started after him then stopped, letting him be the first to embrace the man who had become like a father to him. My heart soared as I watched my brother throw his arms around him, weeping into the feeble man's hunched shoulders.

Unable to hold back, I sprinted to them. "We thought you were probably dead," I said, panting.

In a thin, fragile voice Mr. Merriweather said, "I told Old Man Death I had a funeral to attend," he attempted a chuckle that turned into a cough, "but it wasn't going to be mine."

"But you had a heart attack. The doctors kept telling us you weren't—"

"Oh pooh! What do doctors know anyway?" Gonny said as she wrestled Maudie's wheelchair out of the trunk.

A moment later Pastor Wilson was beside her, helping ease Mr. Merriweather into it. He checked his watch then scanned the road leading into the cemetery. "Do you think anyone else will be coming?"

"No sir, I think it will just be us," Mr. Merriweather replied.

"Are you sure? We could wait a bit longer if you'd like."

"I'm sure."

The funeral lasted an awkward ten minutes consisting of an opening prayer, followed by a halfhearted eulogy that dealt more with man's sin and God's forgiveness than anything about Rosen's life.

As we walked back to the willow tree, the policeman who had driven us met us in front of Gonny's car.

"Will you be driving home with your grandmother?"

"Yes sir," Drew said.

He held his hat tight against his chest, turned and walked a few steps, then slowly looked back. "I wanted to say we're sorry about the other night. We were only doing our jobs. We didn't know that boy was so crazy." He rolled his eyes. "I mean who could ever believe seeing the future from a coffin! I mean really!" He glanced over at Mr. Merriweather as Pastor Wilson and Gonny helped him into the car. "Please tell him we're sorry and that we never meant to cause his heart attack."

"There's no need," Drew said. "You had nothing to do with that."

The policeman feigned a smile. "Would you still tell him?"

"Yes sir. I will."

When we returned home, Mary Lib and the rest of the gang had already departed for the pecan orchard for what sounded like a game of tag. As we wheeled Mr. Merriweather onto the front porch, I could hear Peeps squawking about being tagged unfairly while Cackles heckled him between bouts of her high-pitched laughter.

"I'm going to make some lemonade," Gonny said. "Do you want me to bring it out back for you and the other kids?"

"No ma'am, I'm gonna stay here with Mr. Merriweather," Drew said, pulling up one of the rockers beside his wheelchair.

"Me too," I replied.

Gonny nodded. "I'll be back shortly then."

Mr. Merriweather let out a long sigh. "It's been quite a day, hasn't it?"

I blinked. "A day? Heck, what about a week, a month— shoot, the past two years!"

He chuckled. "I stand corrected."

Drew studied him. "It's a miracle."

"You mean how Rosen saw his own funeral?"

"No sir, that you survived a heart attack."

He shrugged. "What can I say? God still has plans for me."

"What'll you do now?" I asked. "The coffin factory's being sold. Will you and Happy be moving?"

"Please don't go, sir," Drew begged. "If you do, can I come with you? I-I'll be out of school soon. I could go with you or meet you later. I could—"

"Now, now," he said, laying a comforting hand on Drew's arm, "we're not going away just yet."

"But you can't make coffins anymore," I said. "There's no place to do it."

"What about that big ole building there?" Mr. Merriweather said rearing his head back toward the factory.

I shook my head. "But it's for sale now."

"And your point is?"

I scratched my head. "I just figured nobody would buy it, or they'd tear it down or something." I could feel my face flushing red with embarrassment. "I-I guess I'm not sure what my point is."

"Cody," he said softly, "I understand exactly." A smile etched across his face. "What if I told you I spoke to the new owner this morning?"

Drew jumped from his chair. "There's a new owner—already?"

"That's right. And he'd like the business to continue as is."

"That's awesome! Did he offer you a job?"

"He did indeed. In fact, he wants to promote me to president. But there's one stipulation. I have to hire a replacement for my foreman position before we can open back up."

Just then Gonny came out carrying a tray with lemonade and cups. "Here you are, fellas." As she was about to begin pouring, the phone rang. "Shoot, let me get that. You men help yourself." She tilted her head toward Mr. Merriweather.

"But don't let that one lift a finger. The doctor said he should be taking it easy."

"I suppose she's right," he said. "After we finish the lemonade, I may need to take a rest."

"You can do that here. You can have my bedroom," I said.

A minute later Gonny yelled from down the hall. "Drew, would you come here please?"

"I'll be back," he said and ran inside.

I took a sip of lemonade. "Do you think I can keep coming to the factory?"

"I don't see why not. It's going to take some time to get my strength back and with my new responsibilities I'll need more help with Happy."

"Yessss!" I leaned over and gave him a hug. "Thank you for not dying!"

He belted out a craggy laugh that left him wheezing.

"I'm sorry, sir. I-I didn't mean to—"

"My dear boy," he said patting my knee, "you bring such joy to this old heart of mine."

For the next few minutes, we sat in silence, enjoying our lemonade and the simple pleasure of one another's company. What had started out as such a wretched day had turned bright and wonderful. A tender breeze whisked the fallen leaves across our yard, pushing them into piles against the trunks of our maple trees. On the other side of the driveway, a half-dozen men had begun milling about the rubble from Maudie's house, raking leaves into piles and shoving them and the debris into large bags.

"Who are those guys?"

"My guess is they're the men the new owner hired to do the cleanup," Mr. Merriweather said.

"Cleanup?"

"That's right. The owner said he didn't want an eyesore across the street from his new business, which is why he bought Maudie's lot."

My jaw dropped.

"That's why Gonny couldn't take you boys to the funeral this morning. After she picked me up from the hospital, we had to go to the bank to do the paperwork."

"So is he going to build a parking lot like Mr. Rosen wanted?"

"Oh no, something much different." He smiled, teetering on laughing. "By Christmas you'll be enjoying Burlington's newest municipal park."

"Wha—"

"As soon as the purchase was made, he immediately donated the land to the city with the stipulation that only a park could be put there. It won't be big, but it's going to be beautiful."

Just then Drew walked out.

"Wait'll you hear what those guys are doing at Maudie's," I said.

"They're cleaning up."

"You bet they're cleaning up. They're cleaning up to make—"

"A park," he said.

I flashed a look at Mr. Merriweather who had inched his way to the edge of his wheelchair, his eyes darting between Drew and me.

"Wait a minute—how'd you know they're gonna build a park?" I said.

He stood grinning, holding back his reply, relishing the information he was withholding.

"Would someone please tell me what's going on?"

"Cody, it appears your brother has just been on the phone with the factory's new owner."

"Wha-what?"

Drew bobbed his head.

"Who?

"Slate!" Drew said, eyes alight with excitement.

"Our Slate?"

"Of course. What other Slate do we know?" He took a deep breath before diving into his conversation. "At first, I was talking to PaPa. He was telling me about their trip, how Uncle Jake was doing and how Slate really liked it there and all that stuff, but then he put him on the line." He paused, catching his breath. "I don't know all the details, but it appears everything that was Mr. Rosen's has been left to Slate, including his car which he's already had demolished, his house—and the coffin factory!"

I turned to Mr. Merriweather. "So Slate's your new boss?"

"Yep," said Mr. Merriweather. "There's still a lot of legal things to be done, but I'd say within the next few weeks, we'll be chugging along just like before. The only thing I have to do on my end is find my foreman." He put his hand on Drew's shoulder. "So what do you say? Would you like a promotion?"

Chapter 42

By Thanksgiving the factory was operating at peak capacity, and the lumber business was in full swing a few weeks later. Drew was loving his increased responsibilities along with a matching paycheck. As for me, I didn't give a hoot about being paid for what I did there. I had the best job of all—I got to take care of Happy. Mr. Merriweather also had Mary Lib supervise decorating the little park that now stood where Maudie's house once was.

The week before Christmas, while helping Mary Lib hang lights on a twelve-foot fir tree, she asked me, "Do you think Slate will come back to celebrate with us?"

"I don't know. He really likes it on my uncle's ranch. Drew said he's taken up fishing and loves it a hundred times more than baseball."

"But you'd think he'd be okay to come back for a visit since his father's not around anymore."

"Who says he's not around?" I arched a single eyebrow. "Drew said he's heard some of the workers say they've seen him and Grandel's ghost walking the halls of the coffin factory."

"He has not!"

I nodded and widened my eyes for added effect. "He's come back to claim the insurance on him."

"Would you stop it? That whole idea of his father wanting to kill him for insurance money is just a bunch of old hens making up stories because they don't have anything better to do."

I went back to hanging lights. "Yeah, I know. But it sure makes a great ghost story."

"I guess." Her eyes grew misty. "He really should come back though."

Christmas Eve came and as we expected, Slate was absent. In his place, though, was the first snow of the season. Although it was only a light flurry, with less than a half inch covering the ground, it was enough to add to the excitement of our celebration. After a huge turkey dinner, our gang met us at the house and together we walked the streets singing carols to our neighbors. The only adult with us was my mother who played conductor to our tone-deaf group of crooners. On key or off, after every song she managed to praise a different singer.

After the final carol and an obvious over-the-top compliment to Peeps, it was time to head to our new park for the inaugural Christmas tree–lighting ceremony. No more than an oversized garden with a walking path winding through it, the park was nevertheless beautiful, especially given that Mary Lib had every plant, bush, and tree adorned with lights. There were big-bulbed-colored ones, tiny ones, ones that blinked and twinkled, and everything in between. The only thing not lit was the Christmas tree in the center of it all.

"I bet ya could see us from outer space," Reubin said, arching his head back and sticking his tongue out to catch a snowflake.

"I don't doubt it," Mr. Merriweather said, shuffling down the path to us. On his shoulder Happy sat clapping and bouncing with excitement. "Would you look at this!" He held out his hands to Mary Lib. "My dear, what an incredible job you've done. Everybody, can we please give a round of applause for our talented decoration supervisor for this wonderful display?"

As everyone was clapping, I snuck a Pez onto her shoulder and Happy immediately pounced on it. With one hand he hugged her neck while munching on the candy with the other.

"I taught him that this week," I said, grinning.

She blushed. "Thanks, everybody, and thank you, Mr. Happy."

"Okay, gather 'round," Mom said, motioning us to the unlit tree. "We're going to give the honors of the first lighting to someone who helped make it all possible."

We all turned to Mr. Merriweather. As she handed the electric plug to him, he tilted his head skyward, his eyes seeming to follow a single flake as it fell at his feet. As his gaze lingered downward, we waited in hushed reverence. The corners of his eyes crinkled as he began.

"In a way this tree and the park represent the year we've had. It's been dark at times, but here we are, surrounded by all this beauty, with all this light and with all this love." He cast a quick smile at me. "We've all grown in many ways." He turned to Drew, his smile growing bigger. "And we've found how to fill the holes in our hearts. This park is in memory of a wonderful lady we all knew and loved. I'm blessed in my memories of her and am grateful for this place to help remind me of how special she was." He looked at us, not as a group, but as individuals. "And I'm thankful for each of you." He took a step back. "And on behalf of all of us, I'd like to say how thankful we are for the one who actually made it all possible." He turned to face back down the path. Out of the darkness walked Slate, his arm in a cast and a huge grin on his face.

Mary Lib blew past me only to run up to him and freeze with her hands hanging by her sides. "You—You came back!"

"Well, don't just stand there like an idjit," Cackles shouted. "Give the boy a hug!"

Mary Lib threw her arms around Slate, spurring the rest of us to rush in, cheering and shouting. For a solid five minutes we rejoiced at a homecoming I would never have thought possible months earlier.

"Excuse me," came a small voice from behind me. Using his little arms to wedge his way through the crowed was Irvin-Dell.

Slate looked down on him and smiled. "Hello, little buddy."

Irvin-Dell stretched his arms wide and flung them around Slate's leg.

The lighting ceremony that followed was accompanied by another round of cheers and ended with a soft rendition of "Silent Night" and a prayer of thanksgiving from Mom. With her final *amen* there was no outburst or joyous revelry, only quiet reflection as we stood gazing at a simple fir tree that had transformed into a memory that would forever be with us.

Mom clasped her hands together. "Who's ready for hot chocolate and Christmas cookies?"

"We are!" went up the unified response.

"Good," she said, tucking Mary Lib's arm under hers, "then follow us to Gonny's."

Mary Lib looked over her shoulder to find Slate and Mr. Merriweather talking in front of the Christmas tree. "Aren't you coming? Mrs. Edwards and I made the cookies special this year."

"We'll be there in just a minute," Mr. Merriweather said. Then catching my attention, he waved at Drew and me to come back.

"That's one beautiful tree," I said, walking up beside them.

"Slate has something he wanted to say to you boys."

His eyes fell to the cast on his arm as he nervously ran his hand up and down it. "I know I said thank you that day at the festival—" he swallowed, "—but I don't know if I'll ever be able to truly thank you enough. My life has been so much better since then. And it's all because of your kindness, Drew. And if it wasn't for your crazy plan, Cody, I'd never have made it out. Your uncle is an incredible man. He's honest, and so caring. I don't think I've ever met a man as kind." He glanced at Mr. Merriweather. "Well, maybe he's the second-kindest." He lifted his cast. "You know he paid for this. He didn't have to, but he did." He laughed. "He said if we didn't do it now, by the time I got his age, I might not be able to handle a rod and reel and he didn't want to lose his fishing buddy."

"Do you think you'll be staying with him?" Drew asked.

"I-I'd like to. That is, if he'll keep me around a little longer."

I poked Drew's arm. "Go ahead and tell 'im."

My brother's cheesy grin was a dead giveaway. "He absolutely will. PaPa told us last week he hopes you'll consider it your new forever home."

"My *forever* home?"

"That's what he said!"

Just then Gonny's back door swung open and out came Peeps, bumbling through the darkness carrying a thermos and a stack of paper cups. "Here ya go," he said, handing it all to Drew and me. "Gonny said if you knuckleheads were gonna chat it up out here in the cold, you might need her hot chocolate to keep warm." He took off his glasses, wiping the lenses as we filled our cups.

"You got something wrong with your peepers, Peeps?" I snickered.

"No," he said, squinting toward the coffin factory. "I just thought I saw something."

We all turned. "At the factory?"

"Yeah. Through one of the upstairs windows. I thought I saw a light."

"What kind of light? Like a flashlight?"

"Just a light," he said, putting his glasses back on. "Listen, I gotta go. Reubin's giving out his marbles as Christmas gifts." He started for the house. "You guys need to hurry back in before they're all gone."

Drew shook his head, laughing.

"What so funny?" Mr. Merriweather said.

"Reubin giving out marbles."

"What's wrong with that?"

"Nothing's wrong with it. I was just thinking about how

I thought Cody had lost his when he first rattled off his plan to bring back Kennedy."

Slate jerked his head at him. "He had a plan to do what?"

"To bring back President John F. Kennedy by coffin-jumping."

Slate dropped the thermos.

Mr. Merriweather shrugged. "Well, you might as well tell him."

For the next few minutes, I watched as my brother laid out the details of the plan while I fidgeted with my Styrofoam cup. By the time he finished, I'd dug a hole in the side and hot chocolate dripped down my hand.

"So there it is. Crazy, huh?" Drew said.

Slate stood slack-jawed, staring at him. "You were really gonna do this?"

"Up until all the stuff with Maudie and your father and, of course, finding out about the consequences."

For a minute Mr. Merriweather seemed to vanish in thought with a blank expression that ever so slowly transformed into a smile. "It could work though." His smile grew wider. "It absolutely could."

"Sir?" Drew said.

His eyes brightened. "Seriously. It's all possible. It would be a hard sell, but it *could* work. And where this country is headed, having him back would only make things better."

My cheeks began to ache from smiling.

"Are you guys coming in or not?" Gonny shouted from the kitchen window.

"We're on our way, ma'am," Drew yelled. He spun back to Mr. Merriweather. "Are you suggesting we—"

"I'm not suggesting anything. All I'm saying is Cody's plan could work…but there are the consequences."

As we made our way to the house, we passed Irvin-Dell sitting on the back steps. His head was tilted in a curious way that held me up from following the others inside. I sat beside him. "You okay, buddy?"

"Hey, Mr. Cody," he said, squinting.

I leaned over in front of him. "Is everything alright?"

He blinked. "Oh, yes sir."

"What're you doing sitting out here in the cold all by your lonesome?"

"Just watchin' the fireflies."

"It's winter, Irvin-Dell. They aren't out this time of year. Do you mean snowflakes?"

"No sir. Them's fireflies. Two of 'em. They're over yonder in the coffin factory."

I followed his eyes to the building's dark silhouette. "I don't see anything."

"Give 'em a minute."

"It's started to sleet a bit. I think what you're seeing is light reflecting off that."

"There goes one!"

"Where?"

"At the windows. They're on the inside."

"But I don't…" I squeezed my eyes tight, trying to filter out the snow. "Wait…is that…"

"Do you see it?"

"I see something…"

"See it bobbin' around?"

"It's hovering. That's a—"

"Firefly. I told ya, Mr. Cody!"

"That's no firefly. A firefly's light doesn't flicker." I

swallowed hard. "That's a candle flame." My breath left me as I watched another one appear just behind the first. For a moment they hung in midair, side by side as if being held by some invisible force looking back at us. A second later they passed from the window, their quivering haze fading out into another part of the coffin factory.

The End

A Personal Note from the Author

If you read *Twelve Coffins* I would like to say a heartfelt thank you for sharing your time with me. If you enjoyed it and have time to post an honest review, I would greatly appreciate it. And if you'd like to contact me directly, feel free to email me through my website below. I love making new friends!

For more info visit:
LewisPennington.com

Other Books by Lewis Pennington

Visit www.lewispennington.com

About the Author

Lewis Pennington graduated from East Carolina University in Greenville, North Carolina with a degree in Graphic Design and Marketing. Upon graduation, he moved to New York City where he began his career with the now defunct Science Fiction Magazine Omni Magazine. After decades of navigating through the corporate marketing maze he is now focusing on his next chapter in life—providing readers with inspirational fiction. Lewis and his family live in Asheville, North Carolina.

www.ingramcontent.com/pod-product-compliance
Lightning Source LLC
Chambersburg PA
CBHW020906060726
47591CB00004B/1110

9781736423981